KNIGHT'S REDEMPTION

KNIGHTS OF HELL SERIES

SHERILEE GRAY

Cover Design by Cover Couture

bookcovercouture.com

Editor: Andrea McKay

ISBN:

Epub: 9780473454241

Print: 978-0473454234

Prologue

Lazarus glanced up as Scarlet and Tobias walked into the control room.

"You flying or riding?"

Lazarus's retrievals went a whole hell of a lot smoother now that Scarlet partnered with him. She had a calming effect on people, an ability Lazarus lacked and then some.

She screwed her face up in the same way she'd been doing since she was young, since he found her alone and scared in an alley way. He couldn't help but smile.

"Man, I'd love to take my bike out, but I think I'd be cutting it fine," she said, looking disappointed.

Tobias tugged his mate into his side. "We'll take the bikes out when you get back."

Scarlet wrapped her arms around Tobias's waist. "Sounds perfect."

T leaned in...

"I don't need to see that," Lazarus said, more out of habit than anything else. He'd accepted his brother had mated and completely fallen for Scarlet a long time ago.

Tobias smirked at him. "Jesus, you're uptight. No wonder you're still unmated."

"I'm uptight? You're the one with a stick permanently lodged up your..."

"Okay," Scarlet said. "That's enough, you two."

"Tell him there's nothing lodged anywhere, baby," Tobias said, eyes dancing. He turned to Lazarus. "I mean, she'd know."

Scarlet groaned and rolled her eyes.

Lazarus flipped off Tobias. "It's like you want me to kick your ass again." He grinned at his brother's scowl then turned back to Scarlet. "Come on then, kid. We better make a move."

He strode out the double doors to the balcony, and Scarlet joined him a moment later, her eyes sparkling with humor, Tobias right behind her. "How old do I have to get before you stop calling me that?"

Lazarus shrugged.

"I'm far from a kid."

He dragged off his shirt and tucked it into the waistband of his jeans. "You'll always be my kid, doesn't matter how old you get." He glanced at T. "Or how long you're mated."

She smiled at him. It was teasing, but her eyes were brighter. "Love you too, Daaad."

Scarlet was teasing him, but he liked when she called him that. She knew it, too.

She turned to her mate and kissed him goodbye then started toward Lazarus, but T tugged her back. He buried his face in her hair at the crook of her neck and breathed her in before kissing her again. Something he always did.

"I'll have the bikes warmed up when you get back," he said as Lazarus scooped her up in his arms and unfurled his wings.

Scarlet grinned and waved as Lazarus took flight, not looking away from Tobias until he was out of sight.

———

Lazarus strode across the kitchen, locking eyes with the demi-demon they'd come for.

The guy stumbled back a step. "Stay away from me."

Scarlet instantly reached for the guy, but he reared back out of her reach.

"Don't touch me, you crazy bitch."

It was obvious no amount of talking would get through to this guy, and they didn't have time to wait for Scarlet to do her thing, so Lazarus went for him before he threw himself through the window to get away.

Scarlet cursed. "Give me a few more minutes, Laz."

"There's no time."

The demi swung, his fist barely missing Scarlet. Little shit didn't know what was good for him. Lazarus took him down to the kitchen floor, immobilizing him.

Scarlet yanked on the back of Lazarus's shirt. "This isn't helping."

The guy bucked and kicked then spat in Lazarus's face. "Get the fuck off me," he shrieked.

Lazarus's temper flared and before he realized what he was doing, he'd pinned the demi to the ground by his throat. "We're trying to help you," he gritted out.

Scarlet growled and yanked harder on his shirt. "Jesus, calm the hell down and get up off the—" Her words were cut off with a startled hiss.

Lazarus spun around. Her hold on his biceps was so tight her fingernails cut into his skin.

Her eyes were wide. "Laz..."

Crimson bloomed in the center of her chest, like petals unfurling in a sickening rush.

Her legs gave out and she crumpled to the floor. He dove

for her, dragged her into his arms, and did his best to staunch the blood pumping from the gaping wound.

The Orthon demon responsible didn't hesitate. It went straight for its target, the demi cowering on the floor behind them, and dragged him screaming from the room.

Lazarus let them go.

All that mattered was Scarlet.

He brushed her wild red curls away from her precious face. "You're all right, Scar. You're going to be all right." He'd never lied to her before, but he knew he was then.

The striking gold flecks in her soft brown eyes dimmed, muted by pain.

"Don't leave me, sweet girl. I need you here with me. Tobias needs you." Her mouth opened and blood bubbled up between her lips, cutting off whatever she was trying to say. He held her to him. "No. Please, God, no."

She rattled out her last breath—and then she was gone.

Lazarus scooped her up. He was taking her home. He needed to take her home.

He landed on the balcony a short time later with Scarlet's lifeless body clutched in his arms, and pushed through the doors into the control room.

Tobias stood on the other side, pale and shaking so hard his teeth chattered. He'd felt it, her loss, like all mates did. God, Tobias felt it. T stumbled forward and took her from Lazarus.

His friend's knees gave out then and Lazarus stood, tears streaming down his face, feeling fucking broken, helpless, as T rocked his mate in his arms, a sound coming from the male that shook Lazarus to his core.

Tobias looked up at him, the desolation in his eyes hard to look at. "This is your fault," he said. "You were supposed to look after her. You promised me you'd keep her safe."

Lazarus stumbled back a step, but he knew it was true. Scarlet was dead because of him, because of his loss of control.

The agony in Tobias's eyes turned to hatred. "I'll never forgive you for this." He stood, still holding Scarlet, and shifted to his demon form, his clothes falling in tatters at his feet.

Then he strode from the room, diving off the balcony and taking flight.

One

Lazarus sensed the demon before he saw it, could smell the toxic shit coming off it, could feel it prickling over his skin like a chemical spill.

The wind picked up speed, whipping at his hair and face and pulling at his wings. He rode it, gliding above the busy Roxburgh streets, scanning the humans moving below, swarming like ants, in a hurry to get to their next destination. Unaware of what moved among them, of the danger they were in.

There.

The demon had chosen his camouflage well. A human male, small in stature, plain clothing—unthreatening, unassuming. He was anything but, and at that moment the woman it stalked was in serious danger.

Flying lower, he tucked his wings into his back and dropped the last ten feet to an alley floor. His boots crunched on broken glass and other shit littering the ground. His wings vanished when he tucked them into his back, and he grabbed the shirt he'd shoved into the back of his jeans and yanked it on. The acrid scent was more intense at street level. There was definitely more than one.

The thud of two of his brothers dropping down behind him came next and he turned toward Chaos and Gunner as the warriors approached.

Kryos and Rocco were back at the compound and fuck knew where Zenon was. The male preferred to keep his own company. But the three of them were more than capable of putting out the trash.

As Knights of Hell, they'd been created to keep evil off these New York streets. And Chaos was the poor bastard they'd chosen to lead them. The male tucked in his pale gray wings and jerked on his shirt as he strode forward. The streetlights glinted off the tattooed side of his head, and there was a sneer on his lips. "My guess, at least half a dozen."

Gunner rubbed a hand over his buzz cut, the scowl twisting his mouth emphasizing the deep scar through his upper lip. "That shit isn't normal."

It wasn't. The only times demons tended to travel in packs were when they made their escape from Hell. After that they tended to scatter, making them harder to find.

Lazarus led the way out of the alley and onto the street. People rushed past, clearing a path for them like they always did, their flight instincts well and truly kicking in, their subconscious knowing a predator when it sensed one.

Ignoring the stares and gasps of the people around them, they followed the trail, the pungent stench of demon. It took them away from the busy streets, which was not surprising. No one, not even the demons invading Earth, wanted their existence to become public knowledge, not yet anyway. It was an unwritten rule, and the only thing Heaven and Hell agreed on.

The scent grew unbearably strong as they approached a parking garage. A woman's cry echoed off the concrete walls.

They moved in, not wasting another minute, and jumped the stairwell to the lower level.

Standing in a circle were six Sitri demons, laughing as they surrounded the human female. Sitri were known as mischief-makers, lovers of disorder and mayhem. In Hell, they moved in packs; on Earth, they were forced to stay apart, but it looked like these assholes had formed a support group and decided on a night out on the town.

They turned as the knights walked in, instantly baring their teeth and crouching into fighting stances. The woman didn't wait for an invite; as soon as the demons turned their backs she bolted for the exit. Psychos that these particular demons were, they didn't do the same and run for their lives. They grinned...then they ran at them.

Chaos drew his sword and Gunner palmed his Glock. Lazarus let one of his knives fly, the blade burying in a demon's shoulders. Chaos and Gunner were now cutting through the others as Lazarus strode toward the bastard screeching on his knees.

He reached for the knife still buried in the demon—

Fuck.

Lazarus dropped to his knees when what felt like three thousand volts shot up his spine and hammered him in the back of the skull. The demon in front of him took the chance he'd been given, yanked the blade from his shoulder, and buried it in Lazarus's stomach.

Lazarus hissed and fell forward as that same force nailed the base of his spine a second time. He dropped like a sack of rocks, his face making nice with the asphalt. He tried to get up. But nope, moving wasn't an option just yet. His spine torqued as the next wave came, attacking every nerve ending, lighting him up like he'd just taken a seat in an electric chair.

The demon came at him again but was pulled off him by Chaos. Its shriek echoed off the walls a moment before it was cut off by a wet gurgling and the thump of its body hitting the ground.

Lazarus had no choice but to lay there in shock, blinking at the blue Corolla parked beside him while blood leaked from him like a sieve.

Somehow, he knew exactly what had just hit him, the thing that had dropped him to his knees, and he didn't mean the blade that had been buried in his gut.

The powerful instinct couldn't be denied.

He didn't fucking want it. He sucked in a rough breath and tried to sit up. Nope, moving was still a no-go.

This can't be happening.

But it was.

He'd prayed, he'd bargained, he'd wished on a fucking shooting star that this day would never come. Turned out no one gave a fuck what he wanted, and the fates had decided to give him a mate anyway.

And she'd just unknowingly sent him a message.

Now he had no choice but to go get her.

"Let me the hell in!"

Eve peeked around the turquoise and white polka-dot curtain covering the window. Her ex-boyfriend, Eric, was standing there, scowling at her front door. She winced when he kicked it.

Her car was out front. She was obviously home. Hiding wasn't going to work.

She cursed under her breath. "Just leave."

He shouted her name and thumped on the heavy wood for the millionth time. "I'm not going anywhere, not until you talk to me."

He meant it, ignoring him certainly wasn't working. She

hadn't answered any of his calls or texts, and now he was standing at her damn door trying to knock it down.

Their relationship had been toxic from the start. Eric seemed to equally dislike her and want her at the same time. Eve didn't understand it, but she'd had enough, of being treated badly, of this weird love/hate obsession he had with her.

Gritting her teeth and straightening her shoulders, she yanked the door open. This had to stop.

His dark blue eyes flared, latching onto hers as soon as he had her in his sights, then dropped to her breasts, like they always did. "Finally. Jesus Christ, Eve." His tone was one a parent would use on a disobedient child.

Crossing her arms over her chest, she attempted to hide her body. She hated that he could still make her feel worthless. His out-of-control ego had taken a beating when she'd ended their relationship and he was having trouble letting her rejection go.

Eric hadn't started out like this, but over the course of their relationship, he'd changed. At first, she'd brushed off his behavior, coming up with excuses for his hurtful comments, happy that someone actually wanted her. But along the way, he'd turned from a shy, sweet guy into an obsessive, cruel jerk. His treatment of her had gotten progressively worse. He wanted her in his bed, but the rest of the time he was just angry. Everything about her seemed to piss him off. And when he got rough with her in bed as well, she knew it was past time to get out of the relationship.

She looked him in the eyes. "You need to listen to what I'm saying, and you need to hear me..."

Eve gasped and grabbed for the door, squeezing her eyes closed as noise flooded her mind.

Stupid bitch. She should be grateful I put up with her fat ass.

Eve's eyes shot open. "What did you just say?"

Eric frowned. “Not a damn thing. You were about to lie to me, and yourself, about ending our relationship.” His eyes dropped to her chest again and he licked his lips.

God, I want to bury my face between those massive jugs.

She was hearing him, *his* voice, clear as day, but his mouth was shut. Shit, she really was losing her mind. Over the last four weeks, she’d had...attacks. That’s what she’d been calling them. Words whispered in her mind, thoughts that weren’t her own, flying through her head.

Maybe I’ll get her on a diet. She’d be so much prettier if she lost ten pounds.

She clutched the side of her head, pain pounding through her skull.

“What the hell’s is wrong with you?” Eric said, taking a step closer.

Yeah, she’s fat, but I don’t need to take her out in public, as long as I get to keep fucking her. God, I want to wrap my hands around her throat, choke her while I do it, slap her, watch her cry while I pound into her.

“Stay back,” she gasped.

He kept coming. “I don’t know why you’re resisting this.”

Eve shook her head, unable to get her mouth to work. More jumbled thoughts sliced through her mind, words, a voice that wasn’t her own.

He ran a hand over his blond hair, gaze raking over her. “God, look at you,” he bit out, mouth twisting. “Do you think there’ll be guys lining up to ask you out?”

If it wasn’t for those magnificent tits, I probably wouldn’t bother either. I want to hurt her, want to make her scream. Christ, what’s wrong with me? It’s not me. It’s her. She made me feel like this. I was fine until I met her. God, I want to fuck her.

She jerked back as he reached for her, but she was too late. His hand curled around her wrist and he yanked her forward.

She crashed into his chest and his arms came around her, squeezing her tight to him.

His mouth went to her ear. "You want this, Eve, I know you do. No more playing. No more teasing me."

She shoved at him. "Let me the hell go."

He didn't budge, his hold getting tighter as he struggled with his temper for a second then tried to soften his tone when he spoke again. "Come on, baby. You're overreacting, you realize that, right?" He pressed a wet kiss to her temple. "I know you love pushing my buttons, but you need to stop playing me like this. You're seriously starting to piss me off. I want you, and I know you want me. I know you do." His eyes slid back down to her chest.

Damn, look at those big, soft, round...

Eve shook her head trying to make the voice stop. The other times this happened it hadn't been this bad. She was either going mad or, somehow, she was hearing Eric's sick thoughts.

He took advantage of her loss of concentration and pushed her against the doorframe. It dug into her back and she cried out.

"Please go," she whispered.

He shook his head. "I can't...I can't walk away. You're mine..."

A deep sound rolled across her yard, building in volume.

They both stilled, staring into the darkness.

A low, vicious growl came next, so loud it lifted the hair on the back of Eve's neck.

Eric stumbled back a step and Eve took advantage, shoving him away and slamming the door shut. Eric pounded on it again.

She grabbed for her phone, about to call the police when his yelling and knocking was cut off abruptly.

Pulling back the curtain, she peered out into the darkness.

Her porch light lit up some of the front yard and she gasped when a huge shadow moved away from the light, melting with the darkened edge of the garden.

Oh God, had Eric been attacked by something? An animal?

The sound of his car starting reached her, followed by it speeding off a few moments later.

Eve released the breath she'd been holding, dropped the curtain, and threw the deadbolt.

Two

Lazarus scowled. He hated these little towns. True, they made his job easier with fewer witnesses and a hell of a lot less ground to cover. But today he could have been anywhere. It wouldn't have made a difference. He could have located who he'd come for blindfolded.

Despite his distaste for places like this, a day ago the tiny West Coast town might have offered a much-needed change of pace, with its sea breezes and trees and flowers and shit.

But not now. Not today.

The building in front of him was small and sickeningly cheerful. A shock of color beside its more sedate neighbors. He shook his head. Jesus, the place looked like Rainbow Brite threw up all over it. The chill wind picked up, whipping through his hair, stinging his skin, and sent russet-colored leaves tumbling from the trees and spiraling past the shop's sunny yellow door. A door he couldn't seem to go through no matter how long he stood there.

The warring sides of his DNA had never felt more at odds than they did at that moment, which was saying something after everything that had gone down recently. His angel half wanted to protect, do what was expected—do the right thing. But his demon half—well, the demon wanted something else entirely. It screamed louder, fought harder to get free. Jesus, his skin itched with the need to shift into his Kishi demon form.

That scared the shit out of him. He couldn't loosen his stranglehold on the dark fucker writhing inside him, not when he was so close to possessing the key to his salvation and the only way he could win that war.

And she had no idea. No idea who she was or what she was.

Now the only things that stood between him and his mate were wood, glass, and a few cracked feet of pavement.

His gut churned and he clenched his fists against the little zaps of electricity that continued to shoot through him. Shit.

He'd only gotten a glimpse of her last night at her door, and then that human male had put his hands on her, had hurt her, and Lazarus had seen red. The growl that had left him, shit, that had been torn from him, had surprised him more than anyone. But he hadn't been able to hold it back.

He grunted. He hadn't meant to go after the fucker or knock him out. Breaking his nose definitely hadn't been on the night's agenda. Lazarus had been forced to drive the weasel home then wait for him to wake up so he could scrub his memory. The whole thing had messed with his plans, but after the scare that female had, knocking on her door right after all that drama and introducing himself probably wouldn't have been a great idea. Instead, he'd gone back and watched her place until morning. He'd let her enjoy the last night she'd spend in her house.

In her life.

A seabird squawked overhead, jarring him from his thoughts. The breeze increased its efforts, tugging at his shirt.

God, he hated this. Hated that he was about to shatter the fantasy this female had been living.

Yeah, she'd pulled the short straw, because he was here to smash that illusion into a thousand tiny pieces.

He caught a brief glimpse of dark hair and bright pink clothing through the window, then she was gone, his view obscured by a large bookshelf. Another wave of volatile energy washed over him and he gritted his teeth. She didn't have the ability to block all that untamed energy she was sending out, and the female's newly acquired power hammered against his defenses. Calling to him. The strength of it still shocked him. Its effects caused pins and needles to lift the hairs on his arms, sending power arcing through his nerve endings and tingling across the surface of his skin.

At least now he could stay upright. He was adjusting to her presence quickly, and thank fuck for that. He may heal quickly, but that knife to the gut still hurt like a bitch.

He couldn't wait any longer. It was time to make a move, but his feet felt rooted to the pavement. He'd stood there like a damned statue for too long already and some of the yokels had stopped to stare. Dammit, he couldn't screw this up. Schooling his features, he ran a hand over his hair, and before he could change his mind, gripped the handle and pushed open the door.

The tinkle of a little bell announced his entrance into The Book Worm. The place was small and warmly lit. Paperbacks covered every available surface. They lined the walls and filled the overflowing bookcases that crowded the limited floor space.

Books were this female's passion and her love for this place was stamped in every corner of the room. From the mismatched bookshelves painted in bright, cheerful colors to the striped overstuffed couch in the corner and the chunky antique counter with its equally ancient, carefully restored cash register perched on top.

Everything about this room screamed soft, feminine...delicate. He glanced down at his worn leather jacket, scuffed boots, and battle-scarred hands. What did he know about soft and feminine? As for delicate, he was more a bull-in-china-shop kind of male. His stomach did another lurch and he wanted to growl his frustration. Shit, if he had any other choice he would turn around and walk back out that door.

There weren't many things he had been certain about in his long life, but when it came to this female, a female who had created her own little piece of heaven—a place of calm, of solace, of joy within these four walls—he knew a few things with one hundred percent unwavering certainty.

He didn't deserve her. He could never give her what she needed. And in the end, he would hurt her.

But despite all that, he would continue on this course regardless.

He had to. There were bigger things at stake than injuring this female's feeling.

Moving farther into the room, he sidestepped the shelf blocking his path. Though he couldn't see her, it wasn't necessary to search for her. He knew exactly where she was. He glanced up, and halfway up a ladder, his demi-demon busily transferred a stack of books from the uppermost step to one of the higher shelves. Her position, slightly bent forward, caused the pink dress she wore to cling to her curves and highlighted a soft, voluptuous figure.

It was rare for the weaker human genes of their mothers to be dominant. More often than not, the hybrids favored the sturdy physical build of their demon sires.

But this female's figure was all human.

"I won't be a minute," she called over her shoulder and started to climb down.

He cursed under his breath when, with each tentative step she took, the fabric pulled taut over her rounded hips and ass.

He couldn't tear his eyes away, and before he realized what he was doing he'd taken several steps in her direction.

Slamming on the brakes, he barely resisted the urge to go up the damn ladder after her. As she got closer, he had to jam his hands in his pockets so he didn't do something stupid like reach for her. He hadn't believed it, but there was no denying it now. The physical connection was as strong as he'd been told it would be.

She stepped onto the floor, straightened her dress, and turned to face him with a welcoming smile curving her full, dark pink lips. "Oh...sorry!" She took a startled step back.

Not surprising considering he was damn near on top of her. Lazarus sucked in a sharp breath, locked his knees, and fought the blow that followed. No fucking way was he falling on his ass in front of this female.

She was attractive—Christ, beautiful—but what had him damn near hypnotized were her startling pale blue eyes. They held him immobile, called to a part of him he never knew existed, a soul-deep connection he never thought he'd find. Had never wanted to find, and would have been more than happy to leave buried.

The drag on his already deteriorating control escalated, and he had to force his lungs to get back to the whole *oxygen in, carbon dioxide out* routine. A meet-cute had never been on the cards, but swooning at her feet wasn't what he'd envisioned either.

The off-balance sensation persisted and he struggled, and failed, to restore his equilibrium. Probably because all the blood had evacuated his head and taken up residence in his now aching groin.

When a demi's powers reached their peak, his kind were alerted by way of a kind of internal alarm. If it hadn't knocked him on his ass, the fact he was the only one able to sense her would have told him exactly who she was.

Lying on that parking garage floor, he'd only felt dread. And whatever he'd imagined he'd feel coming face-to-face with her for the first time—it wasn't this, this almost violent flood of emotion.

Because he knew her.

It was base and primal and fucked up, but he *knew her*.

He curled his fingers into a fist. He felt torn in two, couldn't decide if he wanted to fall at her feet and worship her like some pathetic, groveling fool, or turn around and run like a pack of hellhounds wanted a chunk out of his ass.

All he knew for sure at that moment was he fucking hated it, this sudden loss of self-possession. He'd rather face an army of Orthon demons than the woman standing in front of him and what she represented.

Like a besotted idiot, he watched, captivated, as her tongue darted out to lick her lower lip then bite down on the plump flesh. He lifted his gaze, and soft pools of blue stared back, round and questioning. Right then, the only thought he could summon was how badly he wanted to taste her.

He took an abrupt step back, man enough to admit that the curvy little demi standing in front of him scared the living shit out of him. Mind sluggish and tongue refusing to work, he stood there, gawking like a damned idiot. The silence had stretched on and her cheeks turned pink.

Her gaze darted toward the closed door then back. "So... was there a specific book you were after? I have a pretty wide selection here."

His stomach clenched at the sound of her sweet, slightly husky voice, and with a great deal of effort, he kept his gaze fixed straight ahead instead of wandering lower. He flexed his fingers, positive he could already feel those lush curves she had in abundance, her soft warmth under his palms. Scowling, he attempted to shake off his messed-up reaction to the female blinking owlishly up at him.

Words would be a great idea about now, dipshit.

"Perhaps if you tell me what type of books you usually read?" She tried again, but this time her smile faltered and she tugged on the front of her dress several times before crossing her arms over her ample breasts.

Great, he was freaking her out.

"I, ah...I don't read much," he forced out.

She jerked back and hugged her arms tighter around her waist. Dammit, he should have kept his mouth shut.

Now he'd startled her, but considering he'd just growled the words at her, he wasn't surprised by her reaction. What the fuck was up with his voice? He sounded like he was gargling nails.

Afraid the skittish female was about to run, he attempted what he hoped was a reassuring smile. It felt awkward and wooden on his face and going by the way her eyes widened in alarm, the pearly white routine wasn't conveying *trust me I'm one of the good guys* but instead *all the better to eat you with, my dear.*

He needed her to trust him, but it wasn't hard to figure out the mute pervert approach wasn't the way to go.

With no other option, and before she bolted for the door, he sent a gentle rush of power to her. It was designed to create calm, to wash away the fear in her eyes, and make this whole shit show a lot easier on both of them. It also gave off a pleasant scent, because good things smelled nice, and bad things smelled like shit, right? He guessed that was the theory behind it.

But before he had a chance to recite the speech he'd memorized, the bell jingled above the door and an elderly woman walked in. She glanced at them briefly before making her way to one of the shelves in the autobiographies section.

His demi released a relieved breath, happy she was no longer alone with him. "Good morning, Mrs. Jensen," she called to the other woman.

Tongue-tied, confused, and without doubt fucking up badly, he forced his brain back into gear. His kind searched their entire lives for what stood within his grasp. Yeah, he wanted it like a bullet to the back of the head. But there was no alternative for him, for either of them. So, clearing his throat several times in an attempt to loosen his damn vocal cords, he tried again. "I need to speak to—"

"Excuse me?"

Dammit.

She turned to face the old woman. Lazarus scowled. He hadn't even heard her approach, so fixed on the female in front of him.

"How can I help you today, Mrs. Jensen?"

The woman didn't reply, and his demi's smile faded as she rubbed at the goose bumps that broke out across her arms. A chill blasted Lazarus, its bite enough to break him free of the hold she had on him. The hair at his nape prickled right before the unmistakable odor of sulfur surrounded him, heavy and cloying like toxic gas. The old woman's eyes flashed to a colorless milky white, and hissing, she lunged, grabbing for the female at his side.

Wrenching her out of the way, he planted his boot in the creature's chest and sent the Orthon sprawling. The savage breed of demon was relentless and wouldn't stop until it had captured or killed its target.

The demon staggered to its feet, gaze darting between him and his female. Before it had time to make its next move, Lazarus ran at it. The form it had taken was heavyset and slow, and instead of trying to escape, it struck out. Lazarus dodged the blow and returned it with a strike to the creature's throat then swept the fucker's feet out from underneath it. Before it could get vertical, he pulled his blade free, grabbed a handful of its soft gray hair, and removed the demon's head with one brutal slice.

Breathing heavily, he looked down at the lifeless creature, at the thick black sludge that oozed from its neck onto the floral carpet.

That had been close, too damn close.

It didn't matter who this demi was to him, or the circumstances. He'd been careless. He'd allowed the intensity of his reaction to cripple his powers. It wasn't the first time he'd lost sight of his duty, had allowed his emotions to rule. Only last time the consequences of his carelessness had been devastating.

He cursed and straightened.

A new demi's powers reached a peak exactly one month after they developed, when all that unstable energy could no longer be contained and escaped in a rush. That energy acted like a kind of beacon for them and helped pinpoint their location. But he and his brothers weren't the only ones able to sense it, and that made the hybrids one hell of an easy target.

Demi-demons were a valuable commodity in the demon world, bought and sold, kept to exploit their unique abilities. If Lazarus hadn't got to her first...

He needed to pull his head out of his ass, and fast.

Still, as adrenaline pumped through his system, heating his blood like it always did after a kill, he couldn't stop himself from turning to her. As soon as he set eyes on her, he was hit by an all-consuming hunger. So fierce he had to lock his knees again or risk falling to them.

Anticipation tingled across his scalp and slid down his spine, but he gritted his teeth and tried to ignore it, tried to shake it off. Whether Lazarus liked it or not, he needed her. If he let her slip through his fingers now, he wouldn't be the only one to suffer the consequences.

Disgusted at himself, he ignored the roar of his body, and

that's when he registered the horror on her face. She was watching the Orthon as its headless body convulsed in violent, jerky movements on the floor. It had transformed, shifting back to its natural state. The thing was large in size, its leathery skin grayish in color, and jagged spikes protruded from its spine like some kind of giant reptile.

Its head had rolled to a stop at their feet, lips pulled back in a snarl revealing sharp yellow teeth, and its cloudy eyes were still open, staring blindly up at her.

That's when the screaming started.

Three

One of the behemoth's giant hands curled around Eve's arm, and he hauled her up against his body, causing hers to collide with the solid wall of his chest. *Oh God*. He was huge. She tilted her head back, taking in his hard features, and her gaze slid higher, locking with startling green eyes.

Her jaw dropped, mouth opening and about to let loose another scream, when his other hand came down over her mouth, cutting it off before she could get it out.

Panic surged through her veins, and she reached up to clutch her attacker's thick wrist, yanking and scratching like a wild cat in an attempt to loosen his grasp. The giant didn't budge. Instead, his grip tightened, holding her immobile in his massive arms.

He decapitated Mrs. Jensen.

His hand still over her mouth, he tilted her head back, forcing her to look at him again.

"Be still," he rumbled. "Think about what you just saw." His voice was deep and rough, more a growl than anything else.

Her mind tried to register what had just happened, what

was happening. And an image of white, colorless eyes flashed through her mind. She squeezed her eyes shut, tried to make sense of what she'd seen.

She dragged a panicked breath in through her nose. Whatever the hell that thing was, it hadn't been the sweet old woman who'd been coming to her shop for the last few years.

Her eyelids snapped open, her gaze shooting back up to his. This guy, this huge, terrifying mountain of a man, had shoved her out of the way, had protected her, hadn't he?

Eve tested his hold, tried to pull free, but still he wouldn't let go. She glanced back up at him. He was watching her, a fierce expression on his face, and those extremely green eyes felt like lasers trying to get inside her head.

She was going to die.

This was how it was going to happen. Some insane, knife-wielding lunatic was going to cut off her head and there was nothing she could do to stop him.

An eerie calm washed through her, taking all her fight with it.

Maybe she was going into shock. She guessed that was a good thing.

Several long seconds crept by, but he made no move to grab that wicked-looking knife. The heavy thud of his heart seemed to pound right through her, like a ticking time bomb counting down—to what she had no idea—while he held her to him, his body unnaturally still.

That feeling of time moving in slow motion, of being submerged, began to lift. She pushed through the haze, struggled to the surface, and her mind began to clear. A muffled sound filled her head and she realized the strangled, frantic sounds were coming from her. His rough, hot palm still covered her mouth, smothering her screams. Her throat burned from the effort, and tears tracked a heated path down her cheeks.

Maybe she was suffering some kind of psychotic episode and all this was some terrible nightmare? But it only took one glance to the floor to know what she'd seen had been no dream.

The creature's remains were still there, right in her line of vision. The corpse was smoldering, flesh bubbling, releasing thick tendrils of acrid smoke. She'd never seen a dead body before, but she was pretty damn sure dissolving wasn't normal. The pungent odor invaded her nostrils and burned a path to her lungs as she attempted to suck down much needed oxygen.

She felt claustrophobic with this giant's oversized paw covering her mouth, and she tugged harder on his fingers. Warm lips pressed against her ear and she stilled.

"I can feel your heart pounding like a frightened rabbit. You need to calm yourself, demi, before I can release you." God, that voice. It was pure gravel.

Calm herself? She wriggled, managing to jerk her head to the side and let out a muffled scream.

"Be still," he hissed.

Like hell. She fought harder, and his grip on her tightened to the point of pain. She couldn't hold back her whimper.

He cursed. "I don't want to hurt you."

Her gaze automatically traveled to the remains on her floor, now nothing but a sooty ash-like residue, the clothes still lying in the shape of a body that had moments ago filled them.

Eve jumped as his mouth brushed against her ear again. "When I remove my hand, you will not scream," the guy growled. "Do you understand?" His warm breath skittered across her cheek, and the deep, raspy timbre of his voice worked its way down her spine, causing her to shiver in response. She nodded, with little choice but to obey.

"Good, that's good, demi," he murmured and eased his hand from her mouth.

She stumbled back a step and stared up at him, getting a better look at his hard futures. His green eyes were unnaturally bright and deep-set, his nose long and straight, and his square jaw in need of a shave. The muscle there jumped as her gaze dropped to his full lips.

The size of the man would intimidate anyone, but coupled with his harsh, almost cruel features, he looked like the brutal killer he was. Panic and confusion caused her pulse to race double time.

Her gaze darted back to the floor. "W-what was that... thing?"

"There's a lot you need to know, but we don't have time for long explanations." He scanned the quiet street beyond her shop's window. "There'll be more trackers coming for us soon. We have to leave."

Her stomach lurched. "Leave?"

"We can't stay here, it's too dangerous," he said.

Eve shook her head. "I don't know who you are, or...or what you want, but there's been some kind of mistake. My name's not Demi. I'm not...I'm not who you're looking for."

His beautiful yet terrifying eyes locked with hers. "There is no mistake."

She shook her head. "I don't understand."

"You will." His brow creased, gaze moving over her, doing a quick scan from head to toe and back. "You're cold."

She blinked up at him. "What?"

"You're shivering. I can hear your teeth chattering."

Eve stared up at him as if he were speaking in tongues. And he stared back, she guessed waiting for a response. She couldn't form one. His fingers flexed lightly around her arm before he released her and slipped off his jacket, revealing a brightly colored tattoo that covered his entire right arm, or what she could see of it at least. She flinched when he reached around her and draped it over her shoulders.

He made a low growling sound. "Put your arms in the sleeves."

She did as he asked, because...well, what else could she do? He zipped the warm leather up to her chin. The gentle action was so completely at odds with what she'd witnessed moments ago, all she could do was stare. God, that weird sense of calm washed over her again, and alarmingly, she felt herself sway closer to him.

The jacket was far too big but, damn, it smelled fantastic. The wonderful scent rose up to surround her, and she couldn't help taking several deep breaths. Heat seeped into her skin from the worn rawhide and managed to ease the bone-deep chill that had gripped her.

Cocking his head to the side, he gave her another once-over and, obviously happy with what he saw, he took hold of her wrist and started toward the door.

His earlier words shot through her head again. "No, stop. I'm not going anywhere with you." As she struggled against his grasp, her gaze landed again on the mess scattered on the floor, and a hit of pure fear spiked through her. She needed to run, to get away from this man, from what the existence of that creature meant.

Without a word, he stopped in his tracks and spun to face her. Grabbing her chin, his lethal gaze collided with hers. "I'm not going to hurt you, but we have to leave." Tilting his head in the direction of the ashy remains, he added, "We sure as hell don't have time for this."

He started dragging her toward the rear exit again.

Never let your attacker take you to a second location—she'd read that somewhere. But the panic swamping her made it impossible to think, let alone come up with some clever way to escape. She tried to pull her hand free from the fingers clamped around her wrist, but it made no difference. He was too strong. Eve tried a different tactic and went completely limp. She was no lightweight, and dragging her feet should definitely have slowed him down...

He didn't even break stride, simply slipped an arm around her waist and carried on.

In a last-ditch effort to save herself, Eve grabbed onto one of the bookshelves and kicked out as hard as she could. He grunted when her foot connected with hard flesh, but still he didn't let go.

Eve clung to the wood for dear life, her nails scratching off flakes of bright yellow paint as he tried to yank her free. When that didn't work, he reached back and tried to pry her fingers loose. His free arm still circling her waist, holding her in place as he worked. The tug of war caused the shelf to topple over with a loud crash and her precious books tumbled all over the floor. Before she could find something else to grab on to, he hauled her toward him and lifted her off the ground as if she weighed nothing.

"No. Let me go."

He jerked her higher, and her face smooched against his shoulder. He held her up with one powerful arm under her butt, manhandling her like she was nothing but a rag doll. As she kicked and struggled, another lungful of that unique scent of his assaulted her, but this time stronger. It filled her senses, spicy and potent, almost drugging. Stilling, and without conscious thought, she inhaled deeply, desperate to take in more.

What the hell am I doing? She couldn't believe she was actually *smelling* her attacker.

Fight, her mind screamed, but her arms were useless, trapped against her sides in his viselike grip. With no other weapon at her disposal, Eve lifted her head and sank her teeth into the exposed flesh between his neck and shoulder. Hard. A snarl rumbled through his chest, and he dropped her back to her feet, his fingers an unbreakable band around her upper arm.

"Stop fighting." He swiped at the wound she'd caused and looked down at the blood on his fingers. "You need to calm the fuck down. We don't have time for this. You're only making it harder on yourself."

Was he serious? "Oh, well, sorry about that," she fired at him. This guy was nuts if he thought she was going anywhere with him. "I wasn't sure about the correct etiquette for a kidnapping." She motioned to the door. "Please, Mr. Giant-Homicidal-Maniac, lead the way."

His eyes narrowed and he cursed under his breath, that death grip he had on her arm loosening a little. "Look, I don't—"

Pressing her palms against his chest, she took advantage and shoved as hard as she could. It was like trying to shift a brick wall. The guy was on her before she'd taken two steps toward the door. One of his huge arms wrapped around her, pulling her in close to his hard body.

"Fucking hell, female. Don't you understand? I'm trying to help you."

"What I understand is that some lunatic, hopped up on steroids, decapitated...well, I have no idea what that thing was, and is now trying to abduct me."

Eve clutched the forearm that surrounded her waist, the muscle bunched hard as stone beneath her palm. She was no match for this man. He could kill her with one flick of his thick wrist and there was nothing she could do to stop him. His warm hands slid from around her middle and drifted up her sides, leaving a hot trail of gooseflesh in their wake. Gripping her shoulders, he turned her to face him.

He looked down at her, brows drawn, determined eyes boring into her.

Suddenly she was a deer caught in headlights—right before impact. And any hope of escape she'd stupidly had sprouted wings and flew out the window with its tail tucked between its legs.

When he spoke, his voice was low, cold, filling her with dread, "Right now, I am the only thing standing between you and life as some sick fuck's slave. So unless you want to wait here for the next Orthon demon to track you down, then, after he's used you in ways that will leave you begging for death, deliver you to your new master, I suggest you come with me quietly."

Demon?

As much as she wanted to reject what this man was saying, close her eyes and convince herself this was all some crazy nightmare, she couldn't.

"Why would it want me?"

"Because you're...special," he said, voice raspy.

The hair on the back of her neck lifted. "What does that even mean?"

His expression softened a little. "I think you have an idea. Something recently happened to you? Something you don't understand, something that scares you?"

"Yes." *Oh God*. "Does this...does this have something to do with me hearing people's thoughts?"

It was the first time she'd said it out loud, and yeah, it sounded even more ridiculous than when she said it in her head. He stared back at her for a moment, opened his mouth like he was about to say something, but then he nodded again.

She swallowed hard. "You're telling the truth, aren't you?"

The muscle in his clenched jaw jumped again and he dipped his chin.

Her limbs went weak, and if it hadn't been for the guy's quick reflexes, she would have ended up in a pile on the floor. His arms came around her, strong and sure, holding her gently against his side. This time she didn't fight him off; she didn't have the energy to. Her mind swam, trying to sort through what was happening, what this all meant. Weirdly, the thought that came through the loudest was how nice it felt to be held.

The last person to touch her had been Eric, and going by his chaotic thoughts, he'd hated himself for wanting her. Had hated her even while he wanted her in some sick and twisted way.

"You good? Or do I need to carry you?" His voice was kind of terrifying, and so damn deep she felt it all the way down to her toes. Shaking her head, she stepped out of his arms.

The adrenaline racing through her blood had burned itself out, and with its departure came a kind of clarity, highlighting the enormity of her situation.

Her choices were limited. And as terrified as she was of this guy, and right now he was up there with the bogeyman, she didn't think she had any other option but to go with him.

Maybe he knew what was going on and what had caused the changes in her. She needed answers, and at that moment he seemed the lesser of two evils. That creature had tried to hurt her, and if it hadn't been for the behemoth standing in front of her, it would have succeeded. That had to count for something.

If more were on the way, she didn't want to be here when they showed up.

Still, it didn't mean he wasn't capable of removing her head the minute her back was turned, but considering the alternative? She swallowed hard, looked into his direct gaze, and searched those harsh features. Yeah, he scared the crap out of her, but he was a better prospect than the thing that dissolved into ash on her shop floor.

Swallowing down the fear still threatening to choke her, she lifted her chin. "Okay...let's go."

Four

"Wise decision." Then he was on the move again.

Eve tugged on his arm. "Hang on. First you have to promise you're not going to hurt me."

He arched a brow. "You want me to...promise?"

"Yes." Okay, she guessed that did sound kind of stupid. Like a killer's promise would mean anything in the first place.

"Jesus." He shook his head, looking frustrated. "I promise I will never physically hurt you."

"Right...well, that's good, then."

"Can we go now?"

"I don't really have a choice, do I?"

"No." The bolt on the front door slid into place as if by an invisible hand behind her.

"What the hell are you?" she whispered.

He grabbed her bag off the back of the chair, gave it to her, then took hold of her hand again and led her to the back door. "I'm a demon hunter, a warrior."

She swallowed, her mouth suddenly dry. "A demon hunter?"

He nodded and tilted his head to the side, taking her in.

The movement reminded her of something she'd watched on Animal Planet, and left an invisible trail tingling across her skin. She sucked in a sharp breath, and his gaze darted up to hers. It was intense, probing, and—God—hot. Warmth enveloped her, and to her complete horror, her body responded to the heat in those eerie green eyes. The sensation heightened further by her acute awareness of his rough, dry palm against hers.

His eyes seemed to darken oddly.

Jesus, he was big, and there was something about him so, so damn wild and terrifying like there was a monster lurking underneath, and yet as scared as she was, she had this weird compulsion to trust this...this *demon hunter*, this warrior.

He cleared his throat and motioned to the parked cars. "Which is yours?"

She pointed out her red Honda Integra. "Where are we going?"

"Give me the keys."

Digging around in her purse, she found the keys and handed them over. He led her around to the passenger side and she climbed in. He jogged around, adjusted the seat back as far as it would go, and squeezed in behind the steering wheel. It didn't make much difference; his impossibly long legs were still scrunched up in her small car.

"Where are you taking me?" she asked again.

His long fingers flexed around the steering wheel several times, and his fierce expression seemed to soften a fraction. "I'm taking you somewhere you'll be protected, until you're capable of cloaking and controlling your powers. Somewhere safe." He started the car and pulled out into the quiet street.

Powers?

"There must be another way. This whole thing is crazy. I can't just disappear. What about my business? My home?"

How could he expect her to leave everything she'd worked so hard to build?

"I know it's hard, but it's not safe for you here anymore." His voice was hard as granite, leaving no room for argument.

Was this really happening? The coastal landscape tilted and warped through the windscreen. "So you just expect me to...to leave and never come back?" she whispered.

"You don't have a choice. Do you have family, friends here?"

There he went, randomly changing the subject again, catching her off guard.

"Do you?" he asked.

She shook her head. "Um, no, not really. No one close anyway."

"Good. That's good. No one to miss you, not for a while at least."

No, she didn't have anyone. Her parents were gone, and the few friends she had throughout her life—well, acquaintances really—had never stuck around.

It wasn't much, but it was her life, and she didn't want to just walk away.

The reality of her situation hit with sudden and frightening force. Her head swam and her throat constricted like invisible hands were trying to squeeze the life out of her. Gripping the door handle, she struggled for oxygen. Black spots dotted her vision. She was in the grip of a full-on panic attack and moments away from passing out.

"I—I can't..." Her lungs felt bound. She tried to take a breath, but a tight band gripped her chest. The car jerked to an abrupt stop, her shoulders taken roughly. Hands moved up to cup her face, forcing her to look up.

"Christ, you need to calm down. You're doing yourself harm, demi." His thumb gently brushed back and forth across her jaw, and she focused on the contact. One big hand moved down to clutch hers, enveloping her fingers. Warmth radiated from him, making her skin tingle.

"Take slow, deep breaths. That's it. In and out. Good girl." His tone was gentle, and after a few minutes of listening to the deep, raspy timbre of his voice, her heart rate slowed. That intoxicating, spicy scent hit, and she gasped down a much-needed deep breath. It overrode the fear and somehow broke through the terror.

His expression was still hard, but his jaw wasn't clamped shut and his eyes had softened slightly.

She pulled her hand from his, needing space. The way he affected her was almost as terrifying as the man himself. "My name's Eve. Not Demi."

"Okay," he said, watching her carefully.

The hand that had been holding hers dropped to one of his jean-clad monster thighs, and he rubbed it against the denim like he was trying to rub her touch away.

"Why do you keep calling me that? Why are you here and what's happening to me? Please, I don't understand any of this."

He searched her features for several long seconds, unnerving her. "There is a reason you can hear people's thoughts. You are more...you are...different." He shifted in his seat. "Demi is not a name. It's what you are. A demi-demon. Half-human and half-demon."

What?

She shook her head in denial.

No.

How can that be?

Yes, she'd always known there was something different about her, in the last few months more than ever. But a demon? No.

She shook her head. "Demons aren't real. They don't exist." The logical side of her brain tried to argue, but she'd seen one with her own two eyes, hadn't she? Right there in her shop.

The memory of that disgusting creature caused her to shudder. He was telling the truth. There was no denying it, no matter how badly she wanted to.

She hadn't let herself believe she was truly hearing people's thoughts, but the voices, the words that flew through her mind, they hadn't been hers. And after last night with Eric, she knew it was the truth.

"Mrs. Jensen was a demon?"

"No. Orthon have the ability to take on other forms."

This new bit of information threatened to throw her back into full panic mode. "Orthon? I'm one of those awful monsters?"

He took her hand awkwardly, again like he didn't really want to touch her. "They're a special breed, born trackers. They're lower level demons, the vermin of the demon world. You're not one of them."

"What am I?" she forced out, not even sure she wanted to know.

"I can only guess. But your sire was most likely a Pathos demon. They sense and are drawn to high emotion, usually suffering."

"Oh God." Her stomach churned. "Will I...will that happen to me?"

"No, Eve." Her name rumbled from his chest in that deep, coarse voice, and she shivered. "Demon DNA mutates when mixed with human. In your case, you developed telepathy." He trapped her with his stare. "Your power makes you very rare in the demon world. No full-blooded demons possess your ability. And only a handful of demi have ever been born with your gift."

"That's why I'm being hunted?"

"Yes."

"This isn't a gift. It's a curse."

"You'll learn to embrace it," he said with certainty.

The idea of living with this thing without going insane—she wasn't convinced. "And you're here to...what? Protect me?"

"Yes. And I promise I won't let anything hurt you. But you have to do as I say."

She didn't have much choice but to trust him. "Are you a demon, too?"

"I'm half demon."

"So you're half-human, like me?"

"No."

Okay, by the cold don't-even-go-there look on his face, he wasn't about to share. That was fine with her. The fact that there were demons running around in the first place, and she was one of them, was more than enough to take in for now.

"Your name? You haven't told me your name." A sudden need to know in whose hands she'd placed her life seemed extremely important.

His throat worked before he spoke, Adam's apple sliding up and down his thick throat. "Lazarus."

Tingles danced across her scalp at the way he said it, the sound of that voice. And she felt breathless again for some unknown reason. She cleared her throat. "Lazarus," she repeated, letting it roll off her tongue, liking the feel of it. "I suppose I should thank you, then, for helping me."

"That's not necessary." He looked more than a little uncomfortable.

Why should her thanks make him uncomfortable? The urge to reach out and touch him, to soothe the frown lines creasing his brow was almost too hard to resist.

Eve ignored the crazy impulse. Despite his having saved her life and calming her during her panic attack, she couldn't let her guard down. Lazarus continued to watch her closely, silently. No doubt afraid she'd flip out again. The silence pressed in around her. The only sounds were coming from the street, muffled inside the enclosed space of her car.

That's all.

Her mind was utterly silent.

"I can't hear you," she whispered.

A dark brow lifted in question.

"Your thoughts, I mean."

"I'm immune. My job is to find your kind when they come into their powers, get them to safety, make sure they're not captured. I couldn't do my job if, for example, you could hear what was going on in my head right now."

The look he aimed at her was so different from the fierce expression he'd had plastered on his face since walking into her shop, and what she saw in his eyes should have terrified her. But alarmingly, what she felt was quite the opposite.

"I can see how that could be a problem." The tightness in her shoulders eased despite all the unguarded intensity he was throwing her way. "I have to admit, the silence is nice."

Although just then it would have been useful to know what he was thinking. Her mind had been crowded for the last month, full of things she could have happily gone the rest of her life never knowing. She'd been positive she was losing her mind.

"Until you're able to control your power, and as long you're beside me, I can block it for you."

"You can do that?"

"Yes."

That kind of freaked her out. What else could he do? "So you're pretty powerful, huh?"

A small nod.

She glanced out the window, took in the familiar scenery, and pain sliced through her. "What will happen to my store, my house?"

"Eventually we'll set you up with everything you need to start a new life." His gaze skittered away. "Maybe once you've mastered your power you can have another bookstore somewhere," he said as if that would fix everything.

"But not here." Her heart squeezed. Leaving her store and never coming back to this place, a place where she'd created a happy, if lonely existence, physically hurt. Once again her life was out of her hands and she was at the mercy of someone else. "Can I get some of my things?"

"It's too dangerous."

Eve turned back to him, desperate for him to understand, and reached out, resting her hand on his forearm. She sucked in a breath as little tingles shot up her arm. Lazarus's eyes flared and the muscles under her fingers bunched hard.

His gaze dropped, zeroing on where she touched him.

She quickly pulled her hand back, curling her fingers into a fist. "Y-you can't expect me to just leave everything, to just walk away without a backward glance." His gaze lifted back to hers, intense, his mouth a hard line. He was about to refuse her again. "Please, Lazarus."

He continued to stare at her, and his knuckles turned white as he gripped the steering wheel. Finally, he muttered under his breath, "Shit." He started the car again and pulled into the street. "We have to be quick."

Her shoulders sagged in relief. "Thank you."

They pulled into her driveway a short time later.

"Wait here." Lazarus took the keys from the ignition and opened the door, but paused, turning back. "And, Eve, don't try to run. You'd be putting yourself at risk, and I'd have to chase after you. That would piss me off. You don't want to do that."

No. She most certainly did not want to do that. He didn't move, continuing to watch her, she guessed waiting for some kind of confirmation from her. Unable to do anything else, she gave a jerky nod. With that, he climbed out, jogged up to the house, and went inside. He was gone less than a minute before he reappeared and motioned her in. She got out and hurried up the path. As soon as she stepped inside, he ushered her toward the bedroom.

"Be quick." Somehow he managed to make his rough voice sound almost gentle.

Sadness overwhelmed her as she entered her room. But she swallowed it down ruthlessly. She couldn't indulge in her misery just yet because once the pain broke free, she wasn't sure she'd be able to rein it back in.

Slipping off Lazarus's jacket, she laid it on the bed, grabbed a bag from the top shelf of her closet, and got to work stuffing in as many of her clothes as she could.

She was coming out of the bathroom when she spotted the thick stack of photos on her dresser. Among them was her favorite, taken two weeks before her parents died in a house fire. Whoever had taken it had captured so much joy, so much love between them it was still hard to look at all these years later.

God, she missed them.

From the doorway, Lazarus cleared his throat. She glanced up. Tension lined his brow and creased the corners of his eyes and mouth, conveying the need for haste without saying a word.

"Right, sorry," she murmured. "I was just...my parents." She held up the photos.

He moved closer and looked at the pictures over her shoulder. "I thought you didn't have a family?"

"They died when I was a kid."

He frowned, those creases between his eyes coming back. "Who took over your care?"

"My aunt took me in for a little while, but they passed me on to someone else pretty quickly. I spent my childhood being passed from one foster family to the next." She turned to look up at him. "It was the demon thing, wasn't it?"

He shoved his hands in his pockets. "It happens sometimes, humans sensing it in children, that there's something different about them, something that keeps them at a distance. Usually in children who end up with powers like yours."

"Like mine?"

"All powers are different, some are just more potent." His expression softened slightly. "They wouldn't have understood their...aversion to you."

Eve smiled at his attempt to sugarcoat the fact that her aunt and her family had hated to be around her, the same for the foster families she lived with. It had been hard—God, it had never gotten any easier—and once or twice throughout her life, in her darkest moments, she'd even contemplated ending it. "I always thought it was because I was adopted, because I wasn't their blood that they sent me away. I guess I can't blame them for their reaction to me now. They had a demon in their home."

It explained the changes in Eric, why he'd acted the way he had around her. As a kid, she hadn't understood why nobody liked her. She'd spent all her time trying to please people. If she was a good girl, if she did as she was told and never made waves that maybe they would love her, that they'd keep her. It never happened. She'd spent those lonely years sitting at the edge of the room, watching from the outside while everyone else had fun—usually with a bag of cookies in her hand. Food became her comfort. Eating something delicious made her feel good, filled the emotional void in her life. Still did to a certain extent.

When she looked back up, the tenderness softening Lazarus's expression startled her.

"They were assholes," he said. "Whatever way you look at it, they shouldn't have treated you that way. I don't give a fuck how they felt."

Oh god, she'd blurted everything out loud, about her loneliness, her issues with food. Her face heated. "It's okay...I..." She swallowed whatever she'd been about to say, then a thought occurred to her. "Why didn't my parents have the same aversion to me? They loved me, Lazarus, I know they did."

He watched her carefully. "My guess? At least one of your adoptive parents must have had demon blood. They would have easily sensed it in you as an infant."

"They were like me?" Stunned, she stared at the picture in her hand.

"That's my guess."

Would they have told her who she was? Helped her through this transition? God, how different her life would have been.

Carefully, she placed the photos in her bag. "I know this sounds crazy, but knowing that, somehow it...helps." She smiled at the big male standing in front of her. "Thank you."

He stilled, unnaturally so. His gaze dropped to her mouth for several long seconds then darted back to her eyes. He looked conflicted, God, tormented.

Her hand lifted, was moving to him before she knew what she was doing. She wanted—no, needed—to touch him, had the insane compulsion to try and ease the torment rolling off him in waves, to make some kind of connection.

Impossibly, he stilled further when she pressed her hand to his biceps. He was hard as steel beneath her palm, like he'd been honed from marble. And like last time, something happened between them. Tiny zaps of electricity seemed to flow from his body to hers, lifting goose bumps all over her skin.

His eyes looked different, had somehow changed. She felt...God, trapped, unable to look away from the luminous, swirling pools of emerald. The color flickered dark then light, like a flashlight being switched on and off behind his irises.

She moved closer.

He shook his head, silently telling her to stay back. "We have to go," he ground out.

Captivated, almost mesmerized by the unearthly green staring down at her, Eve jumped and cried out in alarm when her phone started ringing. Lazarus's big frame went still. The vibrant emerald depths holding her frozen darkened, slowly eclipsed by midnight, causing the whites of his eyes to stand out in stark relief.

"Ignore it."

His quietly spoken words had the same effect as a gunshot, breaking her from her trance. Tension radiated from him, and the way his jaw had hardened, it was like he was fighting for control. He was back to being the warrior, and it was terrifying.

And as much as she wanted to turn and run as far and fast she could, she ignored the urge, no matter how tempting it was. Because she believed him. He was the only one who could keep her safe.

At the moment, this man, demon, whatever he was, appeared to be her only hope.

And the longer they stayed, the more danger they were in.

Five

Eve's little pink tongue darted out again, moistening her lower lip. He inwardly groaned.

Jesus. All she'd done was touch his arm and he'd been close to jumping her. The curvy little demi in front of him called to his demon, like she'd tuned into the fucker's frequency and was calling him home to the mother ship.

His need to mark her, to claim her, had reared up, taken him by the balls, and he'd been damn close to giving in to it, to throwing her on that bed and taking what was his. Just her touch had lit up every molecule in his body. Christ, it had turned his limbs to mush.

His craving for this female was illogical in its intensity, but then from what little he'd seen of the mating process, logic wasn't a factor when a warrior found his female.

Lazarus willed his heated body to cool, more than a little unsettled by his reaction to Eve. Going by the expression on her face, he wasn't the only one.

Her lips were kind of puffy from her biting at them, and he licked his own, imagining her taste, the warmth and feel of them against his.

He gritted his teeth, stifling another groan.

The urge to claim her came from a primal place deep inside. A part of him that recognized her as his, and it was screwing with his head, not to mention his body.

Hell, maybe he should just fuck her and get it over with?

Taking her now would solve a lot of his troubles. His cock definitely had no problem getting behind the idea and strained painfully against the stiff denim of his jeans.

Eyes bright, cheeks flushed, Eve gazed up at him. Her lips slightly parted, begged to be sucked and nibbled. Hair like silken ebony waves tumbled over her shoulders, and he barely resisted the urge to reach out and touch it.

Was this how she'd look in his bed after he'd fucked her? Images flooded his mind, and this time a groan did slip past his lips.

Her eyes widened and she stepped away from him. "Lazarus?"

Good work, asshole. Now she's back to being frightened of you.

One touch from her and he'd lost focus again.

This wasn't how this was supposed to happen. He'd been with her for less than an hour and already he was struggling to keep his shit together and had put her in danger. As tempting as she was, he had to remain fixed on his original path. He couldn't allow this force between them to win. Because this wasn't for him. He couldn't keep her.

"We have to leave," he said before putting even more space between them. Keeping his head straight was getting more and more difficult around Eve. He needed to conduct the rest of this mission as he always did—with cold efficiency.

She nodded and went back to biting her damn bottom lip.

He tore his eyes from her, not sure how to handle this, any of it. How was he going to explain what she was to him? How did you tell someone they were the key to your salvation, your only hope? That your future and that of the free world depended on her leaving everything she'd ever known and accepting him as her mate.

A mate who would leave as soon as he'd taken what he wanted.

A mate who could never love her.

Eve would not be another sacrifice to this war. And that's what would happen if he kept her. If he allowed her to get close.

People who got close to him suffered for it. They got hurt.

He'd do whatever it took to prevent that from happening again.

He glanced over at her. Keeping his shit tight wasn't going to be easy. Besides having to deal with his overwhelming physical attraction to her, he feared his possession was moving at a faster rate. Time was almost up, and he had to find a way to explain the reason he'd come for her without sending her running.

What if she refuses you?

He couldn't think about that now. Getting her to safety had to be his number one priority. The shadows had crept in earlier, the darkness trying to take another piece of his soul. Eve had seen it, the difference in his eyes as he fought to restrain his demon. He just had to hold off for a bit longer.

And hope like hell she'd accept him.

Ignoring her questioning gaze, he collected her bags and headed for the door. She looked around her home for the last time, faltering as they passed a large bookshelf, gazing up at the tattered, well-read books.

"Some of them belonged to my mother," she whispered, like she could hear his unspoken question.

Lazarus didn't bother with false platitudes. Nothing he could say would soften the blow. As much as it hurt now, she'd get over it. She had to.

Swallowing down guilt, an emotion he knew all too well, he steered her back out the front door. Eve climbed into the car and stared out the window as they drove away. He guessed she was attempting to absorb every detail of the small coastal town she'd called home. But eventually, no matter how hard she tried, most of the memories would fade. Over time they would lose their sharp lines, become fuzzy and distant. They always did.

An image of Scarlet entered Lazarus's mind. Small and scared. A mass of wild red curls around her grubby face. She'd stared up at him in awe, and instantly stolen his heart. He'd vowed to protect her from that moment on. Even after she'd grown into a strong, independent female—even after she found her own mate—he'd still seen her as his little girl. She might not have been his blood, but she was his, his child in every way that mattered.

She always would be.

He was wrong, some memories never faded, and he was grateful for the cutting reminder. He couldn't afford to make the same mistakes twice.

Any rogue demon could have sensed Eve's powers and come after her. Lazarus should have expected the attack from that Orthon. He should have damn well been prepared.

Tobias would be keeping tabs on him; he had no doubt about that. The male wouldn't back off, not until he had his revenge. He'd once been their brother. In Lazarus's heart, he still was, even though he was lost to them, lost in his own darkness.

Lazarus ignored the inevitable slice of pain that rode shotgun with memories of Tobias and Scarlet; let it settle, cut deeper. It was his price to pay.

He deserved to suffer for what he'd done. For failing them.

Eve didn't, though, not for his sins.

He gripped the steering wheel tighter. What if Tobias had

gotten close? He could have figured out who Eve was to Lazarus. So far, the other male had been messing with him, biding his time. This was all some sick game to him. But if he had the tiniest notion that Eve was his mate, his fallen brother wouldn't hesitate to use her to get to him.

Tobias had turned his back on them long before Lazarus or his brothers knew what he planned to do. After Scarlet's death, after Tobias lost her, his mate, their brother had willingly embraced the demon half of his DNA, letting go of that part of himself that held compassion, a sense of right from wrong—the ability to care for another being. He chose darkness, walked away from his family, and in doing so declared war.

After Tobias left, Laz and his brothers had done their best to block the connection that still tied them together, but that connection worked both ways, and the evil shit he was sending back was seriously fucking with all of them, was tipping the scale toward darkness. The only way to sever it permanently was death, and since they couldn't find him, blocking it, or trying to at least, was their only option.

What they'd managed to do had hindered his ability, but it wasn't enough. He was using their connection to help him source the demi he could no longer track on his own. If he found out who Eve was, she'd be that much more desirable to him. Shit, the Orthon back at her shop could have belonged to him.

He glanced at Eve. She had no clue just how important she was.

She sat rigid in her seat, eyes wide as they passed a sign asking them to *visit again soon.* And dammit, he wished he knew what to say to make this easier for her. But anything he said would be a lie, because as bad as it was now, it was only going to get a whole lot worse.

She took a shaky breath and turned to him. "So where to now?"

The female was strong, a quality she'd need to draw on more and more over the coming weeks. "We have a plane to catch."

She shifted in her seat. "Where are you taking me?"

"Roxburgh, New York."

Her fingers tightened on the armrest, her only outward sign of distress. "Why are you taking me there?"

"We have a compound. It's secluded, outside the city." He glanced over at her. "Away from prying eyes."

"We?"

"My brothers and I."

The color in her cheeks drained, some of that fire he'd seen in her along with it. Defeat, and though she tried to hide it, fear, was now clear in her eyes. "What will you do to me there?"

Yeah, he'd more than earned her distrust and she'd be wise to remain wary of him.

But as she stared up at him, lost and frightened, he heard himself say, "Have I hurt you? In any way?"

She flinched at his harsh tone and shook her head.

"And I don't plan to."

Her eyes hit his. "You're right. I'm sorry."

He wanted to kick his own ass. She was afraid of him. Just because he felt the pull of this screwed-up connection didn't mean she did. And, boy, did he feel it. Deep down he knew guilt fueled his words, because hurting her was exactly what he'd have to do.

Moderating his tone, he tried to reassure her. "I can help you, Eve."

She sent him a look so full of hope and fragile trust that he wanted to take his own eyes out. It hurt to look at her when she stared at him like that, and before he could stop himself, words were tumbling from his mouth without thought. "I promise I will never do anything that you don't want me to." His voice had turned harsh as images of exactly what he did want to do flashed through his mind.

He dragged a hand through his hair.

Why had he said that? Made her a promise he might not be able to keep.

She remained quiet for a few seconds, eyes downcast, staring at her fingers as she twisted them in her lap. "I'm glad I have you here to help me through this." Her cheeks turned a pretty shade of pink. Then she smiled at him, tentative and sweet.

An erratic thumping sensation stuttered to life in the middle of his chest. The feeling was so foreign it took a moment to work out what had caused it. Any minute now Frankenstein would jump up from the back seat and start yelling, "It's alive! It's alive!"

He clenched his teeth. *Unacceptable.*

The useless damn organ had shriveled to nothing long ago, and that's the way he liked it. The way he intended to keep it. Dead.

Unable to look at her another second, he concentrated on driving.

She remained quiet the rest of the way, besides the odd question about the compound and what to expect when they arrived. He couldn't help but be impressed with the way she was handling the situation, a situation that most took a hell of a lot harder than the feisty, intelligent female sitting beside him.

He was so fucked.

Six

Numb. There was no other way to describe how Eve felt.

Though, one good thing had come from this nightmare. For the first time in a long time, her mind was utterly silent.

Since Lazarus had come for her, she'd enjoyed relief from all that noise, the multitude of thoughts stomping across her battered psyche, and it gave her hope there might be another way. That she might actually be able to gain control over this thing.

The busy Roxburgh traffic thinned as they moved out of the city. A guy named James, also a demi-demon, had been at the airport waiting for them with a car when they'd landed. Lazarus had barely greeted the guy before he'd taken the keys and gotten behind the wheel. He hadn't said a word since. The plane ride had been much the same. He'd not said more than two words, and scowled the entire flight.

"I'm one of the trainers," James was saying. "Once I mastered my powers the hunters were so heartbroken at the idea of me leaving, they offered me a job." He turned to face the back seat and grinned at her. "Grown men crying...never a pretty sight. What choice did I have? I stayed."

Lazarus growled.

Eve smiled back. James seemed nice, not terrifying at all. Maybe this wouldn't be so terrible.

She'd given up wishing this was nothing but a nightmare. What she'd seen of Lazarus's powers so far—along with her close encounter of the hideous, freaky-eyed monster kind—pointed away from a psychotic episode and made all the crazy stuff that had happened to her impossible to deny.

So she'd made a decision during their flight. She would handle this like any other move she'd had in her life, which had been numerous while growing up. She would accept her new circumstances. Fighting or crying wouldn't help, it never did. She could do this. She had to do this. She would adapt, like she always did. No problem.

Being forced from her home, taken to a new city by a man she didn't know anything about—while on the run from demons—which it turns out would like nothing more than to make her their slave.

Yep, cakewalk.

Information overload didn't cover it, and surprisingly, it was Lazarus's strong, silent presence that had kept her mind from short-circuiting. It was crazy, and she had no idea why exactly, but she trusted him to keep her safe.

They drove for another twenty minutes before the scenery changed and they entered some kind of industrial area. They passed old warehouses and empty lots. The whole area looked postapocalyptic, or at least what she imagined it would look like. No signs of life, everything abandoned and run-down.

At the end of the block, the car turned into a short road and they carried on until Lazarus pulled to a stop in front of a set of steel gates. They were at least ten feet tall, and there was a security camera mounted to the side aimed at them.

He slid down the window and pressed his thumb to a small pad.

The gates jolted loudly then groaned into action.

As they slid open, Eve strained to see what was hidden behind the monstrosities.

Oh…wow.

And not a good *wow*; a where-the-hell-have-you-brought-me *wow*. A turn-me-around-and-take-me-anywhere-else *wow*.

The building on the other side was like something from a horror movie, where the serial killer took his victim to torture them before he finished them off. Besides varying shades of gray, the only other colors she could see were streaks of rust bleeding from large steel framework and washed-out green from the dust-covered weeds struggling up between the cracked concrete that surrounded the place.

Eve shivered. The huge, multistory building loomed ahead, casting an ominous shadow that seemed to stretch toward them like a monster about to devour its prey. Eve actually sucked in a breath when they moved from the light and into the darkness.

She tilted her head back, looking all the way up. The windows had been boarded, and some of the iron cladding hung loose, swinging drunkenly in the breeze, squeaking loudly then clattering against the building.

"What is this place?" she whispered.

"Home," Lazarus said without looking back.

Her stomach flipped, and the nerves already tying her belly in knots tightened. Doors slid open in the wall ahead of them and the car tilted forward down a steep ramp into the bowels of the place.

Sensor lights flickered on moments later. They were in a parking garage. Several SUVs like the one they were in were parked there, and a couple of large dangerous-looking bikes were against the far wall.

Lazarus climbed out, came around, and pulled her door open. When he motioned her to follow, she realized she'd just been sitting there, too afraid to move.

Eve scrambled out and had to power walk to keep up with his long strides. He stopped in front of an ancient elevator she guessed wouldn't meet any type of safety code, and she and James walked in after him. He pushed a button, for what floor she had no idea since all the numbers had worn off, and the elevator jarred into action. She stumbled, grabbing for the wall. Lazarus's hand shot out, catching her arm to steady her so fast the movement was almost blur.

There went those weird little zaps again, right where his hand touched her.

She ignored them and focused on the numbers above the doors as they lit up. It ground to a halt on the fifth. Lazarus stepped closer, his hand moving to the small of her back. God, the immense heat radiating off his palm seemed to sear an imprint of that big paw right into her skin through her dress.

"Home sweet home," James muttered as the doors slid open.

It took her brain several seconds to register what she was seeing. The interior was nothing like the shabby exterior. It was clean and modern with a lot of chrome and glass. The floors were a shiny black, and a subtle hint of lemon floor cleaner scented the air. It had an institutional feel and made her nervous all over again.

Several computers were set up around the room, and there was an entire wall covered with monitors. She recognized some of the images from the outside of the building and the underground parking garage.

The three of them stepped out of the elevator. "What is all this?" She turned toward the silent male beside her.

"Our main control area. Besides security for the

compound, we also have a visual link to most of Roxburgh and the surrounding areas."

"Why do you need cameras?" He'd told her how his kind tracked the demi-demons they saved. He'd called it a sort of built-in alarm. All this seemed...well, she didn't know what to make of any of it.

"Bringing in demi isn't all we do." He motioned to the cameras. "Sometimes we need modern technology like everyone else."

That cryptic answer told her nothing, but Lazarus seemed tense and she got the feeling it wasn't the time to push for more.

"Are there other demi-demons here like me?"

"The second and third floors house our demi. First, we have a training area, gym. Above the control room, there's a common area and cafeteria of sorts for those who wish to socialize. The fourth floor is apartments, mine and my brothers." He turned to her then, finally looking at her again. "You can find me there if you need me."

His voice had deepened when he said the last, and the gravel in it had her shivering again.

She nodded, unable to make her mouth work all of a sudden.

That intense gaze moved over her. "Are you cold again?"

Eve swallowed and forced herself to answer. "No, I'm not cold."

His head tilted to the side in that animalistic way, gaze boring into hers, and whatever he saw caused it to darken.

She quickly looked away. The fierceness in his eyes made her heart race and her head swim in a way she did not understand.

"Your room," he said suddenly. "I'll get someone to show you to your room."

Lazarus led Eve out of the control room, trying to keep his reaction to that little shiver, the way she'd been looking at him, on the down-low. Maybe what he'd been feeling wasn't totally one-sided? Maybe not. Whatever that was, no way she'd understand it, and no way would he take advantage of it.

No matter how much of a game-changer it would be in the war with Tobias. Mating her when she was confused and without all the facts wasn't something he was comfortable with. Not one fucking bit.

He ignored the throb of his groin and steered her out into the hall, more than a little pleased that all his brothers hadn't been there for a meet and greet when they arrived. They were intimidating individually; confronted with more than one of them at a time would have freaked Eve out.

And, shit, if Chaos had seen that little shiver, the way Eve had looked at Lazarus, the prick would have locked them in a room together, mated by morning, and have Lazarus out hunting Tobias by nightfall.

The sound of boots hitting the stairs as they approached them echoed up the stairwell, and he gritted his teeth, sensing his brother before the doors opened. Thankfully, it was Kryos and not Zenon. With his angelic blond curls, warm brown eyes, and handsome face, Kryos was by far the least threatening of them all, at least in looks. Being mated helped. Not only did mating mean he had control of his demon, he at least knew how to talk to a woman without scaring the hell out of her.

He smiled. "Laz." His gaze slid to Eve. "And this is?"

"Eve," Lazarus said.

Kryos's smile turned to a grin and he held out his hand. "Nice to meet you." His gaze slid back to Laz. "I hope my surly bro here is making you feel welcome."

Eve chuckled.

Laz scowled at the bastard. "Is Meredith here? I thought she might she show Eve around." His brother's mate would do a better job of making Eve feel welcome than he could.

Kryos frowned a little. "I thought you might..."

"Can she or not?"

"Yeah, sure. I'll get her to meet Eve downstairs in a few." Kryos met his gaze. "Have you told her everything she needs to know...about how we do things here?"

Laz stared back, not missing what his brother was asking. "No, there'll be time for that later. I think she's had enough information for one day."

Kryos lifted his chin. *Message received.*

At least he'd keep his trap shut. And as soon as Eve was safe in her room, he'd be sending out a mass text to the others to keep their mouths shut as well. He needed to do this his own way, and he sure as hell didn't need a reminder that time wasn't something he had a lot of.

Kryos left to get his mate, and Lazarus led Eve to the stairs.

An hour later, Eve was in her room, Meredith still with her, and Laz was in his apartment, wearing out a strip in his carpet. What the hell did he do now? What was the best way to approach this: take her somewhere, like a date? Try and win her over?

Christ.

He clenched his fists. Winning her over wasn't the goal here. He didn't want to trick her into this, make her believe they were something that they weren't. Make her think he could give her something he knew he never could. Honesty was his only option. He needed to just lay that shit out and hope for the best.

"Hey, Eve, you're my mate. That means you'll be tied to me

for eternity, but I don't actually want you for more than one night. So yeah, wanna come back to my room and fuck?"

Who wouldn't fall at someone's feet after that declaration?

The knock at his door was not unexpected. The only surprise was it hadn't come sooner.

He yanked the door open and Chaos, their unofficial leader, walked through and prowled across the room.

Chaos stopped in front of Lazarus. "Does she know?"

"Not yet."

"So you're not mated?"

Lazarus stiffened and barely resisted the urge to decorate the guy's face with a matching pair of black eyes. "Can I have more than a goddamned day? I'd like Eve to get used to me before I fucking jump her."

The persistent hum he'd woken up with vibrating in the back of his skull, plus the uncontrollable craving for the female now in this building, made him aware of how naive he'd been.

He thought he could take her, make her his mate, then leave. But it wouldn't be that easy, not any of it. His life was not his own. The greater good, it always came first. He'd been created to fight, to protect mankind. His *feelings* never came into it. It had always been that way.

Which meant he hadn't even factored Eve's feelings into any of this, how this fucking nightmare would affect her.

Chaos visibly tensed. "We don't have time to fuck around, and until you finish this, we're all at risk. Diemos and his brethren are just waiting for their chance."

By finishing this, Chaos meant making Eve his mate. His brother was even blinder than Lazarus when it came to duty. The male was made of stone.

As for Diemos—the most powerful male in Hell—Lazarus would do whatever was necessary to keep his brothers away from that sadistic bastard. The guy had once been Lucifer's most trusted confidant, his right-hand demon, his favorite.

Until Diemos betrayed him and cast Lucifer out. Word had it Lucifer refused to kill him, fuck knew why, and instead decided if Diemos wanted the throne so badly he could have it.

The king of Hell was currently MIA.

Lazarus knew it was hopeless, but he had to ask. "There's no other way?"

"You know there isn't." Chaos's gaze held an unyielding determination and a grain of pity that set Lazarus's teeth on edge. "Diemos already has Tobias on the payroll. And the way our brother wants you hurting, you know he's coming for you next. We can't let that happen."

Yeah, T wanted him next, and Lazarus deserved that and more. Shame he couldn't let Tobias have at it. But that wasn't an option. He wasn't the only one that would suffer if he didn't do this.

Chaos's gaze locked on his. "I know how tight you and T were, and I know this is gonna fuck with your head, but we need to sever the bond Tobias has with us before he takes the rest of us down with him. I don't know about you, but I don't get off on the idea of being Diemos's new plaything."

Lazarus rested his hands on his hips and stared at the ground. It had to be done, there was no other choice. But the idea of breaking that bond with their brother fucking killed him. T would still be with them if it wasn't for him. Scarlet would have walked through those doors to greet Lazarus's mate with open arms and a wide smile on her face.

Eve could have been his.

Instead, his brother was lost forever. Scarlet was dead. And Eve's welcome was a ticking time bomb of a mate who she'd end up hating when all this was over.

"Suck it up," his brother said. "How bad can it be? Kryos seems happy enough. That bastard's always mooning after Meredith."

Kryos was the only mated male among them. His demon

was leashed, which meant Tobias's deflection didn't pose a risk to him. He'd found Meredith close to fifty years ago, and the pair had been loved up ever since.

Lazarus shook his head. Chaos had no idea he planned to leave after he and Eve were mated. Lazarus didn't need to live there at the compound to do his job, but his brother wouldn't see it that way. "Right."

Chaos shrugged, actually grinning. "I've never heard him complain."

"You'll wanna be next then?" Laz said, knowing the answer before Chaos spoke.

The guy's grin disappeared.

"Yeah, that's what I thought."

"Look, if that female can help keep your shit under control, your head straight, long enough to take out T?" He shrugged again, but Laz didn't miss the pain that flashed across his features with those words. "I figure it's a small price to pay."

Lazarus didn't comment. It felt like a fucking mammoth price to pay to him. He truly didn't give a shit what happened to him. Not anymore. But Eve, whose life he was about to destroy, that was another matter.

Chaos clapped him on the shoulder. "You have no choice, brother."

"I know," he gritted out.

"Good. Don't fuck it up."

"You'll be the first to know."

If he screwed this up, they'd all be a pack of mindless, bloodthirsty demons and Diemos's new playthings within a few weeks.

So, yeah, fucking this up wasn't an option.

Seven

Lazarus groaned and rolled to his back. Fuck, his eyes felt gritty and dry, his body on fire, limbs achy. He hadn't slept more than a few minutes at a time—how could he when he felt Eve just a floor below him? His demon had mentally paced all night, roaring and whimpering, trying to take the driver's seat and go to her.

He rubbed his hands over his face and jerked back the covers. And then there was this...

He looked down his body and winced. His dick lay against his stomach and was so pumped full of blood it was fucking purple. He didn't think he'd ever been this hard in his life. Christ, his balls throbbed as well. He couldn't leave his room like this.

Fuuuuck.

The ache intensified, and he groaned again.

Eve had just woken up.

He knew it. Somehow, he just knew it.

The surge of power that came from her had him undulating on the bed, teeth gritted, his damn eyes rolling back in his head. He dropped his hand to his cock, hissing when he wrapped his fingers around it. He felt like molten steel under his fingers. He squeezed tighter as another wave reached him. He spread his legs wider, kicking the covers away. They felt like sandpaper against his skin. One foot hit the floor with a thump, the other dug into the mattress as he stroked his dick hard and fast, desperate for release.

The waves of power kept coming and it kept him right there, hovering between pleasure and pain, grunting and straining, sweating all over his sheets, close to losing his damn mind.

Then another surge came, so damn powerful his spine torqued and a roar tore from his throat. He came in powerful spurts of scalding hot come, splashing his stomach and chest and seemed to go on and on until he was shaking so hard his fucking teeth were chattering.

When he was spent, he collapsed back, gasping for breath.

What the fuck?

Christ, something had caused her power to do that, those intense surges. Was Eve all right?

His mind instantly conjured up all kinds of scenarios, most of them bad. Lazarus quickly cleaned himself off with the sheet and stumbled out of bed on shaky legs, shoving on his clothes.

He was out the door and in the elevator a few minutes later, and banged on her door as soon as he reached it. Her powers had calmed now. Had died down from a raging storm to gentle waves, and the feeling of biting down on exposed electrical wires had dropped to pleasant tingles over his skin.

He reached down and adjusted his dick when he heard her moving toward the door. Not surprising he was hard again. He'd been hard since she came onto his radar.

The click of the lock came next and he stood straighter when the door opened.

Eve stood there looking flushed and disheveled, her eyes wide and glassy, lower lip red and swollen.

"What the fuck just happened?" Lazarus said, pushing his way into her smaller one-room apartment. He strode to the bathroom and shoved the door open. "Has someone been in here? Did they hurt you? Frighten you?"

She didn't answer and he spun back to her, finally taking in the rest of her. She was wearing a robe, the belt tied tight, enhancing her bountiful curves. His gaze moved back up to her face, the color on her cheeks, the way her lower lip was darker, puffy from biting it, the way her black hair was down and a little wild.

She looked recently fucked.

A growl tore up his throat as he spun to the bed, to its rumpled covers, the pillow knocked to the floor. She'd been with someone? There was no room for anyone under the bed. He strode over and checked the small closet. Empty.

His demon snarled, hating the thought just as much, and reared up, scenting the air. Only one. Eve. Then it hit him, a scent so fucking tantalizing, so intoxicating it almost knocked him on his ass.

Sexual desire.

He spun back to her still by the door, face pink with embarrassment, and he knew.

She'd just come, hard. Just like he had.

Those delicate fingers, currently gripping her robe closed, had been between her thighs, had moved over her slick, hot flesh, bringing her to orgasm at the same time as he had one floor above her. And he'd felt it. Christ, had he felt it.

She cleared her throat. "I..." She swallowed. "I don't know...there's nothing...nothing wrong."

Lazarus's demon fought harder, so hard he felt the stretch and pull under his skin, with the desire to shift. He needed to get the hell out of there.

"I just, I thought I heard something. I'll go." He strode to the door, moving toward her, and another wave of her scent hit him, stronger. She was still turned on. What he wouldn't give to lay her on that bed and bury his face between her thighs, to taste her, to make her come against his tongue over and over before he finally sank inside her.

"Lazarus?" He jolted and looked down at her. He was right in front of her now, hand poised about to touch her, and he barely remembered taking the final steps to reach her.

"Are you okay?" she asked, a slight rasp to her voice that didn't help one fucking bit.

His hand shot out and he grabbed the handle, yanking the door open. "Yeah, fine." *Leave before you do something you shouldn't, before you take her on this floor right damn now.*

Before you shift into your demon form and scare the hell out of both of you.

Lazarus strode out of the room, took the elevator to the control room, and yanked off his shirt as soon as he reached the balcony. The equinox was fast approaching—that had to be it, the reason his control was slipping. He needed to get away from here. Now. His wings sprouted from his back, allowing himself to partially shift, and he dove off the side, taking to the skies.

He flew for hours, but no matter how far he went he could still feel her.

What the fuck was he going to do?

"You're doing great, Eve," James said, smile encouraging. "Now let's try again, okay?"

Eve wasn't so sure. She felt like she sucked at this. They'd been there all afternoon and still she couldn't block him.

"Close your eyes," he said. "That's it. Can you see the door?"

"Yes." She envisioned a solid wooden door with heavy iron bolts and hinges, one she could close and lock, as his thoughts filtered into her mind. He was reciting the alphabet. Listening to him was so different than when she'd had Eric in her head. She didn't know if it was a human/demon thing, but James's thoughts were crisp, focused, not jumbled and scattered. They didn't make her want to scream, so that was a plus.

"Okay, now I want you to start closing it. I want you to block that doorway and lock it shut. Lock me out, Eve."

He finished the alphabet and started on something else; she had no idea what it was. She opened her eyes. He had a book open in front of him, and he grinned and flashed her the cover. Science fiction by the looks.

Eve closed her eyes again and shoved the door closed as hard as she could, but something stopped it. She curled her fingers into fists and mentally pushed against it harder. James's voice continued to fill her head, it dipped in volume several times, cut off for a few seconds, and then she had to let go.

Pain sliced through her head and she gasped.

"Eve, are you all right?"

James got out of his seat and came around, crouching beside her. She nodded, but that made her head hurt more.

"Shit, nosebleed," James said and rushed to a cupboard across the room.

Blood dripped onto the table where she sat. "I'm sorry."

He grabbed a box of tissues and put them on the table beside her. "Here, use these, and you have nothing to be sorry for. I pushed you too hard for your first try—"

The door across the room banged shut and she glanced up. Lazarus was striding across the room, a scowl on his face, eyes furious.

"Yeah, you pushed her too hard. She's fucking bleeding," he said.

James planted his hands on his hips. "This isn't unusual, Laz. You've seen it yourself—"

"Leave us."

Eve stood. "Lazarus—"

"I said go," he said to James.

James muttered something under his breath, offered her a reassuring smile, and strode from the room.

Eve shook her head. "He wasn't wrong."

Lazarus was in front of her, staring at her like he expected her to fall to pieces in front of him. "About what?" he grunted.

"You really are surly."

One of his brows lifted. "You haven't seen surly, female."

The look in his eyes, the way the bright green had darkened, made her belly warm. Then she remembered earlier that morning, and what he'd almost walked in on. Her face heated and his eyes flared like he was the one who could read minds.

She quickly looked away and the sudden movement had her clutching her head.

He cursed and scooped her up, lifting her off her feet like she was weightless, which she was *not*.

"What are you doing?" she said, feeling even more embarrassed.

"Taking you somewhere you can rest."

"I don't need to be carried."

He ignored her and strode out the door and down the hall. Eve didn't know what to do with her hands and in the end, rested one on his shoulder. The heat of his skin seeped through his shirt. God, he was hot. And his heart pounded against her, faster than what was normal. But then, maybe that was a demon thing as well?

She was so focused on every move, every shift of his muscles, the places their bodies touched, she hadn't noticed when the elevator opened that it wasn't on her floor, not until he shoved a door open and strode into what was obviously his apartment.

He put her on the couch and stepped back as if she'd shocked him then paced away and shook out his hands, like he had in the car the day before right after he'd touched her.

He stopped suddenly and turned to her, looking edgy as hell. "Drink?"

The question threw her. "Um...sure."

He strode to the small kitchen off to the side, grabbed a bottle of water from the fridge and a couple of kitchen towels he'd dampened under the tap, and came back.

"Here."

"Thanks." She took the water from him and used the towels to clean up while he watched her, again from a distance.

"I'm fine, if you'd rather I leave," she said.

"I don't want you to leave."

The way he said that was so low she was surprised the ground didn't shake. "Is there a reason—"

"Are you still in pain?" he asked, talking right over her.

"It's almost completely gone."

"Good, that's...good." He stood, solid thighs braced apart, hands at his sides, fingers curled into fists. He was anything but relaxed. Everything he said was at odds with his body language. "Hungry?"

"No," she said at the same time as her stomach rumbled so loudly there was no way he'd missed it. Cue more blushing. She'd been so nervous about her first training session she'd skipped lunch.

He frowned. "You're hungry. Why did you lie?"

Eve's mouth opened, but she didn't know what to say.

"I frighten you," he said. "You want to leave."

Yes, she wanted to leave, but not because Lazarus frightened her. He overwhelmed her, though, in a whole lot of different ways. "I'm not afraid of you."

"Right," he muttered and walked to the phone, punching in a couple of numbers. She listened while he asked for food to be brought up. When he turned back, she didn't miss the change in his posture, the way he rolled his shoulders and unclenched his jaw as if forcing himself to relax.

He watched her for several long seconds, then said, "Will you eat with me?" He rubbed the back of his neck and his huge biceps bulged. "I know we got off to a rocky start, and the way I've been acting..." He cleared his throat. "Will you eat with me?" he asked again.

Eve had no idea what was going on, or what this was about, but he was making an effort, for whatever reason, and she couldn't bring herself to say no when self-preservation told her to do just that.

For some reason, she couldn't bring herself to leave. There was this draw, this pull to him she didn't understand, and it was messing with her, big time.

Like the way you got yourself off thinking about him this morning.

Yes, thank God it wasn't Lazarus who could read minds.

Eight

She was looking at him again, in that *way*, cheeks pink, lids heavy.

Every muscle in his body locked up. So much for trying to relax. He thought if he brought her here, ate with her, had a conversation, he could explain what she was to him. He could make it as pain free as possible.

She'd been in his room all of ten minutes and already he was losing it. With Tobias doing his damnedest to corrupt them, as well as the equinox almost there, he was struggling. His demon knew the portal would be opening in a matter of days and it felt the call.

If you were mated to Eve that wouldn't be a problem anymore.

And he could finish Tobias and help his brothers regain full control as well.

She was watching him. He strode toward her, taking the seat opposite. Looming over her wouldn't help his cause, even if sitting still made him want to jump out of his damned skin, especially around her.

She watched him, looking slightly alarmed like she knew something was coming, something she wouldn't like.

Her fingers dug into the couch cushions. "What is it? What's wrong?"

Again, he found himself wanting to soothe her. Searching his mind for a gentle way to tell her how important she was to him, that she was literally his very own needle in a haystack. "I need to tell you some things, about me, about your place here. I just don't know where the hell to start."

She pulled one of the cushions into her lap, her eyes so wide, so full of fear he fucking wanted to roar. The female was stuck with him, a broken male who had no clue how to make this okay for her. Because it wasn't okay. None of this was okay.

"You know I'm half-demon?"

She nodded.

"My other half is angel."

She blinked over at him. "Angel?"

"Yes."

She stared at him for several seconds, then choked out, "Of course you are." She looked panicked. "I guess that makes sense. If demons are real then angels only seem logical. Next, you'll tell me vampires and witches and werewolves exist as well."

He just stared at her.

Her eyes widened, her throat working. "That's...yeah, that's..." She shook her head, at a loss for words. "Just great. Not terrifying at all."

He pushed on before they got sidetracked and he fucking chickened out. "You know what we do, what our job is. But being what we are, that mix of dark and light, good and evil... there's this, this constant struggle inside us. This push and pull. Usually, maintaining control, maintaining balance isn't a problem, but something happened to mess with that balance, and we're...struggling."

"That's...wow, a lot to take in. I can't imagine what you're going through, how hard that must be." She shook her head, her dark waves moving around her lovely face. "So something happened and now you're what? Getting pulled to your...um, dark side?"

"Yeah, that's exactly what's happening."

She was frowning, and he shouldn't be thinking how much that made him want to kiss her.

"What will happen to you? Is there something you can do?"

Eve looked genuinely worried, and there was good reason for her to be. Time to finish this. "There is something I can do, but I can't do it alone."

She sat forward, those beautiful eyes so intent on him his demon was damn near mesmerized by her. "What? What is it—"

Someone pounded on the door, startling Eve and she broke eye contact, twisting to look at it.

"Laz," Rocco called through the door. "You there?"

Lazarus cursed and strode to the door, wrenching it open. "What?"

His bother stood there, dressed to fight, his short sword—the weapon gifted to them by the angels and used by all the knights—strapped to his thigh. "Why aren't you answering your damned phone?" He stuck his head in the door. "Ahhh, right. Yeah, sorry, but we need you. All hands on deck."

"What's going on?"

"A bunch of rogues tearing shit up in the city."

"Rogues?" Eve was standing, her gaze on Rocco.

Like all the knights, his brother was tall and built, but he chose to decorate his face with a lot of metal and wore a short blue mohawk. The guy stood out in a crowd.

"Give me five to weapon up," Laz said. Roc gave him a chin lift and left.

"You're going to fight?" Eve said as he strode across the living room.

He stopped at his bedroom door, hand on the frame, fingers digging into the drywall, pissed the hell off. He had been so damn close, so close to telling her.

"Is it dangerous?" she asked, gorgeous blue eyes full of fear.

Was that fear for him? Did she actually give a shit what happened to him? Christ, he hoped not. "It's what we do. We fight demons and we send them back to hell." He walked away, unable to look at her any longer, and quickly strapped on his weapons.

When he walked back out, she was standing in the middle of the room, looking unsure. "Stay here if you want, until you're feeling better. I'll be gone awhile." It was crazy how much he wanted her in his place, to know that while he was out fighting she was here, safe in his room. His demon liked that idea as well, the bastard close to purring at the image that flashed through Lazarus's mind, of Eve...naked, asleep in his bed.

Ready for him when he returned.

He gritted his teeth and headed for the door, every step feeling weighted, everything in him not wanting to leave her. Shit. He yanked the door open and turned back to her. She was chewing on her bottom lip and he wanted to lick it, suck that full, abused lip so bad his gut ached.

"We'll talk tomorrow," he forced out, voice wrecked. Then he left before she could answer, closing the door tight behind him.

The knights weren't the only ones affected by the equinox drawing closer.

The demons that'd made Earth their home could be equally affected, though Lazarus had never seen anything like this.

The back of the sandwich shop was coated in blood, human remains hanging around the room like twisted decorations—a hand here, a foot there, intestines dangling from the light above—while three naked Leathren demons, coated in blood, fucked on the shop floor, completely oblivious to the company they now had.

Leathren usually kept to themselves, preferred their own company, and were known for their shy natures. They didn't eat human flesh or any other for that matter. The demons fed off other people's pain and suffering, but they never caused it. They were scavengers. In Hell, they hung around torture chambers, absorbing screams and cries. On Earth, they were usually found near the sick or stalked human killers and abusers to get their fix.

This was not in their natures, none of it.

Rocco turned to him, brows raised, just as confused as Laz. Gunner stood on the other side of the ménage looking no less confused.

"What the fuck is this?" Roc said.

"I don't even think they know what they're doing," Gunner said.

He was right. Their eyes were glassy as hell, oblivious to the knights standing just a few feet from them.

Gunner twirled one of his blades. "We can't let them live. They've killed humans."

Laz agreed. "We'll take out two of them and bring one in for questioning. Something is way off here."

They were about to move in when all three demons

stopped what they were doing, lifted their heads, and turned to them, eyes still glazed and teeth bared.

"Creepy fuckers," Rocco muttered.

He was not wrong. He and his brothers pulled their weapons, about to move in, when all three demons jumped up, ran to one of the work stations, and in unison each picked up a knife. Instead of coming at them, though, they lifted them to the base of their throats.

"Fuck." Rocco ran for them.

He didn't make it.

The three demons were ashing out moments later.

"Christ," Rocco said. "What the hell was the point of that?"

Laz shook his head. "Fucked if I know."

Gunner pulled out his phone. "I'll take pictures of this place, show the others. Zenon might know something."

Zenon was their resident expert on Hell and the only one of their brothers who had been there, though he never spoke of it. If this was some kind of ritual, he'd know.

They left a short time later, leaving the place for the human police to find. Their forensics couldn't pick up demon or angel DNA so they were safe.

"You think Diemos was behind whatever that was back there?" Roc said.

"Fuck knows." The ruler of Hell somehow had the ability to communicate with the demons he sent out, but that wasn't a group of demons following an order. That was something else completely.

"I need a drink," Rocco said.

He wasn't the only one.

They ended up at a bar in the center of the city. It was owned by a demi they knew well, and the clientele was varied, in other words not just human, or demon for that matter. But the difference was the demons that came there followed the rules, had been given sanctuary, and knew how lucky they were to be allowed here on Earth. The other beings here were of no concern to the knights and they left each other alone.

Gunner came back from the bar with a bottle of whiskey and three glasses and put it in the middle of the table. Rocco poured.

"So, you mated yet?" he asked, sliding a glass over to Laz.

"What do you think?" He downed the drink and motioned for another.

Rocco sat forward, expression serious. "I *think* you're overthinking this when you know there's no other option. Get it over with. Plus, she's hot. What more do you need?"

"Jesus, you have no fucking clue," Laz said then looked at Gunner. "What about you? Nothing to add?"

His brother shook his head, running his hand over his buzz cut, the scar through his lips twisting his mouth when he smiled. "It's your life not mine, brother. I don't have to worry about that yet, and until I do, I'll take my pleasure where I can find it."

Something moved through Gun's eyes, something he couldn't name. Laz had seen it before, but Gunner didn't like to talk at the best of times. There was no chance of getting the guy to open up.

Gunner stood then and headed toward the group of hell-hounds across the bar. The New Jersey pack was lethal and only came to Roxburgh for business. Gunner had struck up a friendship with a couple of them and because of it, they helped the knights out from time to time. One of their males and his bitch had been watching Gun since he came in. Gunner leaned in, said something in the guy's ear, and then they all headed to the back of the club and the exit to the alley.

"The guy needs to talk instead of fucking away his feel-ings," Rocco said beside him.

Laz snorted. "Besides Zen, I'd say that pretty much

describes every one of us." Though as appealing as the idea of fucking away his feelings was tonight, there was only one woman he wanted, one woman he would ever want now he knew she existed. That's just the way it worked.

And he couldn't have her, not tonight, maybe not ever depending on what she said when he finally explained what he wanted, what he needed from her.

"Yeah, you're right," Roc said. "Best I get on that." He stood and melted into the crowd as well, making a beeline to a group of human females.

Laz stayed where he was. He had a bottle of whiskey to finish.

It was three in the morning when they landed on the balcony to the control room and walked inside. Alcohol didn't affect them like humans—they had to drink a hell of a lot more to get wasted—but Laz had managed a nice buzz. Maybe that would help him sleep.

James was behind a desk, working on one of the laptops, and lifted his head when they strode in.

As they neared, the guy frowned. "What the hell's that smell?"

"Gunner," Rocco said.

James's gaze slid to Gunner. "What is it?"

"Hellhound," Rocco filled in helpfully.

Gunner scowled.

"You were fighting hellhounds?" James looked worried.

"Nope," Rocco said, grinning. "Well, maybe. Fuck knows what they get up to between the sheets." He mock shuddered. "Do they stay in human form?" he asked Gunner. "Or does shit get kinky?"

Gunner growled and ran at Rocco, taking him to the floor.

Lazarus ignored them both, their grunts and James's cry of alarm, because this was nothing unusual. Idiots. He shook his head and left them to it, hitting the hall and jogging down the stairs to his floor. She wouldn't still be there, of course she wouldn't, but the urgency riding him, making him almost run to his door, didn't give a fuck.

Then he felt her, the hum of her so strong he wondered why the door wasn't rattling off its hinges.

She was still there.

He unlocked the door and strode in.

Fuck.

Eve was asleep on the couch. Her body curled in a ball, knees tucked up, hands by her face. Her dark hair was splayed over the cushion under her head and it looked so damn soft he took a step closer, desperate to touch it. Her lashes were thick, the same intense black as her hair, and they rested against her pale skin.

And her lips...

Fuck.

They were cherry-colored and full, and Lazarus wanted to know what they would feel like against his, how they would taste, more than anything in his whole life.

He stood there, unable to make himself move. His demon was right there with him. Eve was in their domain, she was under his roof and under his protection, and both angel and demon couldn't be happier about that.

There was no leaving this spot. He was stuck. If he took another step closer, he'd touch her and he couldn't—not yet, not when he hadn't talked to her and not when he might lose control. But leaving the room, even going to his bedroom, wasn't an option. He needed to be where he could see her.

So he stayed right where the hell he was.

Nine

Eve yawned and worked at opening her eyes.

Her body felt a little stiff, but her head felt fine, like the debilitating pain she'd felt the day before hadn't ever been there. She stretched and that's when she felt the couch at her back. She was still in Lazarus's apartment. Her eyes flew open as she pushed herself to a sitting position.

And gasped.

"Lazarus?"

He didn't answer her, was just standing across from her, features tight, pained. His jaw was set like granite, the vein in his throat pulsing. He was wearing the same T-shirt and jeans from the night before and the muscles in his arms looked carved from stone.

"Are you okay?"

He still didn't answer but nodded jerkily. It was a complete lie. She only had to look at him to see he was in some kind of pain. She stood slowly. She wasn't sure why, but the way he was looking at her, the unwavering stare, like a hawk about to go after a mouse, combined with the way the green in his eyes seemed to move and swirl—she felt approaching him cautiously was for the best.

His nostrils flared as she got closer, and impossibly, those carved-from-stone-muscles hardened further.

She reached out, placing her hand on his arm. Her gaze dropped to where she touched him. His skin felt a million degrees. He was like scorching rock beneath her hand.

A rhythmic vibrating sound started up.

God, it was coming from Lazarus.

Her gaze shot back up to his, and she gasped when the green of his irises was swallowed by midnight for a moment.

Lazarus hissed.

What the hell was going on? Something was happening, something Lazarus hadn't told her. He'd been about to last night, and she got the feeling the way he was with her, this pain or whatever he seemed to be in all the time, involved her.

"What can I do?" She slid her hand up his forearm to his monster biceps, trying to soothe him. God, pet him. Something. Anything. "Tell me, please."

His nostrils flared and he dipped his head, his movements jerky. Then he dropped his face to the crook of her neck and she froze as he breathed in deeply, dragging his nose up the side of her throat, over her jaw, until his lips were at her cheek, so close to her own.

The rhythmic sounds got louder. God, he was purring. There was no other way to describe it.

"Just one taste," he said. "Please...just one."

Eve swayed toward him, her entire body coming alive from the sound of his rough voice, the plea she heard in it. She didn't know what she was doing, but at that moment she didn't care; she'd give him anything he wanted.

She turned her head, and the outer corners of their mouths brushed. Her heart pounded harder. Lazarus growled and turned to her as well, dragging his lips over hers.

Eve opened for him instantly, her fingers digging into hard muscle, trying to pull him closer, wanting more. His big hand moved up to the side of her face, thick fingers sliding into her hair, and he tilted her head. His tongue licked into her mouth, sliding against hers in a way that was frenzied, hungry. More than meeting her own desperate need for him.

The purring grew louder, the vibrations from his chest going right through her. She squirmed. God, she felt it, right between her legs.

His other hand slid around her waist and he tugged her closer so she was plastered against his rock-solid body.

Someone knocked at the door.

Lazarus stilled, panting, chest pumping.

"You there?" Chaos called.

Lazarus was staring down at her, his eyes bright green now. He cleared his throat. "I need to answer that."

Eve nodded, unable to put together any kind of sentence.

His hands slid from her body and she felt their absence immediately. He stepped back, and again his movements were jerky, stiff.

They'd kissed.

Eve lifted her fingers to her tingling lips, trying to comprehend what she was feeling, what it was about him that drew her so strongly.

Lazarus's hand twitched at his side like he was going to reach for her again. But then Chaos pounded on the door and called out again.

He turned away from her, but not before she saw the muscle in his jaw jump. He yanked the door open. "What is it?"

Chaos took them both in, and if he suspected something had just happened between them, he didn't let on. "We need you out on patrol."

Lazarus frowned. "You could have just texted."

"I did, and called as well."

Shoving his hand in his back pocket, Lazarus pulled out his phone and cursed. "It's dead." He thrust his fingers through his hair. "I'm right behind you." He turned back to her when Chaos left. "I have to go."

It was unexplainable, but she wanted to prolong their time together. "I'll walk out with you then I can swing by the kitchens and grab something to eat."

He nodded and she followed him upstairs. There was a new tension between them now, even stronger than before, and it lifted goose bumps all over her skin.

"The cafeteria's on the top floor," he said.

"Okay."

His gaze lingered on her for several seconds, like he wanted to say something more, but changed his mind, and finally headed off in the opposite direction. She watched him walk away. *Would* she see him later? Something was going on, something he wasn't telling her. She needed answers. Maybe they could have a meal together when he got back and talk.

Decision made, she ran after him to ask. Lazarus was already at the balcony doors when she walked into the control room.

He tore off his shirt and shoved as much as he could into his back pocket—

Massive charcoal wings sprung from his back.

She gasped and he spun to face her. His wings moved gently, and as they did, light shimmered across them, catching on flecks of silver.

"They're...beautiful," she whispered.

"Eve..."

Her gaze moved over his ripped chest and ridged abs...and the large bulge at the front of his jeans.

He cursed and took a step toward her, his wings folding in

as he did. They vanished a second later like they hadn't been there. "Eve, I need you to—"

A low, vicious sound came from behind her, lifting the hairs on her arms. She spun around. Two of the others had joined them. Rocco and another male she hadn't met yet. They stood on the other side of the room, on opposite corners.

Both were huge, chests pumping with their rapid breaths, lips curled back, teeth clenched.

And at that moment they were focused on one thing—her.

Lazarus was suddenly beside her, sliding an arm around her waist, pulling her in close to his side. "What the fuck, Zenon?"

The guy she assumed was Zenon was breathing rapidly and his big body seemed to grow with every inhalation. He wore a black T-shirt that clung to his thick biceps and chest. The skin she could see was completely covered in tattoos. His hair was long and pure black and hung forward, obscuring most of his face.

He didn't take his eyes off her and growled. The sound began so quiet she could barely hear it, but as his chest heaved with every breath, it grew in volume until it was almost deafening.

She tried to scramble back, but Lazarus held her in his firm, unyielding grip, stopping her escape. The terrifying male took a threatening step toward them.

"Do not take another step," Lazarus said, voice deadly.

What the hell was going on? Wasn't this supposed to be some kind of safe haven?

"I don't want to," Zenon gritted out. His nostrils flared and the look he sent Lazarus was one of pure hatred. "I can't help it. What the fuck is she?"

"What is wrong with you?" Lazarus seemed genuinely confused by the other male's reaction.

Zenon didn't, or couldn't, answer and continued to pant in harsh, ragged breaths.

A hiss came from the opposite side of the room and Lazarus spun to face Rocco. He shook his head like an angry beast, light glinting off his facial piercings. He looked in pain.

"Something's wrong," Rocco said as his eyes lost all color, like Lazarus's had in her bedroom and became a hollow, black nothingness. "You need to get her away from me...or I'm—" He snarled suddenly and flung his head back. His body torqued violently, every vein and tendon strained, bulging through the exposed skin of his throat and down his heavy arms. After a few seconds suspended like that, whatever had held him let go. He hissed and lowered his head.

Then ran at her.

Lazarus shoved her back so hard her body slammed into the wall behind her. Zenon roared and came at them from the other side, his growls loud enough to rattle glass.

Her heart pounding out of her chest, Eve pressed into the unyielding steel at her back, scrambling to stay upright when her foot slipped, desperate to get the hell away. *Oh God.*

Zenon moved faster than Rocco and as he drew near, Lazarus planted his feet, legs apart, blocking her with his body. She curled her fingers around the waistband of his jeans, pressing herself into his back, clinging to him. His muscles bunched hard as he tensed, bracing for impact. But instead of coming at them, Zenon dove and tackled Rocco to the ground.

The sound of their bodies colliding was horrific. Neither one held anything back as they went at each other like wild animals.

The door crashed open again and Gunner and Kryos stormed in.

Their sharp gazes landed on the pair fighting. "What the fuck's going on?" Gunner growled, taking in the men bleeding and grunting on the floor. He had a buzz cut and a deep scar through his top lip. It puckered when he aimed his stare at her and hissed in a sharp breath.

Kryos moved in, dragging Rocco off the floor, tearing him from Zenon. Panting, Rocco dragged the back of his hand across his bleeding lip then pointed at her. "It's her...if Zen hadn't stopped me..." He didn't finish, didn't need to.

Four sets of eyes slid toward Eve. Three of them were nothing but dark, fathomless pools. Only Kryos's remained warm brown and conveyed only concern and curiosity.

"What is she?" Zenon growled again. His long hair no longer obscured his face, and a scar or burn marred his right cheek. Tattoos covered his entire neck, finishing at his jawline. In fact, besides his face, there wasn't a piece of exposed skin that wasn't inked. Intense hatred oozed from him, and when his gaze landed on her, his lips curled in distaste.

"Do not fucking look at her," Lazarus barked across the room.

None of them moved. Their gazes lingered, intense and terrifying.

"Kryos, get them the hell out of here," Lazarus roared.

Kryos, the only one besides Lazarus who seemed to have control, shoved at the males closest to him, but they didn't budge. Their massive bodies remained unnaturally still, heads cocked with identical expressions she couldn't decipher but turned the blood in her veins to ice. Finally, after another shove, they tore their gazes from her and stormed out.

Lazarus released a shaky breath and shoved his fingers in his hair. "Fuck."

Eve turned to him, confused and barely holding it together. "What just happened?" Her voice shook.

He blew out a harsh breath. "Fucked if I know."

When the door slammed open again, Lazarus crowded Eve, keeping her behind him. Her fingers still gripped his waistband, her body pressed close. She was trembling. It took all his self-control not to go after Zen and Rocco and do something he had never entertained once in his long life. Zenon was wild, some might even say unstable. You never knew where you stood with the guy or what he might do next, but Roc? He'd never seen the other male like that. Eve had triggered their demons' violent reaction somehow. He had no idea how, but his little demi had made herself a target.

Chaos stepped through the door and prowled across the room, teeth gritted. He looked more than a little pissed. In only a pair of faded jeans, there was no missing the Kishi demon he housed rippling and moving restlessly below his skin, desperate for release. Chaos's brown eyes flashed midnight as he stopped in front of him then slid briefly to the female huddled at his back. "I think we need to talk."

James walked in and Lazarus waved him over. "Take Eve out onto the balcony for some fresh air, would you?" Her grip tightened and she shifted around behind him, her fists pressing into his lower back. He reached around and gently eased her forward to stand at his side. She was scared as hell, the pulse in her throat fluttering madly as her gaze darted between him and Chaos. "It's okay, Eve. They're gone, and Chaos won't hurt you."

She gazed up at him, offering him a tantalizing flash of trust. The look in her eyes was so damn innocent it made him yearn for something he couldn't have. He clenched his fists against the guilt that slammed him in the solar plexus with the force of a battering ram, because it was only a matter of time before she discovered the kind of male he truly was.

Their leader flashed a wide, white, somewhat pained grin, and Eve jumped.

"I just need a private word with Laz."

"Right, of course," she whispered.

Chaos's skin twisted and rolled across his shoulders and down his heavy biceps before his eyes flickered to midnight and back to brown again.

"Oh God." Eve plastered her body against Lazarus again. She hadn't let go of him, her fingers now hooked onto the belt loops of his jeans.

"Jesus. Can you put a goddamned shirt on?" Lazarus growled at the other male.

"No." Chaos shrugged, causing another roll. "It's uncomfortable."

Loosening her death grip, he held onto her frozen fingers and turned to face her, using his body to block Chaos from her view. He couldn't help himself and lightly cupped the side of her face. Her skin was smooth and warm, her cheeks flushed. "James is going to take you out on the balcony. I'll make sure no one else goes out there, okay?"

She nodded.

Shit. There it was again, that burgeoning look of trust. His stomach knotted and he turned away, feeling like a bastard. Chaos cocked a brow in question. He ignored him, and with surprising reluctance, handed her over to James, watching as he steered her across the room and out the double doors.

"What the hell just happened here?" Lazarus hissed as soon as she was out of earshot.

Chaos ran a hand over the tattoo covering one side of his shaved head. "Fucked if I know. The autumnal equinox is approaching, making shit a lot worse when we're already struggling."

The equinox was a catalyst, and with a little sacrificial blood to help it along, opened the portal between Hell and

Earth. Leading up to it always messed with each of them, but the whole Tobias situation had made it a whole lot worse.

Chaos put his hands on his hips. "Maybe there's something with her power we haven't unlocked yet? Something that's magnifying the effect? Maybe it's something else, something that calls to our demons. Fucked if I know, but, brother, whatever it is, it's strong."

"You feel it?" Laz asked him.

Chaos's jaw ticked. "Yeah, I feel it."

Going by the roll of his flesh and the color of his eyes, Eve's being at the compound affected Chaos just as much as the others. It was only the sheer strength of his will that prevented him from behaving like Zen and Roc, and the reason they had appointed him their leader.

Chaos cursed, sucking in a breath, and grabbed for the desk beside him.

Lazarus winced as the points of his friend's wings stretched below his skin, rising above his shoulders before disappearing again. With the ongoing struggle to keep their demon halves under control since Tobias's defection to the "dark side" the knights had only allowed themselves partial shifts. Wings only. Chances were good they wouldn't be able to change back from their Kishi forms if they did, and that would suck big time.

"In our weakened state, our demons will continue to try to overthrow us. And I'm thinking the only way to protect her, and us is to make her your mate." He gritted the words out as if nothing had happened, as if his demon wasn't writhing just below the surface, desperate to explode out of his skin.

Lazarus scrubbed his hands over his face. That demon side desperate for escape in each of his brothers had sensed something in Eve, something unknown, something extremely powerful.

Which meant Chaos was right.

"The gateway is thinning as the equinox approaches. Without knowing what it is about her that's affecting our demons, we can't control it, and having her here around your brothers while you're unmated, it's too damn dangerous."

Lazarus's stomach knotted. He'd really gone and fucked everything up. He was the reason his world had shattered into a million shards of utter hell. *His* weakness had kicked off the mess they all found themselves in now, and his brothers were still paying the price for it.

Chaos must have read the look on his face, and thankfully, didn't push. "Take her to your room, put up a shield, and keep her the fuck there until you've claimed her. She's too dangerous to move around the compound."

Chaos took off, and Laz collected Eve and led her into the elevator, hitting the next floor down. She was going to be stuck in his apartment, with him, until they figured this out or they mated, and he didn't know how he was going to keep it together having her that close 24/7.

Eve stayed close by his side as he hustled her toward his quarters. Once inside he could use his powers to veil the erratic energy she was throwing out, and hopefully give his brothers a break. She must have a million questions and he knew she was waiting until she was in the safety of his rooms to ask them. And shit, somehow, after witnessing Roc and Zenon losing it back there, and Eve knowing that Lazarus and his brothers were made the same, that they had the same kind of vicious demon inside them—he had to convince her to mate with him.

Fuck.

A crash sounded behind them followed by Kryos's voice echoing down the hall. "Run!"

He didn't bother to turn around. The sound of growling, of pounding boots sprinting after them, said it all. Scooping Eve in his arms, he ran for the end of the hall and threw the door open to his apartment. It slammed behind him and he threw up a field of energy that should keep his brothers out. The other male didn't make it that far. Another crash came as they hit the floor. Kryos had taken him down before he got there. As the only mated male among them, Kryos was the most stable. Eve didn't seem to be affecting him at all. Proving Chaos right. Mating would solve this, whatever it was. Rocco's hissed protests echoed through the door seconds later as he was dragged away.

At that moment, Lazarus became aware of the warm female bundled in his arms. She'd buried her face against his neck and her rapid breaths tickled his skin, sending tingles across his scalp. "You all right, Eve?"

"No," she said, voice muffled.

Her lips lightly grazed his throat when she spoke, and he fought not to shiver in response. Jesus. He couldn't take much more of this. Now he'd tasted her, he wanted to kiss her again in a way that went beyond desperate. Lowering her to the ground, he took a step back. "I'm sorry if they scared you."

"Scared me? I'm terrified. Why did you even bring me here? You said I'd be safe."

That knot in his gut twisted. "You will be, I promise. I will keep you safe."

She wrapped her arms around herself. "What was that? What's going on, Lazarus?"

"I know you have a lot of questions, and I will answer them."

"When?"

"Soon." Yeah, he was a fucking coward, but he wasn't ready to have that discussion with her, not yet. It was pathetic, and he didn't know why he was torturing himself, but he wanted one more day. One more fucking day of *what if*, of what might have been, before that look of budding trust on her face disappeared for good and turned to fear and disgust.

He craved that look like a starving animal.

Her eyes narrowed. "Lazarus—"

A quiet knock at the door thankfully interrupted whatever Eve was about to say. "Yeah?"

"It's Meredith. Can I come in?"

He pulled the door open and motioned for Kryos's mate to enter. "How's Roc?"

"Ashamed of himself. He sent me to apologize to Eve."

Eve took in the woman in front of her. Meredith was beautiful, tall and slim, and the stunning smile she directed at Eve was kind. "He really is sorry. If it wasn't for—"

Lazarus cleared his throat, stopping the other woman mid-sentence. Frowning, Eve shot him a look. But he'd moved to the small kitchen off the living room and started messing with his coffee machine.

"Anyway." She tucked her hair behind her ear. "You're safe with Kryos and me. Since we're mated, he has all of that"—she aimed her thumb back toward the door—"under control."

Eve frowned. "Mate?"

Meredith's smile widened and her eyes softened. "Yeah, he stormed into my life and swept me off my feet." She chuckled. "I've been waiting a long time for another—"

"Coffee?" Lazarus barked from the kitchen.

They both jumped and spun to face him.

"No. Thanks," Meredith answered, her gaze moving back and forth between her and Lazarus. He wasn't subtle in the least. He was stopping Meredith from telling her something, and Eve wanted to growl in frustration.

"Okay. I better head out. If you need anything, anything at all, I'm just down the hall." She glanced back at Lazarus as she spoke. "I'll come back in...a couple of days?"

He nodded and crossed his arms.

"If you need to talk before then, just ask Laz for my number."

"Thanks, I—" A sudden wave of nausea took Eve by surprise, causing her stomach to roll. Oh God, she was about to throw up. Her vision swam and she reached for the back of the couch.

"Lazarus." Meredith's voice sounded panicked.

"Eve?" Lazarus called.

His voice grew distant, his footfalls muffled. Her vision dimmed, shrouded in darkness like a shadow moving over her, right before she crumpled to the floor.

The last thing she saw was Meredith's worried expression and Lazarus stalking toward her.

Ten

She was so still.

Lazarus wished Eve would fucking move, make a sound, something. But she just lay there pale and motionless. The two times she'd opened her eyes in the last day and a half, she'd stared blindly up at him, not really there. Not back with him.

When she'd collapsed and he'd pulled her into his arms...

A knot lodged behind his rib cage as unwanted memories and emotions flooded his mind. He squeezed his eyes against them, but this time he didn't have the strength to force them back.

"Don't leave me, sweet girl. I need you here with me. Tobias needs you." Scarlet's mouth opened and blood bubbled up between her lips, cutting off whatever she was trying to say. He rocked her in his arms. "No. Please, God, no."

"Lazarus?" Chaos's insistent voice pulled him from the past. The male stood at the door, Kryos at his side. "Are you all right?"

"Yeah." A complete lie. He was nowhere near *all right.*

Chaos narrowed his eyes, seeing it for himself. "Look, Lazarus—"

"What do you want, Chaos?" He was in no mood for a deep-and-meaningful or a fucking lecture.

The big male crossed his arms over his chest, watching him closely then tilted his head toward the bed, toward Eve's still form. "Any change?"

"Not yet."

Laz hoped he'd drop it, whatever was on his mind, but then the guy frowned and ran a hand over his tattooed skull. "We don't have time for this."

Kryos's brows hiked to his hairline. "I'm sure Eve feels terrible that her loss of consciousness is inconveniencing you, brother. You can tell her off when she wakes up."

Chaos scowled. "That's not what I meant and you know it."

Lazarus wasn't interested in listening to their bickering. The two males were polar opposites and butted heads like angry bulls on the regular. Chaos had tunnel vision, always focused on the greater good—more often than not at the expense of everything else, including his own happiness. Kryos sometimes forgot that being a heartless bastard was what made Chaos an excellent leader.

"Enough." Laz stood, reluctantly leaving his post at Eve's bedside.

"We need to talk." Chaos motioned to the living room.

"I'm not leaving her alone. We can talk in here."

That pleased the other male. Chaos didn't even attempt to hide the satisfaction written all over his face, and no doubt assumed Lazarus's unwillingness to leave Eve meant they were close to mating.

Lazarus decided now wasn't the time to correct him.

———

Eve's eyes felt weighted down. Had she ever felt this tired in her life? She tried to move but stopped quickly when pain sliced through her left arm.

Low voices reached her then, penetrating her foggy brain. More than one person was in the room with her. She tried to open her eyes again, but they wouldn't cooperate.

"Is Meredith all right?"

Eve barely suppressed a shiver at the sound of Lazarus's unmistakable deep voice.

"She's worried," someone else said.

This voice held a quiet intensity. It was soothing, nice. She was pretty sure it was Kryos.

"Tobias has left the city, has put distance between us. We can all feel it. He hasn't covered his tracks, at least not his general location. When you get there I'm sure he'll fuck with you. But he wants you to follow."

"He's trying to get Lazarus on his own," Kryos said. "Let me go with him. I'm the only one of us who's stable. Let me go after T."

"Yeah, and Laz has no choice but to follow him. He's not going to reveal himself to any of us. It's Laz he wants. If I send you with him, we'll lose our chance to take him down."

There was a grumbling sound.

"I fucking hate sending you on your own, but it's the only way we're going to get him out of hiding. And with the way your brothers are right now, they're too unstable to be around her. Brent's wards are rock solid. She'll be safe there." This new voice was hard, determined.

"She can't travel, not yet," Lazarus said, low and just as determined.

"As soon as she's well enough to be moved, get her the hell out of here." There was a pause. "Give her this."

"What is it?"

"Silas has decided to insinuate his superior, holier-than-thou ass in our business. We're on the verge of war and *this* he decides requires his fucking attention. I don't like it."

A light jingling sound, then Laz growled. "What the hell do I do with it?"

"You know how mysterious that angel can be. All I know is she has to wear it. He said it's for her protection and will give you the time you need."

Angel?

They talked some more about whatever *it* was, which made no sense whatsoever to Eve. Then Laz said, "She's been in and out of consciousness, but hasn't woken fully. As soon as she does, I'll make the arrangements."

"Good." A pause. "Just remember that Silas's gift, it's not a cure, it's a Band-Aid. You can't fuck around with this."

"You don't think I know that?" Lazarus's deep, rumbling voice carried a note of torment that hit her behind the ribs.

"Once she's out of the compound, things around here will settle back to the usual semi-violent hum. Isn't that right, mighty leader?"

"God, you're a dick," the pissed voice cut in.

"If you say so, oh wise one."

"So help me, Kryos...if you fucking bow to me one more time..."

There was a snort. "Listen, Laz, I know you don't want this, but claiming Meredith was the best thing that ever happened to me."

The room was silent for several seconds then Lazarus said in a low voice, "You're right. I don't want this."

"Shit." There was another pause. "Looks like you got your reprieve. But remember"—there was more jingling—"this isn't a permanent fix."

"You can't claim her yet anyway," someone else said. "Not until she's recovered. The surge of power you send her during the mating could hurt her or worse."

She stiffened. *Claim? The mating?*

"Eve?"

She jumped.

"Are you awake?" Lazarus asked, followed by the sound of someone moving closer.

She blinked heavily, forcing her eyes to open. Her vision was kind of blurred, but she could still make out Laz and Kryos standing a few feet away. Chaos stood behind them, scowling.

"How are you feeling?" Lazarus asked, voice gruff.

She felt weird, fuzzy. But mainly she felt confused.

"Eve…" He took another step closer.

God, she couldn't think when he was near. Her mind spun with everything she'd just overheard. They'd been talking about her. She didn't understand it—or maybe she did, at least some of it—and that scared her all the more. She lifted her hands, panic taking over. "Stay back…I want you to stay the hell back."

The other two males exchanged heavy stares.

"Goddammit, just tell me. Tell me what's going on?" Fear, and she was ashamed to admit, betrayal laced her words. She tried to wiggle back but winced when pain again shot through her arm.

He took a small step back and shoved his fingers through his hair. "You're injured. You need to be still or you'll tear open your stitches."

"Stitches?" She lifted her arm. A thick white bandage was wrapped around it and angry purple bruising peeking out from the edges. "How?"

Lazarus's jaw hardened and the other two exchanged more looks. "You fell when you blacked out. You knocked a glass bowl off the cabinet. It smashed when you landed on it."

Her head throbbed. "I don't understand."

He turned to the other males in the room. "Leave us."

They did as he asked after several more intense looks were exchanged, leaving her and Lazarus all on their own.

Lazarus frowned. "It could've been a lot worse. Do you remember what happened?"

"I felt sick...dizzy. That's all I can remember."

"This ever happen before?"

"No."

His gaze darted away from hers. "Right. Must have been all the excitement. You need to rest. We have a flight to catch in the morning."

Excitement wasn't the word she'd use. And he was still avoiding her question. "Where are we going?"

"Chicago. We'll be staying with a friend of mine there for a while."

"Why?" That wonderful scent of his hit her, surrounded her. He didn't answer, instead watched her closely, and she forgot what was so important that she would rather talk than sleep.

"Rest, Eve." His voice turned velvety smooth and brushed across her skin like a caress. She could do nothing but obey. The sheets were soft and smelled like Lazarus, and she snuggled down, letting her lids drop.

When Eve woke again it was to the smell of food. Her stomach rumbled. When had she eaten last? She couldn't remember.

She flexed the fingers on her left hand and winced. *Ouch.*

The bed dipped and a hot dry palm gentled across her forehead, brushing back her hair.

"Eve, wake up, sweetheart."

For the first time, Lazarus's voice held no anger, no pain, or urgency. He spoke low and soft, and the natural rasp to it made his words a sensual caress.

He'd called her *sweetheart*.

Her belly fluttered and a zing of pleasure shot between her thighs. The feeling didn't let up, quickly becoming a low, insistent throb.

What the hell is happening to me?

His warm, rough fingers brushed her forehead again. "Eve?"

Goose bumps rose across her skin when he said her name. She didn't like the way her body reacted to the barest touch from him. When she opened her eyes, he sat beside her, watching her. His hair was damp. He wore jeans and a black T-shirt, and the heady mix of the soap he'd used mingled with his own unique scent invaded her senses.

"Hey," he said.

She shivered at the sound of his voice, and her reaction annoyed her. She brushed his hand away then struggled to sit. When she couldn't, she sighed and gave up. Her whole body felt weak for some reason.

"How are you feeling? How's the arm?"

"Okay, I guess. It stings a little."

He checked the tape holding her bandage. "It'll only sting another day or so. Can you sit up?"

"I don't think so."

"Let me help." He slid his arm around her shoulders and gently lifted her forward then tucked another couple of pillows behind her back. His fingers grazed her hip as he withdrew his arm and the skin beneath tingled.

She took a moment to take in her surroundings. She'd been in his apartment but not his bedroom. The bed was huge, the headboard dark wood, and carved into it was an intricate design that she couldn't fully see in her current position. It looked like some kind of battle scene. The duvet cover was deep blue and the pillows were blue and gray. Besides a chunky dark wooden dresser and a pair of bedside tables, there wasn't anything else in the large bedroom.

His features were soft, and she couldn't hold his gaze with him looking at her like that. She felt safe in this room, and the idea of leaving was a frightening prospect. "When we leave tomorrow, what happens if another Orthon comes after me?"

"I'll kill it."

The quiet danger in those three words made her pulse pick up speed. He'd kill for her again, would try to protect her like he'd promised. "What if there's more than one, what if—"

His jaw clenched, and all softness dissolved. "You don't need to worry, Eve. I won't let anything happen to you."

She'd made him angry. Again. And unless they had a handbook on how not to piss off giant scary demon hunters, she guessed this was going to happen a lot.

"So what do you have on the tray?" she asked to change the subject. As much as she wanted answers, she got the feeling she wasn't going to get them from him. Not yet anyway. And honestly, she wasn't sure she was ready to hear them.

His big body relaxed. "Chicken, salad, and a baked potato with sour cream, I believe."

"Sounds good."

He lifted the tray from the bedside table and placed it on her lap. He unscrewed the lid from a bottle of water and handed it to her then sat back against the headboard and watched her. Intently.

"Um, have you eaten?" she asked.

"Yes."

His voice was back to velvet. Okay, no more talking. That voice was doing things to her, things she did not want it to do. If he wanted to watch her eat, so be it. After several tries, it was obvious her injury made it impossible to use her left hand, not until the stinging pain stopped shooting up her arm every time she tried to grip her knife.

Lazarus obviously noticed as well, because he scooted forward, and without a word, took the cutlery from her hands. He cut a piece of chicken then topped it with a little potato and salad, and lifted it to her lips.

Her cheeks heated. "No. I can do it."

"Eat," he ordered.

She stared at him, stunned, though she shouldn't have been. She'd already worked out the guy was a control freak. He stared back until she could no longer bear it.

"Bossy," she mumbled.

His lips quirked on one side, not quite a grin, but close. He didn't say anymore, simply held the fork to her mouth, and waited. She was hungry and the chicken looked good, so she ignored her ire at the order and opened her mouth. He fed her like that, his gaze getting darker and hungrier with every bite she took, and she didn't think it was for the food.

By the time the plate was empty her heart was pounding hard and she was light-headed. He lifted the plate from her lap and placed it on the table.

Covered in blankets, she was utterly decent, but as his gaze moved over her face and traveled the length of her body, she swore she felt the path of his stare heating her skin.

He stood suddenly. "Try to stay awake and I'll run you a bath."

That sounded wonderful. The bathroom was off to the right, and Lazarus went and got the water running, then he walked back out, came around to her side of the bed, and without warning, threw back the covers.

Eve squeaked in surprise.

Lazarus paused, eyes fixed on the parts of her he'd just exposed. The shirt she wore had ridden up past her hips, and she grabbed for the blankets, but his big hand shot out, stopping her.

"What are you doing?" she said, voice shaky.

She hated her thighs and ass and right then it was all hanging out for Lazarus to see. Plus, the way he was looking at her was freaking her the hell out.

He didn't respond. His gaze locked on the birthmark on her hip, half concealed by the edge of her panties. A thick finger grazed her waist then slipped under the elastic, easing down the side of her underwear to reveal the strawberry mark.

"You always had this?"

"Yes." Her heart skipped a beat.

He didn't say any more, but slid an arm under her knees and one behind her back and scooped her up, carrying her *again*. Mortified, she tried to protest. "Please put me down. I can walk. I'm too heavy."

He snorted and completely ignored her. She had no option but to hold on and let him carry her. He strode into the bathroom, lowered her to her feet, then bent over the bath. He turned off the water and tested the temperature. When he turned back he reached for the hem of the T-shirt she wore and started to lift it.

She grabbed his wrists. "What are you doing?"

"You can't take a bath in your clothes, right?" He lifted the faded gray tee past her hips.

She stopped him again. "I'm not getting naked in front of you."

He grinned. A full-on wolfish grin that flashed straight white teeth and a sexy dimple in his right cheek. She felt it in her lower belly, and that throb between her thighs increased alarmingly. His harsh features softened when he smiled.

"You're injured, Eve. I promise I won't look if it makes you uncomfortable."

Dammit. She needed help; there was no way she could lift it over her head on her own. "You can help with the shirt, but you have to close your eyes."

His grin widened, but he did as she asked. And she got

mad at herself because all she could think about was how long and dark his eyelashes were resting on his tanned skin.

It took a couple of tries, but after some careful maneuvering, he got her injured arm free. A warm hand moved to her bare back as he lifted the shirt the rest of the way over her head, causing her to stumble forward. Her chest collided with his, crushing her breasts against his body. Her nipples hardened from the contact. She blushed, mortified.

Lazarus sucked in a sharp breath, which meant, yep, he felt it.

Thank God his eyes were still closed.

"You good from here?" he rasped, taking an abrupt step back.

"Yes...thank you."

"I'll be in the other room if you"—he cleared his throat—"if you need anything." He spun around, almost crashing into the wall. He quickly sidestepped, strode out, and shut the door behind him.

Eve didn't linger in the bath long. She managed to dry herself and, with some contorting, put on the clean shirt he'd left for her by herself. Another one of his shirts. It was oversized, like the man himself, and soft. She could smell him on it.

God, that scent of his, it did things to her.

When she walked out, he was sitting on the bed, his bare feet crossed at the ankle, his back against the headboard. He was working on a laptop.

He glanced up from what he was doing when she shut the bathroom door behind her. His gaze slid down to the shirt she wore, and his eyes flared. She wanted to yank it down to cover her fat thighs, but her arms were crossed over her chest, covering her nipples.

Where the heck were her clothes?

"Get into bed, Eve."

She swallowed hard, unable to make her feet move. "Hmm?"

"You need to rest. We have to be up early in the morning." He flicked back the sheet on the other side of the bed and turned back to what he was doing on the computer.

Now she was more alert, not so drowsy, it felt extremely weird getting into his bed, especially when he was sitting on it. They'd shared that one kiss. Maybe it was nothing. Lazarus hadn't mentioned it again. But it was all she could think about, especially now she was about to crawl back into his bed.

Still, she did as he said, because what choice did she have?

How the hell was she going to sleep with him right beside her?

He sat on top of the quilt, wasn't even touching her, but his presence sat heavy in the room and again made her body react in ways she didn't want it to.

She climbed in, pulling the covers over her. He didn't say anything for the longest time. Maybe he thought she'd gone to sleep.

Finally, the bed shifted when he got up, followed by the sound of the laptop being placed on the bedside table. There was a rustle of clothing and she stiffened.

Was he going to get in and sleep under the covers with her?

"Ah, Lazarus..." She turned to face him. He stood by the bed, and the drawer in the side table was open. He had his shirt off and was wearing some kind of leather holster strapped across his chest. He pulled out one knife after another, strapping them to his ripped chest and thighs.

"I have to go out for a while."

His words registered, and she lurched into a sitting position, gasping when she put weight on her arm.

He quickly tugged on a shirt, and came around to her side of the bed, sitting down beside her. He reached for her, taking her wrist, moving his thumb idly back and forth across the pulse there. She couldn't take her eyes off the wicked-looking blades strapped to his large body.

"Eve..."

"You're leaving?" God, she hated the desperate, needy note to her voice.

"I'll be back before you wake, and James is just through that door if you need anything." He pointed to the door that led to the living room. "As long as you stay in my quarters you're in no danger. Do you understand?"

She didn't want him to leave, she wanted to go with him, but instead, she nodded.

He watched her for several silent seconds. "Good, that's good." He didn't take his hand from her wrist, kept on brushing his thumb over her skin, and whispered, "Sleep, Eve."

The last thing she remembered thinking was how good he smelled.

Eleven

The tiny shop was painted black, with cursive script painted on a sign above the door. The Cauldron. Not very original, but that wasn't what Willow had been going for. The witch sold harmless love potions and other concoctions to humans to make a living, but what they didn't know was she was the real deal and the most powerful witch in New York. It was one of her spells that warded their compound. She'd helped them out, which meant she was under their protection, not that she needed it. The woman had her shop warded just as strongly.

"She say what this was about?" Lazarus asked Chaos.

The fighter shook his head. "She didn't go into details."

Willow had no room for a man in her life—her words—but she did take lovers, Chaos being one of them on occasion. Which suited him just fine, saved him from actually having to go out and be civil to another being, and God forbid he was forced to have a conversation with a woman. The male was efficient in all things. Even finding partners to bed.

He knocked and the door opened a few seconds later. Willow looked pissed off, her red hair wild around her face, eyes flashing, and she tilted her head for them to follow. "The back room."

"What happened?" Chaos asked as they strode after her, their shoulders too wide for the tiny hall, forcing them to turn side-on.

"This." She gripped the door handle to her storage room and shoved it open.

"Jesus," Chaos muttered.

Lazarus took in the scene. A demon of unknown breed lay motionless on the floor. Well, its body was at one end and its head was on the opposite side.

"How did it get in here?" Laz asked.

Willow kicked the lifeless demon. "That's what I'd like to know." She turned to them and he was sure he could see flames in her eyes. "Somehow this piece of shit got in. Now I'm going to be up all night strengthening my wards. Do you have any idea how long that takes?"

"What did it want?" Chaos asked.

"There were two." She motioned to a broken window. "The other one got out through there when I was dealing with this one." She pointed to an empty spot on her shelf. "It took something of mine."

Chaos stiffened. "What the hell did it take?"

Her back straightened. "The finger bone of Golath."

"His what?" Chaos growled.

"Finger bone," Willow bit out.

"You had part of fucking Golath and never thought to tell us?"

The ancient demon was the first ever created by Lucifer, and it was his blood Lucifer used to create his handmaids, before the demon betrayed his master and escaped to Earth thousands of years ago.

The story goes that weeks after he escaped, overwhelmed with hunger, the demon killed a group of children, gorging himself on them, then found a cave to rest. The townspeople tracked him with the help of a witch, and she slaughtered him while he slept. She cut him into pieces and fed him to her pigs so he couldn't be brought back to life.

It was said, but had never been proven, that those bones and where they lay were the location and the catalyst that caused the creation of the portal, the gate to Hell that opened on the equinox and solstice, that the knights protected.

"How much power does that thing have?" Chaos gritted out.

Willow paced away and back. "A lot. More than your average lowly demon would know what to do with...more than most witches could handle." She thrust her fingers in her hair. "Shit!"

"You didn't think to put the fucking bone somewhere more secure?" Chaos growled.

Her back straightened and her eyes flashed. "No one has ever gotten through my wards before."

Lazarus rubbed his temples, his damn head pounding. "Golath was a demon. Why didn't he ash out when he died?"

Willow tapped the demon corpse at her feet with the tip of her boot. "Same reason this fucker is still messing up my floor: a binding spell. He won't be going back to Hell the old-fashioned way. I'll harvest every part of this asshole. There are plenty of things he'll be useful for."

"So they're true, the stories?"

She nodded.

"And this witch, she kept Golath's finger?"

Willow drew in a shuddery breath. "I'm a descendant from her line. It was passed down to me by my mother. It's been in this family for thousands of years...and now I've...I've lost it."

"What would a demon want with it now?" Lazarus asked.

Willow stared at the empty space on her shelf, pain etched

on her features, then she turned to them and shook her head. "Nothing good."

Fuck.

They left Willow's shop and walked out onto the street. And a familiar tingle crawled up Lazarus's spine instantly. *Demon.*

"Duck!" someone called from across the street.

A second later an arrow whistled past Chaos, narrowly missing him.

A cry rang out and they spun in time to see a demon drop to the ground behind them.

Lazarus stared down at the flailing demon. "What the fuck?"

The dark figure who had called out the warning, crossbow still in hand, spun and ran off.

Chaos tore off his shirt and extended his wings. "I'll try and catch up with them."

"I'm right behind you," Lazarus said. He quickly removed the demon's head so it would ash out, and then took flight.

Lazarus didn't go to his apartment when they returned to the compound. They were unsuccessful in their search for the owner of that arrow, which had pissed them both off. Something fucked up was going on and they needed to work out what. Or at least his brothers did. He had his own mission.

Tobias.

Head swimming after their search, he'd gone to the gym and trained until he could barely stand then collapsed on one of the couches in the common room. He barely slept because, like every night since Eve got there, since she came into her powers and he discovered her existence, he felt her like a throbbing beat in the center of his chest, beating through his veins, pounding in his head and his gut. And yeah, he knew the only way to stop it was to go to her, to make her his.

"Fuck." He shoved up from the couch and went back to the workout room. The equinox was here. They'd go out tonight, and he planned on avoiding Eve for as long as possible. If he went back to his rooms, Eve in his bed, those big blue eyes on him full of questions, he'd crack, he'd fucking shatter. He'd fall on her like a starving man.

After the fight was over later tonight, after he'd worked off all the volatile energy pounding through him, he'd do it. He'd go to her and tell her the truth.

The distant wailing of sirens and the low, steady thump of bass from the surrounding bars and clubs echoed off the walls around them.

The alley was free of the homeless, and no drunken couples were stumbling down there in search of privacy. No, evil permeated this place. Its sickly malevolence coated everything like toxic sludge, ensuring every living thing gave it a wide berth. Even the rats had scattered.

Humans continued to move about their lives, ignorant of what was about to invade their world.

Lazarus stood silently with his brothers, each male focused on the red brick wall ahead of them—but all he could see was a sleeping Eve. He'd caved and gone to check on her before they headed out. She'd been curled up in his bed, in one of his shirts.

Shit. She wasn't even there in the alley with him and she affected him, weakened him, caused him to lose focus.

The males at his side were subdued, feeling Gunner's absence as strongly as he was. Gunner had been too unstable to join them. No one knew why it was hitting him as hard as it was, and it made an already shitty situation worse. To his left, Rocco bounced on the balls of his feet, twirling his blades, twitchy, spoiling for a fight. Chaos stood a little in front, legs braced apart, unmoving, alert. His short sword hung loose at his side. Kryos stood to Laz's right, throwing knives strapped to his bare chest and a Glock fitted with a silencer rested in his hand.

And as always, Zenon stood apart. Concealed by shadow, his wide shoulders hunched, ready to charge ahead at any moment. His hair hung forward, concealing the brand on his face, his Li Kweis, the twin axes he preferred to fight with, were strapped to his back on either side of his leathery wings, and his short sword was strapped to his thigh, like the rest of them.

He was one of them, their brother, but Zenon had chosen to keep that distance between them. Lazarus knew it was because, unlike the rest of them who had been raised on Earth, sired by Kishi males and birthed by fallen females, Zenon was Hell born, sired by an unknown fallen male to a Kishi female. He hadn't trained with them, and no one had known of his existence until he'd stepped through the portal. He was a genetic fluke, but he was as much a knight as the rest of them.

If only he realized that.

Lazarus gripped his own blade tighter—several more strapped to his chest and thighs—and waited.

Their powers were useless this close to the hell's gate, the gateway to Hell that popped up during the solstice and equinox, spewing out its inhabitants. As far as they knew this was the only portal. And the knights had been providing a welcome party for the demons that came through for centuries.

Some demons left out of curiosity, some to wreak havoc. Others escaped to beg for sanctuary, but most were sent by Diemos, the sick, twisted head asshole of Hell, in his never-ending attempt to grow an army here on Earth. Preparing for the day that he found a way to open the portals for good.

Roc's boots crunched on the loose asphalt as he moved restlessly. "I wish they'd hurry the fuck up. I wanna slice into someone already." He faced the rest of them. "What do you think the chances are of T showing up?"

"He knows how bad we want him. He won't risk facing us all together," Chaos said without looking back. "He'll stay where he is. He knows Laz is coming for him which is exactly what he wants."

Kryos shook his head. "It still feels weird, y'know? T not standing with us."

"He made his choice," Roc snarled.

"We haven't suffered the loss of a mate. We don't know how we'd react." They all shut up at Kryos's quiet reply.

Then Zenon's eerie soft voice drifted from the shadows. "I don't plan on finding out."

Lazarus turned to him. "That's not a choice you get to make, brother."

Zenon reached back and drew his axes, shrugging his big shoulders. "I'm not like you."

Laz didn't get the chance to ask what he meant by that, because the wall ahead shimmered, a ripple of golden light moving across the surface like the brick was liquefying before their eyes. He tensed as five demons of varying breeds stepped through the activated hell's gate. Their hungry gazes darted around, searching for an opening.

"You know, it never ceases to amaze me just how butt ugly some of you fuckers are," Rocco said in a casual tone. "Or how stupid."

Kryos snorted beside him. Rocco wasn't wrong. Even in human form, this bunch made Freddy Krueger look like male-model material. Despite Rocco's casual words, he almost vibrated with rage and a need to fight. This group was nothing but a sacrifice, sent out first to distract them. More would be waiting to take their chances, and as soon as Laz and his brothers were busy fighting, would make a break for it before the gate sealed again.

Two of them were clever enough to realize Roc had just insulted them and growled.

Dropping all pretense of cool, calm, and collected, Rocco's patience evaporated and he lurched forward, his demon writhing restlessly beneath his skin. "Come on, you ugly fuckers. Let's go."

They fanned out, pulling their own weapons. The big one from the back stepped forward, a manic grin splitting its face. They learned why it was so pleased with itself when the mammoth dragged a human female from behind its back. Blood trailed down her neck and other wounds on her battered body. She looked like a walking corpse, her skin bruised and pallid, scarred emotionally and physically from months held below.

She'd been in the hands of absolute evil, her body used mercilessly, and in ways that would turn your stomach.

"Motherfucker," Kryos growled.

For the hell's gate to activate the demons needed to draw blood. Human blood was not necessary, but it was the most powerful. Which meant the gate would stay open longer.

Chaos cursed.

The female's eyes were blank, and she didn't make a sound nor did she struggle. Laz had seen that look before. Her mind had shut down, desperate to escape the unimaginable horrors she'd repeatedly suffered.

The demon fisted her hair and wrenched her head back, dragging its tongue up the trail of blood dripping down her throat. It grinned. "Let us past, Knight, or I'll remove her head."

Before anyone had the chance to answer, a whistling sound echoed above Lazarus's head.

The demons looked up.

Thud.

One of Zenon's axes landed dead center, almost cleaving the fucker's head in two.

"Jesus, Zen," Chaos muttered.

His fugly companions stared, stunned, for several seconds before all holy hell broke loose. The remaining four, knowing their options were limited, rushed them. They weren't particularly skilled and were dispatched with little effort. But more leaped through the portal and kept coming.

Two came at Laz. He took one out on the fly while the other circled him, trying to find an opening. Lazarus's demon rippled beneath his skin, desperate for release. It was a struggle, but he somehow managed to maintain his human form.

The demon struck out with its blade, but Laz deflected it with a kick to the sternum. The demon staggered back just as Chaos spun and swung, removing its head with his sword.

Kryos had closed in on the injured human female and shielded her as he fought. There were more demons than usual, the reason for that he had no idea, but it couldn't be anything good. Lazarus took out as many as he could, but more replaced them as soon as they were down.

He hissed in pain as a blade glanced off his ribs, and swung around to face his attacker. The coward had already taken off, running for the mouth of the alley. The next came at him before he could go after it. While they continued to fight, more were able to slip through and escape.

"There are too many," Chaos roared.

Laz couldn't move from his position as two more came at him. He looked across at Zenon. He wielded both axes at once and was cutting through the demons surrounding him to get to those making a break for it. Zenon managed to create a gap and took off, his heavy boots ricocheting off the brick walls.

They were bloody and pissed off by the time they'd cleared out the alley, crawling out of their skins, vibrating with the need to take their Kishi forms. Zenon hadn't yet returned, so they partially shifted, unfurling their wings and took to the skies in search of him and any escapees. Kryos flew in front of Laz, the injured human cradled in his arms, then veered off, heading for a human hospital. Her memories of her time in Hell would be blessedly wiped by the time she got there.

Laz let the wind lift him higher, the brittle night air ruffling his hair and whipping through his clothes, cooling his overheated skin. He spotted an Ibwa demon, a monster that feasted on the bodies of the dead, running through an empty parking lot. He dipped his right shoulder and made a tight turn, determined to stop it. But before he could get there, Zenon swooped out of nowhere, his leathery batlike wings catching the moonlight before he scooped the flailing, screaming demon off the ground and took it high into the skies.

Its lifeless body hit the asphalt with a sickening thud moments later, then turned to ash, the breeze scattering it into nothingness.

Lazarus sucked in a sharp breath as Eve's call grew in strength. She didn't even know she was doing it. But it coiled around him, holding fast, making his head spin. He was powerless against it and for once didn't fight it.

He let it lead him home.

Twelve

Lazarus woke with Eve pressed against him, and a raging hard-on. Not exactly conducive to the serious conversation he had to have with her this morning. First, he had to explain the heavy gold amulet he'd slipped over her head after she'd fallen asleep.

The piece of jewelry Silas gave them was supposed to help him somehow. Fucked if he knew what it did, but the angel had said "it was for her protection and would give him the time he needed"—whatever the fuck that meant. But they were leaving the compound today and he'd take any help offered to keep her safe.

He probably should have given it to her as soon as Chaos had given it to him, but, yeah, that would have meant questions he hadn't been ready to answer, still wasn't ready to answer.

He just hoped the angel's cryptic words meant what he thought they did, that they could slow things down, could take things at their own pace, but with the way he was feeling, he was having his doubts.

When he'd walked in last night, fresh from the hunt,

desperate to calm the demon within, he hadn't been able to resist climbing in with her, seeking her warmth. The connection between them was getting stronger by the day.

Christ. He felt like he was losing his mind.

With a little mewing sound, she wriggled closer, causing her shirt to ride up. Her soft warm belly pressed against his abs, scalding his skin, driving him insane. It took everything he had not to reach down and squeeze her delectable ass, spread her lush thighs, and bury himself deep inside her. His cock swelled and his hips surged forward of their own volition.

Fuck, he had to get out of this bed now.

But before he could move, she threw a leg over his hip, pressed her cheek against his chest, and burrowed a hand between their bodies, accidentally brushing the head of his achingly hard dick. He hissed and jerked back. "Fuck."

Her eyes blinked open, and she stared up at him in surprised confusion, looking way too damned adorable. *Fuck. No.* Shoving back, he scrambled out of bed and bolted for the bathroom before she got an eyeful of the tentpole in his boxers, and slammed the door.

"Motherfucker." Stripping off, he climbed straight into the shower and turned the temperature to cold. The water hit his skin like icy pinpricks, but did fuck all to cool his heated blood. Fisting his dick, he squeezed the turgid flesh, trying to kill his erection. *Dammit.* No matter how hard he tried to ignore it, he could still feel Eve's body pressed against his, her softness imprinted into his flesh, her scent branded into his senses.

His dick twitched against his palm, and he growled in frustration. He didn't want her in his head. She was fucking with his mind, not to mention his traitorous body.

Lazarus cursed himself for a fool, even as he rested a hand against the wall, gripped his heavy cock, and proceeded to jerk himself off with fast, brutal strokes. Sliding his palm from thick base to swollen head fast and hard. And all the while he thought about Eve's lips on his, the way she tasted, the way she felt pressed up against him. How those soft full lips would feel around his cock. That was all it took.

He gasped, coming in violent spurts, so hard his knees felt weak from it.

Resting his forehead against the cool tile, he took a minute to slow the beating of his heart before shutting off the water. On trembling thighs, he climbed out and tried not to think about the fact that in his mind it had been Eve's eyes watching him, Eve's hand working his dick, and Eve's name hissing through his lips as he'd emptied his balls.

Grabbing a pair of jeans from the laundry hamper, he shoved them on, opened the door, and walked into his bedroom.

Eve was sitting up, still under the covers, and she stared over at him warily. The heavy gold amulet he'd put around her neck last night was in her hands.

"What is this?" She traced the detailed angel's wings engraved on its otherwise smooth surface. "It's beautiful."

He doubted the delicate image was necessary for the amulet to be effective. Angels were just that damned arrogant.

When she looked up, she sucked in a breath. Her gaze locked on his chest, his brand. "Is that a burn?"

"Yes."

"That must have been incredibly painful."

"I barely remember. I've had it a long time."

Her eyes widened as she took in the rest of him. "My God, what happened to you?"

He glanced down at himself. He looked a lot better than last night. The bruising had all but gone, and the deeper slice he'd taken to the ribs was nothing more than an angry red line. He shrugged. "It's nothing."

"You've been hurt."

"I'm fine." He shoved his hands in his pockets. "I think it's time I told you a few things."

She released a shaky breath, but her voice didn't waver when she spoke. "I'd like that. I hate feeling so helpless."

Her inner strength truly amazed him. "That," he said, pointing to the necklace, "you must wear at all times."

"What is it?" He moved to her side and took it from her fingers. It was warm to the touch, heated from her skin. Lifting it, he slid it over her head, resting it between the swell of her breasts. It looked lovely around her neck.

Dammit, focus.

"The amulet is imbued with angelic power. I wish I could tell you exactly what it does. Angels like to be cryptic as fuck, but if they want you to wear this, there's a reason for it."

She tilted her head to the side. "Silas?"

Shit. "You heard us talking? What else did you hear?" The words came out harsher than he'd intended.

She shook her head. "Nothing really. I was pretty out of it. Silas is an angel?"

He released a relieved breath. "Yes." He was their own personal guardian angel, one who spoke in riddles and got his kicks out of confusing the shit out of his charges.

She nodded, and again amazed him with her strength. Her fingers brushed across the shiny golden chain. "Will it help with your brothers and how they reacted to me?"

"I don't know." Fucking Silas. Why couldn't he just say exactly what it did? Why all the damn secrets? "But it provides protection, wards against evil."

"Demons?"

He nodded.

She bit her lower lip. "What about...ah, what about you?"

Is that what she wanted? Something to protect her from him? He wished the amulet worked that way, for both their sakes. But when he woke up this morning, he realized it wasn't going to be that easy. Yes, her power was now masked from him, and the part of her that had made it possible for him to track her like he had when she first came into her power was blocked. And yeah, that was a really fucking good thing. No demon would be able to sense her while she wore it. But that weird tight feeling in his chest, the buzz in the back of his skull, that awareness of her, was still there just as intense as before, which meant, he was shit out of luck. Whatever Silas meant when he said it would "give him the time he needed" had nothing to do with dimming his desire for Eve, or the call to mate with her, like he'd hoped it would.

The amulet was designed for something else entirely. And he guessed for something more than what he'd discovered this morning. He just wished he knew what exactly.

"It doesn't affect me in that way," he said.

She tilted her head to the side. "Okay."

He couldn't read her expression, didn't know if she was pleased, disappointed, or indifferent. He shoved his fingers through his hair, at a loss for words, no damn clue how to proceed with her sitting there staring at him. "Christ, Eve, I'm sorry. I'm so fucking sorry."

"For what?" she said, voice a soft rasp that skittered across his skull.

"For throwing your life into chaos, for dragging you into my fucked-up world," he choked out.

Her fingers unconsciously toyed with the golden disk at her throat. "You had no choice. You saved me, Lazarus."

He cursed and stood, pacing away.

"What is it?"

He cleared his throat. "Just...don't take off the necklace."

She blinked up at him. "I won't."

"Look, I know you're frightened. My brothers, they scared you." Mother of all understatements. "But that wasn't them. I've talked to them, and they feel like shit for the way they acted. There's a lot going on at the moment. Shit that's fucking with us in a big way. Just know that I'll do whatever I have to. I'll make sure you're safe. No matter where I am." Once he and Eve were mated and everything had died down, this would be her home. These were her people. He needed her to trust them or he'd never be able to leave her.

She didn't speak, but watched him with those big innocent eyes. She was so damn sweet.

"Eve? Do you trust me to do that for you?" he asked, needing to hear the words from her.

She gave him an unconvincing jerk of her chin. It shouldn't, but her unconvincing response gutted him. He didn't deserve her trust, but he wanted it all the same.

"Take a shower and pack your stuff. We leave in half an hour." She flinched at his sudden abrupt tone. Jesus. He fucking hated that he frightened her so damn easily. But most of all, he hated that he cared.

Eve sat perched on the edge of a bed in the hotel room they'd checked into earlier while Lazarus stalked about restlessly. The guy really was huge, well over six feet. His hair was rumpled from him shoving his fingers into it repeatedly. The disheveled look didn't help soften him any.

The size of him, coupled with those hard features and lately a permanent scowl, ensured the guy had the same effect as an escaped grizzly when he entered a room.

As he moved, she couldn't help but admire the strength of his body, not to mention his lean hips and fine butt. What would it be like to be with a man like him? The thought had plagued her since waking pressed against his hard chest, his hand resting on her hip, his heavy legs tangled with hers.

She almost snorted out loud at the ridiculous notion.

She'd certainly never find out. It was like their kiss had never happened. When she'd woken, he'd shoved her back like she had cooties then stormed to the bathroom and shut himself in.

Now they were stuck in an airport hotel due to a mess-up with their tickets, waiting for the next available flight. Lazarus wasn't handling this news well.

His jeans hung low, molded to his powerful legs as they ate up the carpeted floor. Heavy black boots carried him to a small table and chairs in front of the sliding glass doors, and he shrugged off his leather jacket, slinging it over the table.

He scowled deeper, crossing his arms, and glared out the window. The plain black T-shirt he wore strained around his biceps, and she couldn't help admire the intricate tattoo that completely covered his right arm. It snaked its way up the corded muscle, disappeared under the sleeve, and reappeared halfway up the side of his neck.

He was like no other man she had ever met, utterly masculine. She shivered at all that barely restrained power. He was so different from Eric it was laughable.

Would he stay with her when they reached their destination, or would he drop her off and go? Anxiety accompanied the thought along with an unreasonable feeling of loss. God, she was confused. Why couldn't she think when he was near? The desire that stirred inside her when she was with him was intense, completely out of her control, and made absolutely no frickin' sense.

That delicious scent of his filled the small room, demanding a response she didn't understand. Her body reacted once again, but no matter how nice he'd been, how well he'd taken care of her after she'd blacked out, how he'd made her feel when he kissed her, she couldn't allow herself to get attached. She didn't know him, not really. She wasn't anything special. This was his job.

"That's an impressive tattoo you have there. Did it hurt when you had it done?" she asked, needing to get out of her own head. Her reaction to being separated from him was ridiculous.

"I was born with it." He rubbed his hand over the large colorful symbols, each linked to the next. "It tells a story. What we are, where we come from. Each knight has one."

She wanted to ask what the beautiful symbols meant, but his closed-off expression made it clear the subject was not up for conversation. He confirmed it when he turned away, staring out the window again, shoulders tense.

"Are we safe here?" she asked.

"I don't think we've been followed. I can't sense any Orthon nearby, but I can't be sure," he said.

"That isn't very reassuring," she muttered.

He spun around, and his gaze pinned her to the spot. "I won't let anything happen to you," he said with a fierceness that made it impossible to doubt. "I promise you that."

She could only nod in answer, once again caught in the emerald depths of his eyes. Her body heated and her cheeks flushed at the reaction.

He turned back to the window. "I used a protection spell to ward the room. If they manage to track us, they can't get to you without doing serious, even fatal damage to themselves. Can you feel it?"

Ever since she'd stepped into their room, she'd been aware of a kind of faint electric current, a slight tingling across her skin. "I think I can, yes."

Without looking back, he said, "Tell me about your power, Eve."

Not a request. They hadn't really talked about her powers since her collapse. Her training sessions had been cut short as well, and now she'd left the compound she wasn't sure how she was going to master them. The sudden change of subject was obviously a way to distract her, to stop her from worrying, but now she just had another thing to worry about.

They had the night to kill before the next available flight out. She'd rather watch a movie than talk about how afraid she was of the demon side of herself, but Lazarus wasn't the kind of man you argued with.

"When it first started, I could only hear a person when they were in my immediate vicinity, but lately it seems to have grown stronger. Sometimes I even get the odd image flashing through my mind," she admitted.

"It's developing. It'll only become more intense over time."

He delivered it in that same emotionless, matter-of-fact way. No biggie. Like the other bombs he'd dropped since he'd stormed into her life.

Because of this thing, because of what she was, she'd already been torn from her life. She couldn't see anything positive in her future if she couldn't master her power. How could she ever have any type of relationship with all that noise vibrating through her skull? Suffering through every one of their negative thoughts, streaming directly into her head, smacking her around the cranium until she was emotionally bruised and battered.

All she could see ahead of her was more loneliness.

At that moment, the fragile walls she'd built since Lazarus stormed into her life crumbled. It was too much. Eve tried to hide her face, horrified when the first sob tore from her throat.

"Eve?"

"Why me?" She shook her head in her hands. "I don't want this. I don't want any of this. I wish you'd just...I wish you'd..." She was unable to say the words.

Footsteps moved toward her. Lazarus knelt and took her frozen hands in his, rubbing them between his large rough ones. He'd seen something in her, had heard it in her voice. "You wish I'd what?" he said, voice low, hard, terrifying.

She didn't want to talk about it. Not now, not ever. "Nothing. Forget I said anything."

"Answer me, Eve. You will finish that sentence." He placed a finger under her chin and made her look at him.

Humiliation colored her cheeks, and her gaze darted away, focusing on anything but the male in front of her. How could she admit to what had been going through her mind? What had gone through her mind more times than she wanted to admit, even to herself?

"Look at me," he growled.

Disappearing sounded like a fantastic idea about now, but he wasn't giving up anytime soon, and last time she checked, vanishing wasn't part of her skill set.

"Eve, look at me. Now."

No. Anything but this. Don't make me say it. As fascinating as the purple flowers on the curtains were, she couldn't stare at them all night. So she lifted her gaze, zeroing in on his chin, and after several seconds trailed up to his lips, lips that made her want things, so many impossible things.

Swallowing down the lump in her throat, she ignored the nerves flapping in her belly and locked stares with him. "I wish...I wish you'd ended all this for me the moment you'd walked into my store," she whispered.

His nostrils flared and his jaw clenched so tight she winced. "You want me to end your life?" he said so quietly she barely heard him.

She cringed. Hearing her own words out loud for the first time made what had only ever been a thought in the back of her mind during her darkest moments, real.

He shook his head and those lips she'd been admiring curled. "I thought you were stronger than that. You're not the only person in the world to have a shitty life, Eve. And believe me, you're not the only person to want to check out and leave it all behind. But I will tell you this right now. You don't get to bail on me. Do you understand? I won't let you."

Anger welled up inside her. "Why the hell do you care?" she yelled. "You don't know anything about me or my life."

His nostrils flared as he dragged in a rough breath. "I want to...on both counts."

She shook her head, didn't want to hear this, didn't want to risk believing in him, or his empty words.

He cupped her jaw. "This new world, it's your world. Where you belong. It won't be a walk in the park, but things will settle down. You'll meet people like you. You will find acceptance...a life worth living. I promise you that."

Hope bloomed, no matter how much she wanted to deny it or try to squash it and protect herself from any more pain.

"I can help you, Eve. It may take time, but you will eventually be capable of blocking your power when you want to. Until then, I'll continue to do it for you."

She searched his eyes. "Really?"

"Of course." He smiled, a small curve of his lips, not like the one he'd given her in his bathroom back at the compound, but his face transformed. His callused hands worked hers, thawing the chill from her fingers like nothing else could, and sent little tingles up her arms as his skin grazed lightly across hers.

Her gaze moved over his features, hard, fierce, then down to his mouth. He would have looked brutal if not for that sensual mouth. He reached up and, using the pad of his thumb, brushed her cheek with tender care. It came away wet.

"I'm sorry, it's just...this is just..."

"Shhh, it's all right. It's going to be all right." He leaned forward and kissed her next tear away, followed by the next. Featherlight presses of those firm lips moved along her cheek, then worked their way to her jaw and across to her mouth.

Their lips met, the heat of his searing hers. Lazarus's big body tensed against hers for a split second, but then he repeated the touch, tentative at first. His tongue eased out, tasting the seam of her lips in a sensual slide that had her opening for him without thought or hesitation, and he swept inside.

Totally lost to the exquisite, drugging sensation of his kiss, the world dissolved around her. He growled low, pulling her in closer, gripping her tighter. She leaned in as well, needing to feel his body pressed against hers, and clutched at his shoulders. A whimper filled the silence, and she realized the needy sound had come from her. Reaching up, she threaded her fingers in his hair and tried to tug him closer, like that was even possible.

What started as sweet and gentle erupted into almost painful hunger. Her body went up in flames. This wasn't a slow exploration anymore; this was hard, urgent, all-consuming. This was madness, but she couldn't stop, didn't want to stop. Something happened when he touched her, and all sanity flew out the window.

She fisted his shirt and moaned into his mouth as he moved forward, looming over her, forcing her back on the bed. His hard body came down on hers while rough fingers tugged at the buttons down the front of her dress.

When there was enough room, he slipped his large hand inside, groaning as he cupped and squeezed her breast, pinching the hard nipple through the silk fabric of her bra. She whimpered as he continued to ravage her mouth. His tongue moved against hers with a sensual onslaught that left her head swimming and her body hot and desperate for more.

Her legs parted and his large body instantly filled the vacant space. The massive proof of his arousal brushed the most aching part of her and he growled again. One of his hands moved down to cup her rear, holding her tight against him, and he rolled his hips.

Eve cried out, both relieved and tortured by the pressure she'd been desperate for. His mouth trailed down her neck, sucking and nibbling, sending her into sensation overload as he ground against her again, the intense contact only heightened further by the lace of her panties moving against her sensitive flesh. She was wet and hot, and his repeated thrusts quickly brought her to the edge.

She shifted beneath him, tilting her hips to gain closer contact. She needed more, wanted everything. "Please, Lazarus," she whimpered. "Please, I need you."

He stilled abruptly, his powerful biceps locking under her palms. His big body shook and sweat beaded on his forehead.

"What is it?" Midnight flashed across his irises. "Lazarus... your eyes."

He flinched.

She reached up, touching his temple. "What's wrong?"

He shuddered and shook his head. "Nothing."

Her mouth fell open when he rolled his hips again.

"Don't stop," she gasped.

He thrust again, his teeth gritted.

Eve cried out, body trembling beneath him. Then she was coming, waves of heat, of pleasure, washing over her so strong all she could do was cling to him.

Lazarus's face went to the side of her neck, puffs of his hot breath tickling her skin. They stayed like that for several minutes. He was still hard.

"Lazarus..."

He moved then, sliding off her but staying close. She tried to keep her eyes open.

"Rest," he said.

She didn't have much choice. She was exhausted all of a sudden, boneless.

Eve woke several times during the night, and each time Lazarus was there beside her. When she finally woke to the morning sun streaming under the curtains she was alone in bed. Lazarus stood by the window, looking out at the streets below.

"You're awake," she said, lifting to her elbows.

He turned to her, a tight, pained smile curving his lips. "Yeah. I wanted to make sure we're safe to leave. I can't sense anything close by."

She held the sheet close to her chest. "That's good."

His gaze slid over her. "It's time to get ready. We need to leave soon."

He turned away, giving her what privacy he could in the small room as she climbed out of bed.

"I'll just go freshen up." She rushed to the bathroom and closed herself in.

Some kind of force was pushing her toward him. She felt it, and it was so incredibly strong. She certainly wasn't acting like herself. She wasn't overly experienced, had only slept with two guys, and now she was throwing herself at a man, a demon, she hardly knew.

He'd gotten her off, but hadn't done the same.

She swallowed, a lump forming in her throat. Did he not want her like that? He'd kissed her twice, but last night he hadn't...

Eve shut down the direction her thoughts were going.

She stared at herself in the mirror, her still puffy lips from kissing him, her wild hair, and cringed. God, the guy had only been trying to make her feel better, and she'd jumped him.

Get it together, Eve.

This was a job for him. Nothing more.

She couldn't afford to forget that again.

Thirteen

Lazarus led Eve to their seats on board the Boeing 737. Christ, he hated traveling this way, but they didn't have much choice. They usually used their own plane for times like this when they needed to travel with their demi, but since Gunner was their pilot, that option was out. Gunner had gotten worse, had locked himself in one of the holding cells below their compound, afraid he'd hurt someone.

Lazarus glanced at Eve. She hadn't met his eyes since this morning, had kept them hidden from him since they did what they had last night.

After the way he'd acted, her silence didn't surprise him. He'd come so damn close to taking her, to sinking inside her and losing his head completely. He should have pulled away, but there was no way he could have left her wanting. Every part of him had rejected the idea.

So he'd fucking rubbed up on her until she got off then he'd forced himself to stop before his control snapped completely and he'd taken more. Fuck, it had left him hurting.

That persistent hum, his constant awareness of Eve had only gotten more intense. It felt like she was plugged directly into his nervous system and sent a continual electrical current straight to his dick.

Shit, having her soft, pliant body beside him had tormented him through the long night, but he couldn't make himself get up and sleep in the chair. She'd wriggled and squirmed in her sleep, had made these breathy little sounds, driving him crazy. He'd barely resisted finishing where they'd left off. Taking what he wanted. What he needed.

The situation was a huge mess, and after her confession last night—that she would rather die, than face this new life—he had to tread very carefully from now on. But the pain radiating from her had damn near killed him.

He scrubbed his hands over his face. His mind whirled, full of contradictions.

What the hell was he going to do? What if he couldn't convince her that mating with him was the best decision for both of them?

And then there was the effect Eve's presence had on his demon, something he hadn't anticipated. Especially since they hadn't mated yet. When he'd touched her, kissed her, his demon had actually calmed. Shit, the bastard had purred. Oh, it still reared and bucked, but only because that dark side of him craved the light it recognized in Eve.

He found he was capable of a level of control over his demon that he hadn't had since Tobias's desertion. Since he found Eve, he'd twice prevented his demon from breaking free and wreaking the havoc it continually screamed for, and both times that had been because of her.

What if they didn't have to mate?

Could sex be enough?

If that was the answer, she'd be able to move on with her life once he'd taken down Tobias. He and his brothers would regain control and she wouldn't be tied to him, not in any way. His desire for her wouldn't lessen, but then he'd already planned to walk away, to face a future craving her and never being satisfied. A price he was willing to pay. Whatever it took to protect her from him.

It would mean deceiving her, but it would be for the best. In the long run, it would be for the best.

He squeezed his eyes shut.

How could he ask that of her? How could he ask her to let him use her body like that? Besides, he wasn't even sure it would work. Was he willing to risk his brothers to find out?

Jesus, he'd lost his goddamned mind.

Until recently, they'd all been tracking Tobias. The situation hadn't been ideal. They still had to retrieve the newly changed demi-demons, like Eve, while hunting rogue demons that escaped into the city. Now they were all unstable, and in Gunner's case, caged like a wild animal. Things couldn't get much worse. His only option was holding off his own demon long enough to find Tobias.

And there was only one way that he knew how to do that with certainty.

Mating with Eve.

Their brother's death was the only thing that could restore the delicate balance between good and evil warring inside each of them. If he failed, the knights would be lost forever, and mankind would become easy prey to Diemos and his demons.

A child's cry brought him from his thoughts and back to the now full plane. Eve was settled back in her seat, still avoiding his gaze, and she continued to do so after they'd taken flight a short time later.

He could feel her fear and had the uncharacteristic urge to provide comfort. He'd never been good with words, or people for that matter, and had no idea how to go about it. But at this point, anything he said would be insufficient.

So he stayed quiet.

He glanced over at Eve again, unable to help himself. She

was dressed in jeans and a blue shirt with the words *Read Books Not T-shirts* stretched across her large breasts. The female looked good, too damn good. Her thick, dark hair sat piled on top of her head in a loose ponytail, and some of it had broken free to frame her pale face as she looked around the plane with wide eyes, biting her lower lip nervously.

Don't look at her mouth.

He quickly turned away.

Time dragged, then halfway through the movie they were watching, Eve asked, "You said demi-demons are trained and released?"

"Yes."

"So how long will I be staying with you? When will I be... released?"

Never, if I have my way. But he didn't say that. Hell, he didn't know where the possessive words filling his head had come from. Instead, he said, "Each demi is different. Once they're trained to shield and control their powers, and we're convinced they've mastered those skills and will be safe in the outside world, we allow them to leave and start their new lives."

She nodded.

"It'll be all right, Eve. You can do this." He shrugged. "You have to do this. Failure isn't an option." He was pushing, trying to bring back the feisty woman who fought him in her store. He hated seeing her this way.

She frowned. "You keep saying that, but it doesn't feel all right." She turned and faced him fully, fire flashing behind her eyes. "I can tell you, from where I'm sitting, none of this nightmare feels *all fucking right*."

There it was: that spirited side of her nature that would get her through this ordeal. She'd been quiet, withdrawn since last night, and it was entirely his fault. He'd acted like an animal in that room.

He couldn't help it; he grinned at her.

Her brows shot up. "What are you smiling about? You think this is *funny*?"

"No. I'd just rather you yell at me than not speak at all."

The corners of her mouth tipped up a little. "It's a lot to take in."

He reached over and grabbed her hand, not just to provide comfort, but because he couldn't help himself. "I know, but it's that strength of yours that will get you through this, Eve. Don't ever forget that."

What the hell? Suddenly I'm a fucking shrink.

She studied his face. "I hope you're right."

"I know I am." He kept hold of her hand. Disturbingly, he was unable to let her go. Her fingers wrapped in his felt good... right.

She dropped her gaze. "I'm glad I've got you here to help me through this."

"I'm not going anywhere." He tightened his grip on her fingers as if to prove the point. "Eve, look...last night, what happened between us..." He ran a hand through his hair. "Shit, what I'm trying to say is..., I acted like an asshole," he stammered out. Christ, he sounded like a spotty teenager.

"After you...after we..." She stopped mid-sentence, apparently having the same trouble.

"Talk to me, Eve."

She looked everywhere but at him. "Something's going on, something I can't explain. I don't usually, you know, dive on guys like that."

Now wasn't an ideal time to explain what she was to him, but then he wasn't sure there ever would be. And so far, all his other attempts had failed. At least this way she couldn't get up and run the fuck away. "There's something I need to tell you."

She looked down. "No, it's fine, really. I understand why you didn't take things further. I just wanted you to know that's not how I usually behave. I know I put you in an awkward position."

She put *him* in an awkward position? "What are you talking about?"

She glanced up at him, puzzled.

"Why do you think I stopped?" he added.

Her cheeks darkened, and she cleared her throat. "You're not attracted to me. You were just being kind."

How could she think that? Words spilled from his mouth like someone else had taken control of his vocal cords. "Jesus, you couldn't be more wrong." He sounded needy as hell, but was past caring. "You cause such a hunger inside me, Eve. As it is, I can barely control myself around you. I want you so bad I can barely think of anything else. And just so you know, right now I'm so fucking hard for you it hurts."

He'd yakked up the contents of his frustrated and confused mind without restraint, and instantly wished he could take it back. But going by the intoxicating, purely feminine scent that drifted up to wrap around his senses, Eve was right there with him.

Her nipples hardened, the peaks straining against her T-shirt. He licked his lips, mouth watering for a taste of her. He might not have wanted to rush her, but being half angel sure as hell didn't make him a saint.

The hard length of his cock burned hot against his stomach. Thank God his shirt was covering all that was going on down there, because the thing had popped past the waistband of his jeans—like it was trying for a look-see at what he wanted so damn bad.

Her cheeks flushed, making him want her even more. She bit her lip, and the innocence that had captivated him the minute he'd laid eyes on her returned in her wide-eyed stare.

"There's more," he said.

She sucked in a breath. "More?"

"Yeah, I just..." Where the hell should he start?

"You're starting to freak me out, Lazarus."

Fuck it. "You're not just a demi-demon, Eve, you are..." He stared into her beautiful eyes. "You are *my* demi-demon."

She blinked several times then blurted, "What do you mean, *yours*?"

Inwardly, he winced at the look of horror covering her face. "You're my mate."

"What? You mean like..." She paled. "You mean like Kryos and Meredith?"

Okay, this was harder than he thought. "Yes. Each knight has a female somewhere in the world." She stared at him, and he shifted in his seat. "She is everything he needs—will ever need. Once they mate, the warrior's strength increases and the demon half of him stabilizes." He reached out, unable to stop himself from brushing a loose strand of hair behind her ear. "And for a demi, mating means immortality...and the protection and devotion of her warrior for eternity."

"Immortality?"

"Yes." The disbelief quickly disappeared from her face.

No, sweetheart, I'm not making any of this shit up.

"And you're my...my warrior?"

Hearing her say those words nearly had him undone. The cabin lights were low for the night flight and highlighted the shadows beneath Eve's eyes. She looked fragile. He wanted nothing more than to pull her into his lap and convince her everything would be all right. But he couldn't, because it wouldn't. "Yes, and you are my female." He barely recognized his voice, the words rasping past his lips. "But nothing is set in stone. In the end, the decision must be yours, Eve."

Her eyes widened. "I...I..."

"You don't need to decide now." He'd have a better chance of her accepting him if she believed she had a choice in this. He just hoped she made the right one.

She blinked up at him. He wanted to say more, to reassure her, but his reply caught in his throat when unease wrapped around him like a dark shadow, so damn suffocating.

"What's going on?" Eve said, picking up on his sudden change of mood.

Lazarus stood, unable to respond, and stepped into the aisle. He pretended to get something from the overhead storage compartment and glanced across the rows of passengers in the front and behind them, searching. Most appeared asleep or watching a movie. He did another pass.

Fuck.

"What are you doing?" Eve tried again, voice shaky.

Pins and needles tap-danced down his spine, right before milky eyes opened and the fucker returned his stare, smiling.

They were still an hour from Chicago, but the Orthon wouldn't attempt anything until they were free of witnesses. He sat back down without a word.

"What is it?" The concern in Eve's voice and etched into her features caused rage to course through his veins. He wouldn't let anything happen to her. "It's nothing."

Uncertainty shifted through her gaze, and she opened her mouth to say more.

"We'll talk more later." Lazarus surrounded her with the compulsion to sleep. He'd used it a lot on her lately and he felt a little guilty, but it was better than letting her freak out for the next hour. She visibly relaxed and made a *hmm* sound.

In a matter of minutes, she'd drifted off to sleep beside him.

The flight seemed to take forever, but finally, their plane touched down. He reached up and collected Eve's carry-on.

"Are we here?" she asked groggily.

"Yeah."

She stood, and he led her toward the exit. First, he had to

get her out of the airport. After that, Brent, another demi, would put them up at a secure location.

He glanced behind them, spotting the Orthon. It was in the guise of a middle-aged male, following and gaining on them quickly.

"What's going on, Lazarus?"

As usual, Eve didn't miss a thing. "We have company," he said with a sharp glance over his shoulder.

Clever girl that she was, no further explanations were necessary. She grabbed his hand and picked up the pace beside him.

Fourteen

Lazarus steered Eve toward a large group of people milling about and pushed his way through the center of the crowd. He turned abruptly, and Eve hung on tight as he pulled her down a short corridor, completely ignoring the *Staff only* sign.

Pausing, he forced her behind his body, pressing her against the wall. Eve peered around one of his thick biceps. A man turned into the hall, colorless eyes trained on her.

Laz swore under his breath.

"Lazarus?" Those weird creamy eyes never wavered from her, and her stomach lurched. This was actually happening. It wasn't a nightmare, and that *thing* was coming for her.

"It won't get anywhere near you."

He pulled her farther down the corridor, following a narrow passage that turned to the left. Lazarus opened the first door they came to.

"In here." He pushed her inside and shut her in.

The *click* of the lock engaging followed.

He'd done that trick using his powers to lock it from the

outside, and she instantly felt that electric buzz over her skin, which meant he'd somehow warded the room.

Silence engulfed the small space.

She was frozen to the spot, adrenaline racing through her veins with no outlet. The silence was filled by her pulse echoing through her skull and blood rushing in her ears.

She couldn't hear what was happening beyond the flimsy door—

A deep growl ripped through the room, followed by a thump that rattled the door on its hinges.

Then nothing.

Time seemed to tick by at a snail's pace, and Eve held her breath, waiting.

When it finally came, the lock releasing was barely audible over her thumping heart. She scrambled back until her heels collided with the wall behind her. Frantically, she searched for a weapon, anything. Standard-issue airport one-ply lined the walls, but she didn't think hurling toilet rolls at a crazed demon would cut it.

The handle turned and the door eased open.

Eve's breath caught in her throat—

Then released on a *whoosh,* when Lazarus poked his head in, eyes downcast. "Wait here. I need to make sure he was alone." Then he was gone again.

He seemed calm, like fighting killer demons in busy airports was an everyday occurrence. How could she do this, live this life? Where monsters were real and didn't just go bump in the night. No, they came out in broad freaking daylight. Thinking about that wasn't a good idea, not while she was stuck in here. She concentrated on slowing her heart rate, which wasn't working since she couldn't stop pacing around the tiny floor space.

A few minutes later, Lazarus stepped back into the room. She looked out into the hall, where the Orthon's ashy remains lay on the ground in a pile behind him. Lazarus closed and locked the door.

"He was alone?"

He didn't answer her.

Eve took him in more closely. His chest was pumping at a rapid pace, and the veins and tendons in his neck and hands stood out on his tanned skin. Sweat beaded on his forehead and he was gritting his teeth as the muscles in his shoulders moved unnaturally beneath his jacket.

He wouldn't look at her.

Oh God. "Lazarus?" She took a step forward.

"Don't." His voice rumbled darkly and lifted goose bumps across her skin. "Stay back."

"What's wrong? Are you injured?"

His head shot up. Eyes black and unblinking stared back. Not even a flicker of green remained.

"Lazarus?"

He shook his head, teeth gritted. God, he looked in such terrible pain.

He wanted her to stay back, but how could she? She couldn't bear to see him like that. He said he'd never hurt her, and she believed him. So she took a step closer, approaching him slowly, like you would a wild animal.

He watched her, or she thought he did; it was hard to tell with his eyes washed in black like that.

When she was standing in front of him, she reached for him. She didn't know what she could do, but she wanted to help with whatever had caused this transformation. She lifted her hand and gently cupped the side of his face.

He hissed, his chest pumping rapidly. The light show started in his irises again, like it had back at her house and at the compound. He moaned and turned in to her palm, pushing into her touch like a contented house cat.

"Lazarus? What's happening?" she choked out.

He lifted his gaze, and with the color trying to break back through, they were easier to read. Need, dark and hungry, stared back at her, freezing her to the spot. He looked almost feral. She wasn't afraid, though. No, instead her body heated, responding to the raw lust burning into her.

Despite all she'd gone through in such a short time, her only thought at that moment was what Lazarus had said to her on the plane earlier.

"You cause such a hunger inside me, Eve. As it is, I can barely control myself around you. I want you so bad I can barely think of anything else."

The enclosed space caused his delicious scent to fill the tiny room. His massive body crowded her, surrounded her. She didn't know what was happening to her, to both of them, and right then she didn't care.

"Don't," he rasped, even as he moved closer, as he rubbed his cheek against her palm.

"I can't help it," she replied, more than a little shocked by her actions.

Demons were hunting her. Who knew what would happen when they walked out that door? If she didn't act now, she might never know what it was like to be with him. Could she live with that? No. She was surprised to realize she couldn't.

Eve had played by everyone else's rules all her life. Time after time her family had rejected her then dumped her like garbage. She'd spent most of her life ignored and unwanted—until now. It didn't matter if it was only a day, an hour, hell, a minute—she would take it. It felt too good not to.

His eyes flared. "Don't do this." He drew in a deep, shuddering breath.

"I can't stop myself. I don't want to." She ran her hands up the ridged planes of his abs and across the solid wall of his chest to push the heavy leather jacket from his shoulders. The thump as it hit the floor sounded loud in the quiet room.

"We can't do this," he croaked. "You deserve better than to be fucked against the wall in a goddamned supply cupboard."

She clamped her thighs together in an attempt to ease the ache. "Please." She pressed closer, desperate to have his hands on her.

His eyes bore into hers. "This force between us...it's too strong. I won't be able to stop this time...do you understand?" He shook his head. "Fuck. I need you," his voice caught on the last word.

"I'm here." She'd die if he didn't touch her soon.

"I won't be gentle, Eve. I can't. If you want to change your mind, do it now," he warned, voice ragged.

She shook her head, liquid heat flooding her sex at his needy words. "I won't change my mind."

His eyes did that thing where they flashed between emerald and ebony. "Then touch me, Eve. Just...I need you to touch me."

The desperate plea kicked her into action. She slid her hands under his shirt, marveling at the smooth hot skin beneath before lifting it up and over his head. His body was magnificent, all corded, sinewy strength.

He thrust his fingers into her hair, and the loose hair tie fell away, releasing the heavy mass. His eyes seemed to stabilize then, but remained a darker shade than before.

He reached down and yanked up her shirt, shoving it over her head, tracking every move like the massive predator he was. The pure unrestrained hunger in his eyes successfully eliminated any lingering apprehension she had about the way her body looked. Instead, she felt bold and sexy for the first time in her life.

Large, rough hands cupped her breasts through the white cotton cups of her bra before he pinched the hardened buds between his fingers. Eve whimpered—she wanted his hands on her bare flesh—and reached for the center clasp. He let out a low moan of appreciation as she undid it, letting her full breasts bounce free.

"Jesus, you're killing me. I have to—" His voice surrounded her, wild and barely in control. Dipping his head, he caught one aching peak between his teeth and sucked hard. She moaned from the sensation of his hot wet mouth on her sensitive flesh and held his head against her. He looked up. His eyes had changed again, were paler. Then rational thought scattered as he moved to her other breast, drawing her hard nipple deep, devouring her. She bit her lip to keep from crying out.

With deft fingers, he undid her jeans then thrust a hand down the front of her panties, sliding through her slick folds, grazing her clit repeatedly. She whimpered and clutched at his heavy arms to stay upright.

Without warning, two thick fingers entered her. She cried out as he pushed inside, driving her higher. Her body moved of its own volition, her hips rolling against his hand.

He rested his forehead against hers. "Jesus, you're so damn hot, so tight and wet around my fingers. I need to feel you wrapped around my cock," he said against her mouth before he kissed her hard and demanding. His tongue moved against hers in an imitation of what was coming.

His other hand slid between their bodies, and he fumbled with his jeans. He shifted back, and his heavy cock sprang free, pre-come already glistened at the head.

He was long and thick, and beautiful.

"I can't wait any longer...need inside you. Need to feel you squeezing me tight, sweetheart."

"Yes." That was all she could manage.

He removed his hand from her panties, but instead of moving his massive body between her thighs, he looked at his fingers, glistening, covered in her, and brought them to his mouth, sucking each finger clean.

His eyes drifted shut and he groaned. "Fuck, Eve. You taste better than I imagined." The next time I have you, I'm going to take my time feasting on you. I'm going to do all the things I've wanted to do since the minute I saw you." He opened his eyes and the uninhibited desire staring back caused another rush of liquid heat between her thighs. "Do you want that, too?" he asked hoarsely.

She managed a shaky nod.

In seconds, he had removed her jeans and panties completely and pressed her into the wall.

"Now, please," she said, not ashamed to beg.

He lifted her like she weighed nothing, and had her wrap her legs around his waist. He fisted his thick shaft, positioning himself.

Holy hell, the guy was huge everywhere. Apprehension must have shown on her face because he gripped her chin and made her look at him.

"I'm big, but you can take all of me. You were made for me. This body was made for me. I'll make this good for you." He slid the head of his cock through her folds, covering himself in her arousal before working his thick shaft inside her. He drew back a little to allow her body a chance to accommodate his size before feeding her another inch.

"Christ, you're so tight...feels so good," he gasped.

"Lazarus...I need..." She stopped talking as he drew out slow then slid back home, fully seating himself. Her eyes drifted closed.

He groaned long and low.

She loved how out of control he seemed and forced her eyes open to watch him. She gasped when their stares collided, his steady gaze already locked on her as he drew back then slammed home. Too much, those eyes of his were too damn much. She tried to look away, but he gripped her jaw, stopping her.

"Don't hide from me. I want to see your face when you come," he said.

With each thrust he ground against her swollen clit, filling her deeper. She was half out of her mind by the time he leaned in and took her mouth in a brutal kiss.

Hungry for more, she nipped his lower lip. When he hissed, she ran her tongue over the abused flesh and sucked, soothing the sting, and Lazarus seemed to snap. His hips slammed forward, going so deep she gasped. His pace increased, taking her hard and fast. His chest pumped, and his breath came in fast pants.

"*Oh God.*" It was too much. Pleasure sent her reeling when he slammed into her next. She stiffened as her orgasm hit, and sunk her teeth into the muscle of his shoulder to stop the scream about to tear from her throat.

One of his big hands slapped against the wall by her head, and he growled.

Her inner muscles tightened, squeezing repeatedly around him. Lazarus shook, his big body almost vibrating as he moved his hands to her ass. He angled his hips, hitting her deeper as he thrust into her. Then he was coming, and so was she. Again.

He snarled—a wild, untamed sound that was anything but human, and dropped his head to her shoulder, shudders still rolling through him.

His skin felt hot and slick against hers, and goose bumps prickled her flesh as he panted, his warm breath tickling her neck.

After a few seconds, he lifted his head. "You okay?"

Was he joking? She'd never experienced anything like that before. She couldn't help it—she grinned. "Ah, you were in this...um"—she looked around—"cupboard with me, weren't you?"

His lips tilted up, offering her the smallest of grins. As he brushed her hair back behind her ear, his expression turned serious. "Is your arm all right?"

"It's fine."

He frowned.

Was he second-guessing himself and what they'd done? Did he regret it? "Lazarus—"

"It's time for us to go." He glanced down at her nakedness and once again darkened his gaze.

Her skin flushed with heat. "Okay."

He stared at her for a long second like he was going to say more, but then let Eve slide to the ground and stepped back.

The moment was over.

Fifteen

Oh yeah, what they'd done had complicated the hell out of things. He rubbed a hand over his forearm. Jesus, he had goose bumps, his skin still tingling, fucking alive.

Being buried inside Eve—nothing had ever felt so good. It'd taken everything he had not to yell *mine* when he'd come. The power of his release had almost knocked him on his ass. He could still feel her, tight and hot around him, gripping him—could still smell her sweet scent.

He shifted, trying to accommodate the hard-on that wouldn't quit, his body aching for more of her already. He needed to get his shit back under control, but damn, it was a struggle. Especially with his demon hovering just below the surface, just as hungry for Eve as Lazarus.

The bastard was just waiting for another chance to break free.

He stared out the window of the cab, trying to keep it together. Not fucking likely when he could hear the way Eve kept shifting in her seat, when the scent of her arousal was reaching out to him, coiling around him. He took slow, even breaths, and did his damnedest to ignore the way she was affecting him. *Like that'll help.*

Lazarus knew better. There was no help for it. Because standing outside that door in the airport, protecting his female and waiting to engage his enemy, had sent his demon rocketing to the surface. He'd become consumed by the darkness, more than ever before.

After he'd dispatched the Orthon and made sure there weren't any others, he'd been desperate to get back to her. And by the time he'd reached that supply room door, he'd no longer been in the driver's seat. It was like hovering above himself, watching from a distance. He'd watched his hand rise to release that lock with no control over his actions.

The demon and not the demon hunter had gone back into that room. With serious effort, he'd warned her, told her to stay back. But instead of keeping her distance, Eve had approached him, touched him, and pulled him from the dark, bathing him in her light and warmth.

Thank God he hadn't lost his head completely.

Kryos had warned him, had told him what would happen when he took Eve for the first time. Still, when that silvery thread had appeared in his mind's eye moments after sinking deep inside her, he'd been stunned—not only by its beauty, but by the undeniable truth that Eve was meant to be his. It had called to him, enticed him. All he had to do was reach out and take hold, and Eve would be his, his mate.

She hadn't even been aware of it. Only a male had the ability to complete the mating. He could have made her his that easily.

Without her consent.

He'd resisted. He couldn't bring himself to do that to her.

He curled his fingers into a fist so tight the skin over his knuckles felt close to splitting. He'd fucked up. Badly. He should have been protecting her, not fucking her. He'd left her open to attack.

Eve didn't know what she was doing. How could she? After all she had been through in such a short time, how could she resist the pull of their connection?

He'd taken advantage of that, of her.

Like a goddamned animal.

But in that dark place in the back of his mind, he knew there hadn't been any other option. He was fast becoming a slave to this constant craving for her. He hated to think what might have happened if he hadn't accepted the gift she'd offered him, if she hadn't been there to pull him from the brink. His demon had all but taken him.

Had there been another choice? Not that he could see.

Like he thought, had hoped, Eve had the power to force back his demon with her body. He knew that without a doubt.

Taking her as his mate wasn't necessary.

The realization twisted something deep inside, and he clamped a lid on it, forced it deep down. He knew the sick feeling—the sense of wrongness he felt at that moment would never leave him. But he could live with that; better that than the alternative. This was how it should be, how it had to be.

Bad things happened to the people he cared about, and he wouldn't allow Eve to be the next victim of his weakness. Part of his heart had died with Scarlet, and what remained had iced over when Tobias gave up the fight and succumbed to his demon.

Tobias was lost, and that was on Lazarus.

"Where are we going?" Eve asked beside him.

Her voice caused another stab of guilt, and he had to force down the bitter pill before he could speak. Dragging his eyes from the city lights blurring past the cab's window, he faced her. He wasn't ready to look at her again, and sure enough, as soon as he got another eyeful of those full lips still swollen from his kiss, her large pale eyes, not to mention her soft curvy body, his own hardened to painful proportions. It was as if she'd reached out and touched him.

"My friend owns a club," he finally answered. "There's accommodation. It's well warded, safe."

As if on cue, the cab pulled over and Lazarus handed the driver some cash before he grabbed their bags and climbed out. He waited while Eve scooted over and stepped out beside him. The place looked normal enough from the outside, like any other club, loud music, half-dressed females, and rowdy males looking for a good night. But this place had a unique difference.

Lazarus grabbed her hand and walked to the front of the queue. The bouncer let him past with a wordless nod.

Eve's body pressed in close to his as they squeezed through the tightly packed humans, driving him fucking insane. He ground his teeth, trying to concentrate on retaining his slipping control. Just the warmth of her hand in his was too much. His nerve endings came alive at the slightest touch of her skin. He hurried toward the bar, pushing his way through the crowd.

"Where's Brent?" he barked, too on edge to moderate his tone.

"Out back," the guy, a shifter, shouted over the music. His eyes trailed over Eve, his appreciation blatant. The growl that ripped from Lazarus was unexpected and loud enough for the guy to hear over all the noise. His eyes went wide before stuttering, "S-sorry, man. No offense, yeah?"

"Don't look at her again."

Eve shot him a sharp glance. Apparently, he no longer had control over what the hell came out of his mouth either. The word *mine* was stuck on repeat in his mind. God, he wanted to smash something.

Without another word, he turned from the bar. He didn't need to push through the crowd behind him this time because people parted like the Red Sea, stumbling over themselves to get out of his way.

Once they were away from the bar, he led Eve toward the back, weaving through the sweaty patrons dancing to shitty music. They finally reached the back of the building and a large male opened a nondescript door. Lazarus led Eve into the small hallway, turning a corner and stopping in front of another stocky male, this one a demi-demon, guarding a second plain metal door.

"Tom," he greeted the guy in charge of security.

"Good to see you again, Laz." He grinned.

The guy looked at Eve, winking at her as they passed. This time Laz managed to contain the growl before it escaped. They entered another hall, this one long and dark. Lights edged the floor, lighting their way. The farther they went the louder the thumping bass grew in volume.

"What is this place?" Eve tightened her grip on his hand and moved in closer. He ground his teeth at the contact, positive he felt a tight, beaded nipple graze his biceps.

"It's a club inside a club." They approached another door, and another security guy opened it for them.

"Welcome to the Jungle" by Guns 'n' Roses blasted from the speakers. Yeah, the song couldn't be more apt. He felt rather than heard Eve's gasp as they stepped through the door.

The dimly lit club was fairly full for this time of night. Barely covered males and females sat at tables or on the strategically placed couches around the room. Some talked, some danced, and though it was early still, some fucked.

Brent had opened the sex club more out of necessity than anything else. The place catered to nonhumans, a place they could come together, where they could have whatever needs they had met. Being the type of demi-demon Brent was, this place was more than just a business, it kept him safe, kept him breathing. Many that came here did so for the same reason.

"Jesus Christ, Lazarus. Where have you brought me?" Eve's hand moved up to clutch his forearm.

He bent down to speak close to her ear and had the sudden urge to dart his tongue out and trace the delicate lobe. "This place is owned by a demi named Brent. His demon side is different from yours. This place provides the cocktail of sex and volatile emotion he needs to keep from losing it." He didn't add that most of the employees and patrons here were *other*. She had enough to take in for now.

"Oh." Her eyes widened as she took in her surroundings.

A Dom passed by them. A leash dangled from his fingers, the strip of leather attached to a collar around another guy's neck. The sub crawled on his hands and knees, cheeks flushed, his excitement obvious as he followed his master to one of the private rooms.

"Is he going to...what do they..." She stopped abruptly, frowning. He guessed she was unsure how to finish her sentence.

"They give each other what they need."

Her cheeks darkened.

"Come on." He approached a waitress, a young demi named Chaya. Brent gave her a job after her release from the compound a few months back. Like Eve, she favored her human DNA and had a curvy build.

A wide smile lit up her delicate elfin features when she turned and spotted him. "Hey, Lazarus, I didn't know you were coming."

"Something came up."

She smirked. "You lot missing me already, huh?"

Yeah, he wasn't touching that one. The female had given them all hell while at the compound, and she'd enjoyed every damn minute of it. "How do you like it here?"

Her low chuckle said she knew exactly why he'd changed the subject. "A girl's gotta pay the rent somehow, right?"

He introduced Eve then asked after his friend's whereabouts.

"He's with someone right now, but he shouldn't be much longer." She glanced over to where the private rooms were located and scowled. "You can wait over there." She pointed to a table.

"Thanks."

"Sure." She spun on her skyscraper heels and disappeared into the crowd.

"So Brent's a...is he a..." Eve started.

Lazarus took pity on her. "His sire was a sex demon."

He led her to the table and Eve sat across from him studying her hands, pretending not to notice what was going on around her. Strobe lights flashed incessantly, irritating the shit out of his eyes, pulsing with the loud music. Each flash revealed a glimpse of writhing, naked limbs tangled in the darkened corners. The smell of sex was thick in the air and heightened his already out-of-control need for Eve. How Brent spent every night in this place, he didn't know.

The music made it hard to talk, and Lazarus was relieved when a door across the club opened and Brent strode out. He was dressed in gray trousers and a black silk shirt, looking sharp as always.

His friend tugged the female who followed him from the room closer, kissed her temple, and sent her on her way. He shrugged into his jacket and took a moment to survey his club.

Brent never let it show, but Lazarus knew the guy still struggled with the demon side of himself and what it demanded of him. But it was either this or...well, it wasn't worth thinking about the condition Lazarus had found his friend in many years ago.

Brent glanced up at that moment and spotted him, his

frown replaced by a wide grin. He made his way over to them, straightening his jacket and running a hand over his slightly mussed hair. "You should've said you were coming. I would've towed out the welcome wagon."

"Sure, you would have."

"You doubt me?"

"Always."

Brent chuckled, his gaze sliding to Eve standing at his side. "You need a place to stay?" he said without looking at Lazarus.

"Yeah, we do."

His dark gaze continued to trail over her and Lazarus wanted to snarl a warning.

The guy smiled when she looked up at him, all charm and model good looks, and extended a hand. "I'm Brent. Nice to meet you. I hope Lazarus hasn't given you too much of a hard time."

Eve giggled. Fucking grinned up at the asshole, and *giggled*. An urge to reach out, grab him by the throat, and wipe that smile off his face nearly won out.

"I'm Eve." She took his hand. "Interesting place you have here." That beautiful open smile covered her lovely face, and Brent sucked in an appreciative breath.

"Would you like the grand tour? The private rooms are... cozy." His friend's voice had dropped an octave, and the charming grin now held an edge of hunger.

Eve blinked up at him. "Oh, I...no. Thank you."

Lazarus decided that perhaps a warning was in order.

He smiled at her when she glanced his way and leaned closer to Brent, like he was trying to talk over the music. "If you take one step with her toward those rooms, I'll make it so you never walk again. Do you understand?" he said in a low voice.

A dark chuckle rumbled from his friend. "I'm beginning to."

Brent was like family to him, but if he so much as touched Eve, he'd rip the guy's hands off at the wrists.

Brent leaned back. "Can you stop with the crazy-assed smile now? I'm trying to run a business here. You're scaring my customers."

The guy was obviously in the mood to mess with him, or had a death wish, because he turned back to Eve, relaxed and still grinning like Lazarus hadn't just threatened to cripple him. "Would you like a drink, Eve?"

She smiled back, and like always he felt it like a sucker punch to his gut. "Sure, sounds good."

Brent turned to him then and the bastard winked. "Get the female a drink, Laz."

A growl built in his chest before he could stop it. Brent's brows rose, and he said in his own low tone, "You would leave your female wanting?"

Brent was fishing, but it didn't take a genius to work out Eve meant something to him. Not with the possessive way he'd been behaving. The other male's eyes widened when, scowling in silent warning, he turned and stalked to the bar. His need to provide for Eve, to give his would-be mate whatever she needed was a compulsion he couldn't ignore.

After ordering their drinks, he turned back to Eve, unable to keep his eyes off the female for more than a few seconds at a time. Brent looked to be chatting amiably, but then Eve flinched and clutched her forehead.

Shit.

With the way her power was growing in strength, the short distance between them must have been far enough for the block he had over her telepathy to drop. By the way her mouth was hanging open she'd gotten a head full of his perverted friend's thoughts, not to mention the rest of the room.

Grabbing the drinks, he stalked back to the pair, and after

strengthening the block, he put down the drinks and pulled her into his side. "All right?"

She smiled, the strain washing from her face. "I am now."

He let his fingers drift across her shoulder and into her hair so he could massage the back of her head and neck where she would feel the most discomfort. She leaned into his touch and made a little moaning sound that hit him right in the balls. More of his waning self-control slipped. It took effort, but he dropped his hand and stepped back.

"Anything you want to tell me, brother?" Brent said.

He had a stupid look on his face, one Lazarus had never seen on the other male before, and didn't much like. Lazarus glared at him. "Yes. In future, keep your thoughts R13."

Brent shrugged. "Impossible."

"She's telepathic."

The guy didn't look worried in the slightest. In fact, he looked amused. He turned to Eve. "I apologize if I embarrassed you, Eve, but you really are an attractive female."

Lazarus growled through clenched teeth. "In future, don't think about her."

"I'll do my best, but I'm not blind."

"Then don't look at her, or I'll make it so you don't have a choice."

Laughter lit his eyes. "For fuck's sake, if you have your way I'll be in a wheelchair with glass eyeballs."

"And no fucking hands," Lazarus added.

Brent laughed harder.

"Not another damn word," he gritted out.

"It's okay," Eve said beside him. "I'm all right now you're back. Anyway, I'm used to it...well, I thought I was." She looked confused, her cheeks flushed.

"Just take us to the room, you sick shit."

Two apartments were located upstairs: one Brent's, the other kept empty for the knights if they should need it.

Brent took them up, and once inside, Lazarus carried Eve's bag into the bedroom. Eve's quiet laughter drifted in from the living room.

When he walked back in, he raised an eyebrow at Brent who was grinning as well. "What are you talking about?" He didn't like that the other male had caused her happiness when he seemed to only cause her pain.

"I didn't say a word." His friend smirked. Shit, as soon as he'd left the room Eve had gotten another dose of Brent's thoughts.

"What the hell were you thinking about?" he demanded.

"A few images of you I thought Eve might find entertaining." Brent shook his head. "Man, the seventies really weren't kind to anyone, were they? Orange bell-bottoms, Laz, really?"

"I never wore orange bell-bottoms, dipshit."

"No, but I have an excellent imagination."

Lazarus shook his head at the guy's warped sense of humor. "Leave."

Brent ignored his rudeness. "It was nice to meet you, Eve. Call down to the bar if you need anything." Then he left them very much alone.

"This is nice," Eve said after a few minutes of silence looking around the small apartment.

"It's okay."

"Is it all right if I grab a shower?"

"Of course. Everything you need should be in the bathroom." An image flashed through his mind of her naked, water sluicing over her pale skin, hands moving over her voluptuous body, nipples dark and peaked and begging for his mouth.

She didn't move right away, but stood there watching him, waiting for something, something he couldn't give her. Her color was high and she bit her lower lip. "Well, okay. I'll just..." She motioned to the bathroom.

He gave her a sharp nod then watched her walk away.

He didn't go in after her, and it almost killed him. If he was honest, his fear of this growing hold she had over him was the only thing keeping him from joining her in the shower and fucking her hard against the cool tile. But after the way he'd reacted downstairs, he didn't trust himself to have her again without forcing a mating.

His stomach churned. Did she believe he was capable of tender feelings, of love?

Why hadn't he told her the truth?

Maybe because I selfishly want her even though I can never love her.

He didn't want to see that trusting look on her face turn to betrayal, the heat in her eyes turn to dread. He shook off the thought and sat his ass on the couch.

He was incapable of giving her what she deserved, what he'd seen between Meredith and Kryos, and—before everything went to hell—Tobias and Scarlet. Love wasn't something he could offer. Not anymore.

The bathroom door opened a short time later, and he couldn't stop himself from looking at her when she walked out. She wore a pair of red boxers with little white hearts all over them and a white tank top. The outfit should have been innocent enough, but on Eve it was the opposite. The top clung to her out-of-control curves and her beaded nipples were visible through the thin fabric. His mouth went dry.

"I'm going to head to bed," she said.

When she walked through the living room, Lazarus stood. He felt like a puppet and Eve controlled the strings. Without thought or control over his actions, he stepped forward, blocking her path.

"Is everything all right?" She lifted her arm and cradled it to her chest.

Shit. What was he doing?

Her bandage stood out against all that smooth, creamy skin. "I, ah, I need to take a look at your arm."

"It's fine, really."

"Bathroom, Eve." He didn't really need to look at it now, though, did he?

She swallowed hard. "It's not sore. I can check it in the morning."

Her resistance just made him more determined. He couldn't be in the same room as her, but he also didn't want her hiding from him. Where Eve was concerned, he was a mass of contradicting thoughts and feelings. Completely fucked in the head over her. "Go to the bathroom, Eve," he heard himself say.

Her shoulders stiffened, but she turned and walked back toward the tiny room.

He followed and tried to ignore the sway of her heart-shaped ass the whole damn way.

She turned to face him and he gripped her hips, lifting her and sitting her on the bathroom counter. She squeaked in surprise, and the soft heat of her curves branded his palms. After gathering supplies from the cabinet, he removed her bandage and began cleaning her injury with methodical efficiency. All the while trying not to take in her scent and the subtle way her breath hitched when he touched her skin. Taking her wrist, he inspected her wounds. Warmth radiated from her body as he leaned in to get a better look. Her breath coasted across his neck and goose bumps broke out across his skin.

"It's healing well."

"That's good," she said in a hushed tone that only made it worse.

He quickly redressed it. "There, all done. We can change them again tomorrow." How the hell would he get through this again tomorrow? Stepping back, he inspected the new bandage.

Her gaze heated.

Nostrils flaring, he drew in a deep breath. God, he could smell how turned on she was.

She confirmed it when her skin flushed pink. Her cheeks, her chest, the tops of her breasts.

So fucking beautiful.

It took everything he had, but instead of moving back in and taking what he wanted, he started for the door. Her body soothed him, tamed his demon, but he couldn't take her just because his dick was hard, just because he wanted her. That wasn't what this was, not now. It never was.

He had to stay focused, he needed to maintain an emotional and physical distance for both their sakes. "I'll let you get to bed."

"Good night," she called after him.

He paused at the door, struggling, desperate to go back to her.

She made the decision for him when she climbed off the counter and slipped passed him.

He tracked her across the room, unable to look away, until she shut the door, closing herself in the bedroom.

Sixteen

Music drifted up from the clubs and bars as the city moved at a rapid pace below. Lazarus looked down from the top of the building he stood on, the wind ruffling his hair, coasting across his fevered skin. It did little to cool his blood. Shit, he was on fire, burning from the inside out, and had been since he laid eyes on Eve.

He needed it to stop.

An image of Scarlet invaded his mind, a memory that succeeded in shooting ice through his veins and putting another crack though his heart.

"What did you get her?" Tobias asked Lazarus five seconds after walking into his apartment.

"A gun."

Tobias grunted and looked down at the jewel-handled blade in his hand. "Well, I'm giving mine to her first."

Lazarus shook his head and scowled at his brother. It was Scarlet's twentieth birthday and there was no way Tobias was going to give his baby girl a present first. The guy had been acting weird lately, overprotective of her, especially since they'd started taking her along to retrievals. They all loved her, but T's behavior seemed extreme.

"What the fuck is up with you?" Lazarus said, starting to get pissed off.

Tobias rubbed the back of his neck and actually winced. "Okay, so there's something I need to talk to you about." The guy stalled out, looking fidgety as hell.

Lazarus straightened. "What?"

Scarlet walked in, a small smile on her lips. "I guess I'll tell you, since Tobias is obviously going to chicken out."

Both Tobias and Lazarus turned to her, and he noted Tobias looked shocked.

"Tobias is my mate," she said, stopping beside the male.

Lazarus went rigid and Tobias stared down at her with his mouth hanging open. "You know?" he said to her.

She smiled up at T, beautiful and open. "Yeah, of course. I've felt something...I don't know...a connection between us since Laz brought me home. It's changed, though, grown stronger the last few months. It's become something different...um...more." She blushed. "Was that the same for you?"

Tobias made a choking, growling sound and nodded.

She chuckled at the male's continued slack-jawed expression. "So are you gonna kiss me now or what?"

"Like hell," Lazarus barked out.

Tobias touched Scarlet's face, with an expression on his own that Laz had never seen before. Awe. There was no other way to describe it. "Yeah, I'm gonna kiss you, sweetheart, a lot," he said. "But first I have to let Laz kick my ass. It's only right."

Scarlet nodded sagely, her lips kicking up in a grin. "Agreed." She motioned to the door. "I'll be down in your room when you're done."

Tobias sucked in a sharp breath, eyes darkening, and Lazarus took advantage of his momentary distraction and tackled him. Yeah, he knew this was out of the male's control, but it didn't change the fact that his friend was about to mate a female he considered his daughter, and Lazarus was going to kick the fucker's ass before he worked at accepting it.

"I'll be down shortly," Tobias called back, then grunted when Laz punched him in the gut.

"Don't damage any of the important parts!" Scarlet called as she walked out the door.

Tobias groaned. "You're totally gonna go for the important parts now, aren't you?"

"Fuck yes," Laz said.

They'd made their peace and Tobias had made Scarlet his mate. The knight had loved and cherished her, protected and respected her, had been the kind of male any father would wish for his child.

Pain sliced through him. And then Lazarus had destroyed them both.

Lazarus felt the angel's presence at his back before the guy made his arrival known.

"You called?" Silas drawled.

Arrogant asshole.

"Ouch," he said, amusement in his deep voice.

Lazarus turned to face him. "Get the fuck out of my head, angel."

Silas stared at him, silver eyes missing nothing, head tilted to the side. Under the moon, his hair looked like strands of spun gold, the black streaks through it such a contrast it was hard to look at. "You have so much anger and pain, Lazarus. Getting in your head isn't exactly a barrel of laughs for me either."

He looked at the angel who'd trained him many lifetimes ago, the male who had branded him as one of Heaven's warriors, and shook his head. "Then stay the fuck out."

He ran a hand through that unusual hair. "I don't like being taken by surprise, Laz. You know that."

He wore his usual uniform—black jeans and tee. The battle scenes tattooed on his arms in black ink were on full display. His gold wings shifted then settled again, arching high over his shoulders. When they were still they looked like they were made of solid gold, like he carried the intense weight of them on his back.

Lazarus held his gaze. "Since you know why I called you here, let's not waste any more time." When Silas said nothing, he knew there was something the fucker was hiding, something Lazarus wasn't going to like. "What is she?" The wind whipped away his words, but the angel heard him. He heard every fucking thing. "Tell me," he roared. Because he knew Eve was no ordinary demi, not after the way his brothers had reacted to her.

"She has the mark," Silas said.

Lazarus clenched his fists. He fucking knew what the guy was going to say, but goddammit, he'd hoped he was wrong. "What mark?"

Sympathy lit the angel's eerie silver eyes. "She has the Beast's mark. She's a descendant of Lucifer's handmaidens." Silas took a step closer to him. "Lazarus, she's a hell's gate."

Lazarus strode away as fear and anger pumped hotly through his veins. Lucifer's handmaids had served only him. Whatever he wanted, they got, which meant they had the ability to move between realms at will. Eve being a descendant, having the mark, meant she also carried the ability to open a gate.

Making her Diemos's number one target.

Fuck.

The demon needed her. When Lucifer left and took his handmaids with him, he'd trapped the other male in Hell.

If Diemos left during the equinox, before he had an army here on Earth, and 24/7 access to the hell's gate, he risked being locked out and losing the throne he'd worked so hard to take.

He wanted control over the portal above all else.

Lazarus shoved his hands through his hair. He wanted to plow his fist into the angel's face, but it was pointless. Silas would see it coming. "That's why she collapsed back at the compound? The equinox affected her as well?"

"Yes."

"Why didn't you tell me?" he rasped.

"She's safe," Silas said. "The amulet, it has the power to mask what she is, block it."

Lazarus turned to him. "It can protect her if she remains unmated?"

Silas shook his head. "I didn't make the amulet for that purpose."

"You didn't answer my question, angel."

Silas sighed and shoved his hands in his pockets. "Yes. Theoretically, it could protect her throughout her mortal life. Render the gate undetectable by demons...until the time of her death."

A wave of grief washed over him so powerful he barely managed to hold his ground and not stagger back. Without mating, her life would be longer than a mortal, but it *would* end.

But then a full mortal life, one full of love and laughter, would be better than an eternity tied to him.

Lazarus fought to control his conflicting emotions. "The amulet, it would protect her, though? She'd be safe?"

Silas's square jaw clenched. "Yes, as long as she keeps it on."

How could he even contemplate this now? Now he knew what she was and what she could unwittingly unleash onto the world. Still, he had to ask. "I'm not certain," he started carefully, "but the way things are progressing, I don't think it will be necessary for us to mate." The roughness of his voice was humiliating. He hated showing weakness, especially in front of this male.

"You can't hide from me," Silas said softly.

"No shit," he muttered.

"Are you sure about this, Laz?"

"No." What was the point of lying? He'd see right through his bullshit.

"I guess the decision is yours. If you can dispatch Tobias before you're taken by your demon, you may have a chance." He shrugged. "If you're successful, and you then choose not to take Eve as your mate, you'll return to the way you were before Tobias's betrayal."

His gut clenched. No Eve. The idea wasn't as appealing as it would have been a short time ago.

"And Eve?"

"The amulet will keep her safe, and once she is trained and released, she can carry on with her life the way she sees fit."

"Right."

"But your connection to her would still be there. You'd feel her. But harder still, you'd have to allow that connection to strengthen. You'd have to embrace it to make sure she was safe, to ensure she never removed the amulet. Lazarus, you'd know when she was happy and when she wasn't. Could you live with that every day? Feeling her living her life, living it with her in that way? Maybe even knowing she was with someone else...someone that wasn't you?"

His demon, who was usually subdued around Silas, shrieked, the sound vibrating through his skull. Its claws pushed at the tips of his fingers, trying to break free. Lazarus hated the idea as much as his demon, but it would be for the best for Eve. As long as she was happy.

And safe, away from him.

"I would think long and hard before you choose this route," Silas said. "Mating with you is the only way to destroy the gate she carries permanently. Also, there's only one amulet in existence, and Eve will have it." He shrugged his wide shoulders again. "Who knows what trials you and your brothers will face in the future?"

His eyes glittered through the darkness. Yeah, the angel knew. He knew exactly what trials they would face.

Fuck.

"Then tell me, what should I do, Silas?" He hated the desperation in his voice, but fucking hell, he *was* desperate.

Silas shook his head, his wings extending, ruffling in the breeze. "It is not for me to say."

In two steps, Lazarus was in front of him. He grabbed the front of the angel's shirt and shoved. Silas staggered back a step. Lazarus knew he'd only managed it because Silas had allowed it.

"Tell me," he roared. "For once, would you just fucking tell me what to do?"

The angel's eyes gentled then he repeated, "It is not for me to say."

Lazarus shoved away from him and walked to the edge of the building, trying to regain his composure.

"You need to forgive yourself, Lazarus," Silas said close behind him. "Scarlet has."

When Lazarus spun back around, the angel was gone.

Brent's thoughts streamed into her mind, and Eve laughed.

Lazarus shot Brent a dirty look.

Brent smirked, his sensual mouth tilting up on one side. "What? I'm keeping it clean."

Laz turned to her, brow raised.

"He's singing the *Teenage Mutant Ninja Turtle* theme song," she said.

"Jesus," Lazarus muttered.

Lazarus was fresh from the shower, his dark hair still damp and a little rumpled from him thrusting his fingers through it. The jeans he wore molded to his powerful thighs, and his faded T-shirt clung to his wide chest and thick biceps. He looked amazing.

A zing fired through her belly when he trained those pale eyes back on her.

Nope. She couldn't look away.

His tongue darted out, swiping across his full lower lip, and she swayed, fighting the urge to lift up on her tiptoes and taste that plump, firm flesh again for herself.

His Adam's apple bobbed and he cleared his throat. "Let's get started."

Eve stood in the middle of the living room in their temporary home. Lazarus announced that morning that they needed to get back to her training. Since this was her first training session with Brent, she wasn't sure what to expect. But Lazarus had promised to teach her to block her telepathy, and because of her lack of any kind of breakthrough at the compound, she was afraid to believe that it was possible, that she might be able to live a normal—well, normal-ish—life after all.

Lazarus moved closer and her pulse sped up instantly. How on earth was she supposed to concentrate with him standing so close?

"Just relax, Eve," he murmured.

Easy for him to say. He didn't go into cardiac arrest whenever she came close.

He moved around and stood at her back. Heat poured off him in waves, radiating from his chest and searing her back through the thin fabric of her dress. Her skin tingled in a pleasant way and made her want to lean back, take more of his warmth. His hands came down on her shoulders and he leaned in closer. Her knees wobbled.

Fingers tightening, he massaged lightly. "Where do you feel it, Eve?"

She squirmed. Where did she feel it? Oh no, she wasn't going there. "I, ah..."

Brent chucked like he was the one that could read minds, and her face heated.

"Just keep singing, asshole." Lazarus's lips brushed her hair when he spoke next. "When you're listening to him where do you feel it?"

Brent's singing continued.

Eve glanced over at him. "I can't believe you know every word of that song."

He shrugged. "I liked cartoons."

Laz gave her another squeeze. "Focus."

"Right. In my head, I guess."

"No, Eve. Where do you *feel* it?"

Eve tried to zone Brent out and focus on the source of her ability, which she'd never done before, and immediately zeroed in on the low buzz at the back of her skull. She reached back and showed him. "Here."

"Different abilities manifest differently. If your ability had been a physical one, for example, you would have felt it here." He reached around and placed his hand against her chest, his palm skimming the tops of her breasts. Her heart hammered faster. He didn't comment, but there was no way he couldn't feel her reaction to his touch. His hand moved to the base of her skull, massaging gently. "This is the point where all psychic powers are felt, and the point you need to visualize when you want to block it. Understand?"

"I think so."

"Up until your first lesson, you would have tried to block your ears to escape others' thoughts, yes?"

She nodded. "It never worked."

"That's because your hearing has nothing to do with the way your ability works. So from now on, I want you to picture this point right here."

More massaging. Firm, but gentle. Goose bumps were breaking out all over her body from his touch. "Okay."

"Now, as much as I'm sure you love hearing Brent sing, imagine this is a life-and-death situation. Your options are block Brent, or I kill him for you to shut out the terrible sound of his voice."

Eve laughed and Brent's eyes narrowed. Lazarus could be funny when he wanted to be. She liked it.

"I want you to close your eyes and visualize a small black hole, no bigger than the tip of your pinkie. That's where your power flows, allowing all that noise, all those thoughts and images to reach your mind. Now I want you to imagine blocking it."

She did as he said, picturing the tiny black hole. "Okay, I see it. What do I block it with?"

"Gum," Brent said. "When I was training, I used to pretend to stuff a big piece of chewed-up gum over mine. Grape Hubba Bubba worked best."

"Good choice," she said, smiling. "Grape's my favorite, too. I can do that."

She was sure she heard Lazarus grind his teeth behind her. "Whatever works," he said, still close behind her. "Now can you hear Brent singing?"

"Yes."

"Excellent. Now you have ten seconds to block him out, or I'll slit his throat."

Eve tried to spin to face him. "What?"

"Ten...nine...eight..."

"No. You wouldn't, would you?"

"Six...five..."

"I'd rather you didn't test him on that, Eve," Brent said.

His singing, still loud and clear, echoed through her mind.

Eve tried to visualize the pinkie-sized hole then imagined stuffing it with gum. All the while Lazarus counted down.

It wasn't working.

"Three...two..." Lazarus's deep voice filled the room.

"Anytime now would be good, Eve," Brent called.

Eve shut everything else out and concentrated on blocking Brent—

Silence.

The kind of silence she'd only experienced since Lazarus stormed into her life.

"One..."

She uncurled her fingers so her nails quit biting into her palms, and released the breath she'd been holding. "Are you doing that?" she asked Lazarus, because how could it be her?

"It's all you, Eve." She could hear the smile in his voice.

"I did it? Oh my God. *I did it.*" She spun around and threw her arms around Lazarus's neck.

Lazarus rested his hands on Eve's waist. She pulled back, arms wrapped around him, and smiled. No, she fucking beamed like he'd just brought her a new puppy. He blew out a breath, the wind knocked clean from his lungs with that one look.

"You did really good," he managed. What else could he say? Hell, he could hardly think, let alone form a coherent sentence with her staring at him like that.

"I did, right?" she said.

Shit, she needed to stop smiling at him like that. She tilted her head to the side. "You really had me going there for a minute."

"Did I?" He wanted to smile back, but fought the impulse into submission.

"Come on, I know you'd never actually kill Brent. Though your rather drastic plan worked."

He reluctantly released her and pushed his hands into his pockets. As soon as she stepped back, he wanted her hands right back where they'd been. "Slitting Brent's throat wouldn't kill him, not the way I'd do it. Besides, he's a fast healer."

"Oh my God, you're terrible." She slapped his arm playfully.

He liked seeing her like this, relaxed, kinda goofy—happy.

She turned to Brent. "Poor Brent. Don't worry, I'll protect you."

Brent pushed away from the wall, that predatory smirk back on his handsome face. "Would you really, sweetheart?"

"You can leave now. You've served your purpose," Lazarus said to him.

Brent sent him a look that was far too knowing and winked at Eve before he left the apartment.

Eve stared at him. "Well, that was rude."

Her defense of the other male did not sit well with him, not at all. In fact, it made him insanely and irrationally pissed. "Was it?"

"Yes."

"And you care why exactly?"

Her eyes widened at his harsh tone. "What's wrong with you?"

He shoved his fingers through his hair. "Nothing."

She went quiet and the silence stretched out.

When he made himself look at her again, her arms were crossed over her chest and she was studying him like she wanted to crawl inside his head, discover all his secrets. It freaked him the hell out that she might be able to see the truth, see the kind of male he truly was.

One thing he couldn't hide anymore was what Silas had told him the night before. She had a right to know what she was. Thinking about how this new bit of information would affect her, terrify her, made him sick to his stomach. He'd do anything to protect her from that.

But he couldn't. It was too important to keep from her. Too damn dangerous to keep from her.

"Thanks for this, for helping me," she said carefully.

"You'll need to practice. The more you do, the longer you'll be able to hold the block. After a while, it won't be any effort."

The worry disappeared and her smile returned, but this time with the wattage cranked way up. "Can we try again tomorrow?"

"Sure." His voice was back to gravel.

The look on her face, all that gratitude, and hope was making it hard to breathe. He didn't deserve it.

She reached out, put her hand on his chest, and the brand burned into his skin there heated, causing the flesh beneath to tingle.

"Lazarus..." Her voice was soft, sweet, a lover's caress. No one had ever said his name like that before, and dammit, he liked it. Wanted to hear her say it again.

He stepped back. "I have to head out."

The smile faded and she crossed her arms again. "Oh... okay."

She looked down hiding her eyes from him. He hated that, hated that he kept on hurting her, but what he hated most of all was that he wasn't even close to being finished.

And then he felt it.

It was unconscious on her part, he was sure, but Eve was reaching out to him, calling to him, and his body responded to the volatile energy she was throwing his way in pulsing waves.

His dick, already hard, stiffened further. Jesus, he wanted her, needed to be inside her again. But he didn't reach for her, even when it was all he wanted, all he could think about.

"I'll see you tomorrow, then?" she said in a quiet voice.

He shrugged on his jacket. "Yeah."

His boots felt heavy as he walked to the door. His body, his demon, was at odds with his mind, screaming at him to stay and take her, make her his once and for all.

No. His only option was to find Tobias and put him out of commission. Then he could let Eve go.

He'd made his decision.

Seventeen

Eve took the stairs down to the club. She needed a drink. Well, that was her excuse, but in reality, she was desperate for company. Even if that company was of the leather-clad and extremely kinky variety.

Besides her training sessions with Lazarus, or as she'd come to think of them, her daily dose of sexual frustration and torture, she barely saw him. He left right after running through her blocking techniques and didn't come back until after she was asleep.

She didn't know what was going on in his head. The male was completely unreadable. He'd told her she was his mate, told her how much he wanted her, but then proceeded to avoid her like the plague. She didn't get it, didn't get him.

Which left her feeling lonely, confused, and kind of pissed off.

Brent had been great. He spent a lot of time with her, helping her with her training. It wasn't easy, but he was a good teacher. Now she could block out the noise on her own, not all day, but for extended periods.

Brent had been hanging out with her a little, taking pity

on her. They'd watched a few movies and sometimes ate together before he headed down to the club, but he wasn't Lazarus, and she felt his absence like a physical ache.

She shook her head. Insane.

The club was quiet when she hit the door, the only sound the low murmur of Brent's voice. He was behind the bar, his staff gathered around him.

The club was empty since it wasn't quite opening time. She'd only come down during the day since they got there, while it was closed, and was surprised at the rush of excitement and flutter of nerves at the prospect of hanging around, maybe staying for a while once it opened.

Being among people who didn't have any hang-ups, who made no apologies for who they were, was exhilarating. They took what they wanted, when they wanted it. Eve envied that.

"We're a dancer down," Brent said.

"I'll do it," Chaya, the curvy waitress she'd met when she arrived, spoke up.

Brent visibly stiffened. "No. You won't."

Chaya narrowed her eyes. "I can dance, Brent."

"I want my customers coming back, and that means having someone who knows what the fuck they're doing. You're working the bar." Chaya flinched and her cheeks heated.

Eve winced. She'd seen another side to Brent over the last week, not so much softer, but more relaxed, a side he obviously didn't share with his staff. Brent didn't seem to notice or care that he'd hurt Chaya's feelings and had already asked another waitress to dance. She glanced between him and Chaya, at the way they were purposely *not* looking at each other.

Eve leaned against the bar and tapped him on the arm. "Hey, um...I can waitress if you're short. I've done it before."

Brent turned and so did everyone else. That slow smile

lifted his sensual lips. "You think Lazarus would be happy about that?"

"I doubt it, but it's not really his decision. I don't answer to him."

Brent raised a brow. "I don't think he sees it that way, sweetheart." He turned back to his gathered staff and waved them away. "You know what to do." He turned back to her.

"Come on. Give me something to do," she pleaded.

He crossed his arms. "It's not a good idea."

"He's not here. He's never here. And if you don't let me help, and I'm stuck in that room another night all by myself, I'll go mad."

"You think you have enough control to sustain your block for a few hours?"

She really hoped so. "Yes. And if I start to struggle, I'll go back upstairs."

He rested a hip against the bar. He looked powerful in his dark suit, his height, and good looks no doubt intimidating to most. "If I let you do this, you have to stick to delivering drinks and clearing tables. If anyone worries you, bothers you, you come to me or one of the guys on the floor."

"Guys?"

"George"—he pointed to a huge man standing by the door—"or Mark." Mark stood against the wall on the other side of the room, his gaze taking in his surroundings, not missing a thing. They were both frightening as hell. "They look out for the staff. You need help, you grab me or one of the guys, yeah?"

Excitement bubbled up inside her. "Is that a yes?"

He still didn't look convinced, but finally said, "I guess it is."

"Thank you! You won't regret it."

A wicked glint lit his dark gaze. "We have a certain image here, and it needs to be maintained at all times. So, if you're doing this, you need to do it right. You need to dress the part. Go get changed."

Did he think that would dissuade her? Eve looked around. Okay, it might. She didn't have anything in her bag that would fit in down here. Who the hell would? "Ah…I'd love to, but rubber gives me a rash."

Brent snorted. "It's not negotiable."

She grinned. "Just when I thought my dreams of wearing a studded collar would never be fulfilled…"

He shook his head at her sarcasm. "If you're determined to do this, go talk to Chaya. You're a similar build. She'll have something you can wear." He was enjoying her discomfort way too much.

"You're loving this, aren't you?"

"I'm looking forward to seeing how you'll look in Chaya's clothes." He chuckled, rough and low. "And what Lazarus will do when he sees you."

Her heart sped up. "I doubt he'll care either way."

His smile turned wicked. "We open soon. Get changed and get your ass back out here."

"Yes, boss."

He walked off, headed to his office, and Eve spotted Chaya on her way back to the bar. "Chaya?"

The other woman stopped in front of her, a wary expression on her face. "Yeah?"

"Um, Brent said you might have something for me to wear. I'm waitressing."

Her eyes slid to the door Brent had just disappeared behind then back to Eve. "Right, come with me."

Chaya wore a short pleated black leather skirt and spike-heeled boots. Her top was red and slashed in strategic places, showing a lot of skin and cleavage, and her long dark hair hung loose, swaying around her waist. Chaya looked gorgeous. No way could Eve pull off an outfit like that.

They entered a room with lockers lining the walls. There were still a few people milling about, talking, and getting ready. "Out," Chaya barked. Surprisingly, everyone scattered without argument.

Chaya flung open her locker and pulled clothes and shoes out. Everything was short and way too revealing, but after some not-so-gentle coaxing, Eve ended up in a short A-line red tartan skirt, black fishnets, and a black sheer tank that showed off the red bra she wore underneath. Eve had never been able to wear heels for any length of time, so Chaya gave her a pair of knee-high lace-up boots with a chunky sole that Eve loved and never wanted to give back.

Chaya stood back and gave her a head to toe. "You look awesome."

Eve looked down at herself. "My fat thighs are out for the world to see."

"We have pretty much the same build. Are you saying my thighs look fat?" Those catlike eyes stared up at her, unblinking.

"No, *you* look amazing. And I..."

"Look hot."

Did she? She didn't know. Dressing like this wasn't really her thing, but she could handle it for a night. It was kind of like playing dress-up, like being someone else. A welcome prospect after everything that had happened.

"What goes on out there? How do you handle being around it every night?" Eve asked while Chaya sat her down to apply a thick coat of charcoal liner around her eyes and fluffed her hair.

She shrugged and planted a hand on her hip. "You get used to it after a while, though I've definitely worn out a few vibrators. I'm on a first-name basis with the woman who owns the adults-only store around the corner."

They both burst out laughing. It felt good to laugh. That

hard exterior Chaya had dropped while they'd played dress-up, and Eve started to think that maybe they could be friends. A little thrill ran through her. She could have friends. There were people like her that understood, that wouldn't be scared off by what she was inadvertently sending out.

People she wouldn't have to hide who she was from. Chaya knew, she understood.

A noise came from the door and they both spun around. Brent stood there, expression dark, controlled. The same way he'd looked that first night when she'd seen him across the club, before he'd seen her and Lazarus. This wasn't the Brent who laughed at cheesy movies with her and ate pizza from the box. No, this Brent was the businessman, the sex demon who knew how to wield his power. A force to be reckoned with.

He took her in. "You look good."

"Thanks, I guess. Not too much?"

He shook his head and the corner of his mouth lifted. "No, you'll fit right in." His gaze slid to Chaya and the barely-there grin slid from his face. "I need you behind the bar now. The place is filling up."

Chaya's shoulders stiffened before she turned to Eve. "I'll see you out there." She stormed out.

Eve stared up at Brent. "What's up with you two?"

He crossed his arms over his wide chest. "Nothing."

Yeah, right.

"You ready?" he asked.

"Yep. All set."

"You remember what I told you?"

"Yes."

"Humor me."

"If I feel worried or if someone creeps me out, find you or one of the guys then go to the apartment."

"The wards are stronger up there. It's the safest place for you if you feel your block dropping." He shook his head. "I don't like this, Eve. And Laz will have my balls if anything happens to you."

"I doubt that very much." She tugged at her skirt, which kept creeping higher. "I'm just clearing tables and delivering drinks, right? What could go wrong? Plus, you're saving my sanity. That has to count for something."

He didn't look convinced. "Just stay alert."

"Will do." She rubbed her hands together. "Time I got to work." She started toward to door.

"And, Eve?"

"Yeah?"

"Chaya was right. You look hot." He winked then led her out to the club.

A couple of hours into her shift, and she well and truly had the swing of things.

The music thumped so low she felt it in her belly, and the lights pulsed along with the bass. It confused the senses, enticed. The surreal sensation made her feel like she was someone else, free to do whatever she wanted.

It wasn't hard to see why this place was so full.

The club had been busy since she walked onto the floor. The heady atmosphere was electric and led its occupants to sin. Made you crave it.

Lazarus had walked into the club an hour ago and Eve was doing her best to ignore him. He hadn't approached her, but Eve had felt his presence the minute he arrived. She didn't know how, but she knew his gaze had never once left her, followed her wherever she went. She felt it burning a path across her skin.

She felt greedy after being starved of his attention for so long. Alive, sexy. Turned on.

Chaya placed two more drinks on her tray. "Over there. The corner," she shouted over the music.

"Okay." Eve weaved her way through the crowd, not

shying away from the hands that brushed her skin as she moved by or the offers whispered into her ear. She took a hedonistic kind of pleasure from it, all of it. For some reason, knowing Lazarus was watching, and saw how others reacted to her, desired her, tried to touch her, turned her on even more.

The lights were dim, but with every flash of muted red light, she got a glimpse of glistening skin and tangled limbs. She stopped by the table and unloaded the drinks for the couple sitting there. Beside them a woman lay on the padded vinyl bench seat, legs spread wide, her skirt shoved up around her hips. The guy she was with had his head between her thighs. He feasted on her, worshiped her body with long sensuous strokes. The sheer carnality of the act caused the ache between her thighs to intensify. God, she wanted that.

She couldn't look away. How would it feel to do something like that with everyone watching? Heat washed over her. She was so turned on by the sight a moan broke past her lips.

The woman turned to Eve, a smile spread across her glossy red lips. "Join us?"

For a split second, she imagined what it would be like to say yes. To let go and just feel.

What am I thinking?

She stumbled back a step. "No...I, ah, sorry." Spinning around, she shoved through the crowd blocking her path and headed to the back of the building and the glowing fire exit sign. She needed fresh air. All the raging hormones in this place were getting to her. She grabbed the handle and shoved the door open. Cool night air hit her skin, and she sucked down a lungful.

But before she could take a step outside, someone grabbed her arm and yanked her back.

Eve squealed and spun around.

Lazarus stared down at her, eyes flashing fire. "Where the fuck do you think you're going?"

"I—I just needed some air."

He cursed and dragged her back into the club. "Have you forgotten what could be waiting for you out there?"

Oh God. "I'm sorry. I didn't think." In this place, she couldn't think straight.

Lazarus pulled her through the club and didn't stop until they reached Brent's office. He threw the door open without knocking and strode inside.

Brent was sitting on the couch in the corner, a woman crouched in front of him, his fingers fisting her hair while she worked his cock with eager, hungry sucks.

"I take it Eve's finished for the night?" he said without looking at her.

Okay, that was way more than she'd wanted to see of her new friend, and didn't resist when Lazarus growled and shoved her behind him, blocking her view. "Put your fucking dick away."

Brent laughed, dark and rough. "Can you kick my ass later? I'm a little busy at the moment."

"Count on it." Lazarus led her back out, slammed the door, and dragged her toward the stairs.

When they reached their apartment, he pushed her inside, pulling her through the living room and into the bathroom. The light flicked on and he slammed the door shut, throwing out a hand, using his powers to lock it. The shower came on next.

"What are you doing?"

His expression was dark, intent. "Washing the stench of that place off you. This"—he motioned to her clothes, her face—"isn't you."

She tried to unlock the door. It wouldn't budge. "How the hell would you know?"

"Get in the shower," he growled.

She took a step back. "No."

His eyes narrowed. "Get in the fucking shower, Eve."

Her palms grew sweaty and her pulse sped up. "Make me." She didn't know why, but she wanted to push him, to see him lose control. She wanted him to want her again, to stop ignoring her.

His nostrils flared and he took a step toward her. "Is that what you want?"

"Yes."

What on earth am I doing?

Lazarus didn't hesitate. He toed off his boots, yanked his shirt over his head, revealing all that beautiful smooth skin and thick slabs of muscle, then closed the gap between them and started stripping her. She didn't fight it—why would she?

"I've been watching you," he said against her ear. "Watching you strut around in that little skirt, showing off these perfect tits." He cupped her breast, squeezing the sensitive flesh, making her gasp.

Oh God, she wanted him.

"Did you like it?" he growled.

"W-what?" She couldn't think straight.

His other hand came up under her skirt, and without warning, he pushed her panties aside and slid two fingers through her drenched pussy. She cried out and he cursed. "Watching people fuck, Eve. Did you like it?"

She moaned and gripped his biceps, her head dropping forward against his chest.

"Tell me," he said.

More. She needed more.

And like she'd said it out loud, he pushed a finger inside her, going deep, hitting the sensitive bundle of nerves there. She sobbed. "Y-yes."

"I saw them touch you, putting their filthy fucking hands on you when you walked by. You like that, too?"

"Yes." *What is wrong with me?*

He took hold of her chin, tilting her head back, making her look at him. Fury lined his hard features, held his big body rigid, and though it was all kinds of screwed up, she loved that he might actually be jealous, that on some messed-up level he might actually care.

He didn't let up, just continued to fuck her with his fingers in a controlled way that made her want to scream. "Did you want to join that couple? Did you want that male between your thighs, tongue buried in this tight, hot little pussy?"

"No," she gasped, his crude words heightening her already out-of-control desire.

"I can feel how turned on it made you, how wet you got from watching that male fuck his female with his tongue. He did this to you. You want him. Fucking admit it."

"No...I don't. I..."

"Say it." His tone was low and harsh and he tightened his grip on her.

"Yes, I liked it," she cried.

He hissed, lips peeling back from his teeth, eyes flickering to ebony.

"But it wasn't him I wanted," she said, close, so close to coming apart.

He ground his erection against her hip. "Who? Who do you want?" he asked, voice guttural.

Gripping his shoulders, she rode his hand. "You. I want you." Then she was coming.

He didn't stop. His fingers continued to move inside her, ringing every last tremor from her body before Lazarus stripped her out of her remaining clothes and carried her to the shower. He climbed in with her, shoved her against the wall, and dropped to his knees. She gasped when he buried his face between her thighs.

Her fingers thrust into his hair, holding on, pulling him closer as he lapped at her, devoured her with deep, hungry strokes of his tongue. He pressed her into the wall, lifting one of her legs over his shoulder, opening her wide for him. Water sluiced over his bare back and drenched his dark hair. Eve couldn't help but fist the glossy strands tighter, close to losing control all over again.

He looked up at her, eyes flashing dark then light, glazed with lust. She loved it, loved that she'd done that to him. That she'd made him so out of control, so crazy for her.

He fucked her with his tongue until she was a writhing, sobbing mess then he wrapped his firm lips around her clit and sucked, sending her over the edge. She didn't hold back—couldn't—and held him to her, grinding against his mouth, lost in sensation. He growled against her, not stopping until she sagged against the wall.

When he pulled back suddenly a few seconds later, she opened her eyes.

Lazarus stood against the tile wall, still in his jeans, the denim drenched and clinging to his hips and thighs. His chest pumped and he gasped out harsh breaths.

Eve took a step toward him.

"Don't." He shook his head. "You can't touch me. Not now. I'm barely hanging on. I'll take what I want. To hell with the consequences."

"Take it," she whispered. "I don't care what the consequences are." She wanted it, whatever it was.

"You don't understand." He pressed back into the wall, his face a mask of pain and longing.

Every muscle strained, every vein and tendon stood out on his tanned skin. She couldn't take her eyes off him. He was magnificent, beautiful. A groan slipped past his lips and he reached down to grip his straining cock, squeezing his hard flesh through the wet denim.

She licked her lips. "Lazarus." His name came out as a plea. She had to see him, all of him.

His hands shook as he popped the button and slid down the zip. His heavy cock sprang free, thick and swollen. A constant stream of pre-come leaked from the tiny slit, running down the shaft, and her mouth watered to taste him. She wanted to drop to her knees and take him into her mouth. "Let me—"

He shook his head, eyes wild, slightly unfocused. "Stay back, Eve. I mean it."

He fisted himself and began to stroke, eyes never leaving her. He leaned heavily on the wall, didn't speak, didn't look away. "*Ah, fuck.*" His fist tightened and his strokes increased in pace.

Eve had never seen anything like it, never seen a more beautiful sight in her life. She slid her hand down her body and slipped her fingers between her folds, massaging her clit, too turned on not to. Lazarus watched her every move, and the sound that left him was full of anguish and need and spurred her on. She cupped her breast with the other hand and squeezed like he had earlier. He moaned low then hissed through his clenched teeth. He was wild, untamed. The solid slabs of muscle in his massive thighs locked up tight.

"What have you done to me?" He groaned and grew impossibly long and thick before he finally cried out her name and came hard. Thick creamy ropes spurted from him, washing down the drain.

Eve leaned against the wall and followed him, coming for the third time against her own fingers.

Lazarus was there before her legs gave out, supporting her weight. He turned off the shower, wrapped her in a towel, and carried her to her room. His hands were rough and economical as he dried her off and squeezed the water from her hair.

He pulled back the covers and put her into bed.

Moments later, Eve drifted into a restless sleep.

Eighteen

Eve woke to sounds coming from the small kitchen and the smell of bacon cooking.

Her stomach rumbled.

Shoving back the covers, she tugged on a pair of shorts and a tank and left her room. Things had gotten crazy the night before. Intense. The way Lazarus had been, the things he'd said.

"You can't touch me. Not now. I'm barely hanging on. I'll take what I want. To hell with the consequences."

What did that mean? She was done waiting for answers.

Her belly flipped when she saw him. He was standing at the counter in only a pair of jeans, a mountain of bacon and eggs piled on plates in front of him.

"Morning," she said, voice still husky from having to yell over loud music last night.

He spun around, his gaze moving over her before coming back to her eyes. His chest expanded sharply.

He licked his lips and cleared his throat. "I made breakfast. You hungry?"

"Ravenous."

Lazarus handed her a plate, and they ate for a while in silence.

"Thanks for doing this."

"I thought that maybe we could talk this morning."

"I was thinking the same thing," she said, suddenly not hungry anymore.

Somehow she finished her breakfast and carried her plate to the kitchen. Lazarus followed her in, putting his plate in the sink.

Eve turned to him, looking up at his strong face, down to that wide chest. She lifted her hand and placed it on the burn there. It had a pattern to it, almost like someone had branded him. She'd been wondering what it was since she first saw it.

"How did you get this?" she asked, tracing it gently.

His nostrils flared. "We were given them when our training was complete. The brand is supposed to prevent us from entering Hell, from being corrupted."

"Corrupted?" Eve stared up at Lazarus, trying and failing to control the pounding of her heart.

Lazarus lifted his hand to hers, covering it, curling his fingers around hers. "Let's sit down."

Her belly flipped at his serious tone. He led her into the small living room and Eve moved to the couch and sat...and waited.

Lazarus paced around in front of her for a few minutes, making her even more nervous.

Finally, he stopped and faced her. "There are things you need to know, about me, about us...about you."

"Okay," she said, clutching her hands together.

His jaw tightened. "It has...it's become obvious that *being* with you...it balances me. It gives me the strength to keep control over my demon, control I've been losing over the last few weeks."

"Being with me? You mean like last night?"

He dipped his chin.

"The mate thing?" she said, pulse picking up speed.

He swallowed, throat working. "Yes."

She wished she knew how to wipe away the anguish lining his face. "Why are you losing control?"

He sat on the couch beside her, rubbing his palms on his jean-covered thighs. "A very long time ago, demons discovered a way to leave their realm and began moving among mankind. The angels were clueless, only learning about it after a demi-demon, new to his powers, accidentally wiped out his entire village. The demons were using human females to carry and raise their offspring, and when they were old enough to be of use, they would reclaim them to use as weapons to gain control and power on Earth."

She could barely believe the horror of what he was telling her. But she knew looking into his eyes that it was all true.

"The heavens couldn't allow such atrocities to occur, so six angels chose to fall for the good of mankind."

Eve rubbed her temples, a slow throb building behind her eyes. "Why did they need to fall?"

"To breed with the very demons they despised, to create a race of warriors. The knights of Hell, they called us. The angels had tried and failed to track the demi-demons on their own, to control the demon hordes escaping hell. But with the addition of demon DNA, it would be possible. They had to prevent the demon offspring from being used as weapons. They couldn't allow such evil to corrupt the Earth. Balance must always be maintained."

"And you're one of the knights?"

"Yes. I have no idea which fallen birthed me; none of us do. We weren't raised like human children, Eve. We were raised to be warriors, weapons in the war between Heaven and Hell."

What he described turned her stomach, made her ache for the little boy he had once been. Yes, she'd suffered repeated rejection by her extended family, but she'd also had many years of nurturing by her mother and father, of feeling loved.

"What happened to disturb the balance?" He kept using that word. It wasn't hard to figure out something had tipped the scale.

"Tobias, one of our bothers, surrendered to his demon after the death of his mate. He chose a life without the memory of her love." He swallowed hard. "Because living without her was just too painful."

She wrapped her arms around herself when a cold, hollow feeling settled in the center of her chest. "How he must have suffered to make such a choice. He's the one you've been searching for?"

"Yes. And because he surrendered to his demon willingly, the possession was gradual. They became one, which enables him to maintain a measure of control, unlike the rest of us. Now he answers to Diemos."

He stood, his back to her. "You see, all knights are connected, a bond that was formed when we were born. It's an added safeguard created by the angels to keep us tied together so we won't be tempted to abandon our purpose, a bond so strong it can only be broken by death. While Tobias lives, he can send his toxic poison to us through that bond. We're absorbing his dark, demonic nature, which is throwing off that delicate balance." He turned to face her. "He's taking the rest of us with him."

The horror of his words and the cold way he spoke them caused her to flinch. "Lazarus, I'm so sorry—"

"No." His deep voice cut her off, startling her. A muscle in his jaw jumped. "Don't be sorry for me."

Anguish transformed his gaze. And whatever had caused the pain and self-loathing she saw there had left a mark on his soul and caused a torment so deep she could see the invisible wound bleeding from his chest. She tamped down the urge to go to him, to comfort him. At that moment he wouldn't welcome it. "What happens now?"

"The angels have taken his actions as a declaration of war. He chose his side, and it wasn't ours. Now you understand the urgency, the reason I need to find Tobias."

She stood and took a step toward him. When he didn't retreat, she moved in close enough to rest a hand on his biceps. The muscle flexed under her palm, hard as stone. "I'll do whatever I can to help."

"You will?" he choked.

"Yes." If being with him helped save him and his brothers, of course, she'd help. How could she not?

"I hate that you have to do this. I hate that you are in danger because of me. But, Eve, I'm also thankful. You don't know how many people you're saving by allowing me to"—he sucked in a sharp breath—"by giving yourself to me in that way." His throat worked several times before he carried on. "Sex seems to provide enough of a calming effect on me that..." He ran a hand over his head before he glanced back at her. "There shouldn't be any need for us to mate fully. I felt it when we were in the storeroom at the airport. And just touching me seems to help a little."

It took effort, but she managed to school her features. Dammit, why did it hurt so much? His words confirmed what she'd already guessed. The idea of being tied to her for the rest of his life was not a welcome prospect. Lazarus would use her body, and when he no longer needed her, he would leave.

She should be used to this by now. Really, she should be as pleased as he obviously was. Even though she knew this was how it must be, it stung. She had grown to care far more than she should for the dangerous warrior.

Realization struck, and her mouth went dry. "That's why you're keeping me close?"

"No." He shook his head. "My main priority has always been keeping you safe."

"You sure about that? Or was it so I could help you control your demon, so you could track Tobias?"

His lips compressed into a thin line. "I had no idea you'd have that effect on me. I promise you that."

The man in front of her was going through hell, doing what he had to for a greater good. But hanging on for dear life while he dragged her through the fiery aftermath wasn't much fun either. Neither was having your life ripped out from under you and treated as nothing more than a means to an end.

The way he was looking at her, she knew that wasn't it, though. There was more. "What aren't you telling me?"

He closed the distance between them and his hand went to her hip, finger sliding into the elastic of her shorts, tugging down the side a little.

Eve watched, confused as he ran his fingers over the crimson birthmark she had there. Her heart rate had picked up speed when she looked back at him.

"This"—another brush of his finger over the mark—"is called the Beast's touch." Eve's whole body jerked and she tried to pull away. Lazarus wouldn't let her, his big hand gripping her hip, holding her there. "As far as we know, only demi who carry this mark can do what you can."

She clenched her fists so tight her knuckles ached. "And what's that?"

"You can open the gates of Hell."

Oh God. She tried to pull away again, but Lazarus wouldn't let her retreat. "How?" she whispered.

"When Lucifer still ruled Hell—"

"He doesn't rule Hell anymore?"

Lazarus's brows lowered. "He was overthrown by Diemos and cast out. No one knows how, or where he is, if he's even still alive."

Eve's head began to pound. "And what does that have to do with me?"

"He had a group of warriors, demons, he called his handmaidens. They were loyal to only him, guarded him, took care of him, and they also had the ability to open and close the gates of Hell." He squeezed her hip. "You are a descendant of one of his handmaids, and as a result, you have inherited the same ability. You're a hell's gate, Eve."

She started to shake. "I'm a what?"

"Demons can only cross from Hell to Earth four times a year—during the summer and winter solstice, and the spring and autumn equinox. That's when the barrier between realms is at its thinnest."

She wanted to block her ears, didn't want to believe what she was hearing.

"And if Diemos captured you—"

"Diemos?"

"He controls Hell now, and his main goal is to take Earth as well, to rule it. Because of his limited access to Earth, Diemos can only send a small number of his soldiers through at a time. He doesn't like that. The gate opens, he sends demons through, the gate closes, and we get time to whittle down the army he's trying to build. It's a never-ending cycle, and the only way to gain unlimited access is to possess a hell's gate demi. With you, he could activate the hell's gate at will."

Eve was suddenly struggling to breathe.

He rubbed her back. "Eve?" He cursed. "Calm down. I need you to calm down."

She shook her head and pushed at his arms with more force. He let her go this time, let her stumble back several steps. "Calm down? Are you serious?"

Lazarus stayed where he was as she paced around.

"Eve..."

She shook her head, trying to take it in. All of it. Her stomach roiled. "I think I'm going to be sick."

"Eve, look at me."

She forced herself to look up, to meet his green gaze.

"I won't let that happen. Do you hear me? Now we have you, they can't use you. No one can get to you here. And while you're wearing the amulet, they can't track you either. Your power to activate the gate won't work."

"Is there a way to get this...this gate out of me, to stop it?" She wanted to claw at her skin, tear it out of her body.

His jaw clenched again. "Mating will render the power useless." He pointed to the heavy gold necklace she wore. "But it's not necessary. As long as you wear that, you'll be safe."

She squeezed her eyes closed. God, what she wouldn't give to be in her little bookstore right at that moment, back to living her quiet, solitary existence. She'd spent her life giving to others, trying to please, only to have it thrown back in her face. No more. She was sick of life happening to her, of being overlooked, of being the girl people walked all over.

She let her anger rise to the surface, anger she had kept bottled up for far too long. A bitter laugh escaped, and she didn't recognize her voice when she spoke. "Lucky you, huh?" She curled her fingers around the amulet and held it up. "I can only imagine your relief that this chunk of metal exists. I mean, I'd hate to put you through the alternative."

"Eve—"

"No, it's fine, really. If jumping your bones on a regular basis is what you need from me..." She smiled, though it was more just a baring of teeth. "Well, that's a sacrifice I'm willing to make."

He stiffened and crimson slashed his sharp cheekbones. "Eve." He took a step toward her, reached for her.

She took a step back. "No, you're right, this is extremely good news. So how does this whole thing work? You start to lose control of your demon, and I—what? Jump on your dick and make it better?"

He flinched. "I promise I won't bother you unless it's absolutely necessary."

Ouch. The blows were coming thick and fast, and she felt emotionally battered and bruised as a result. She didn't want to look too deeply at how strong her feelings had grown in such a short span of time. Since he wouldn't be coming to her unless he absolutely had to, she might get a reprieve from his overpowering presence, maybe get a chance to gain some perspective over her jumbled emotions.

"I'd appreciate that," she said.

He stiffened.

"And once you kill Tobias, I'm free to go? I just have to make sure I wear this amulet...you know, so a horde of demons doesn't come after me, yes?"

"Eve, please—"

"What about pregnancy, sexually transmitted diseases? I'd prefer not to be left raising a child on my own." Obviously, this was something she should have considered *before* they'd had sex, but at the time they'd been in a seriously stressful situation and it hadn't exactly been the first thing that had popped into her head right afterward. She curled her fingers into a tight fist. She'd always wanted kids, someone to love and be loved unconditionally in return. It had been something she'd craved almost all her life. A real family.

"I can't carry diseases of any kind. And pregnancy can only occur between mated couples." His voice was so low she barely heard him.

She shrugged carelessly, despite another verbal slap. "I guess I'm stuck here for a while longer, then. You know, since I'm the go-to girl when you need to get off." Accusation was clear in her voice, but she couldn't stop it, didn't want to. She should have known better than to trust so easily. Would she ever learn? How many times would she extend her hand only to have her fingers bitten?

He stood ramrod straight, his fists clenching and unclenching at his sides. "It's not like that—"

She ignored him and talked right over him. "All my life I've wanted to be special, to be important. Well, look at me now." She threw up her hands. "I got my wish. Turns out I've got a magic vagina." She turned her back on him and headed for the bedroom, needing to get the hell away from him.

He swore under his breath. "Eve, for fuck's sake. Stop."

She paused at the bedroom door but didn't turn around. She hated herself for thinking it, but she wanted him to tell her that wasn't all there was between them, that he cared for her. Even just a little.

The silence dragged out and finally, he said, "I have to go out for a while. Will you be all right on your own?"

Trying but no doubt failing to hide the conflicting emotions stirring inside her, she glanced back at him over her shoulder and shrugged "It's what I prefer. What I'm used to."

His mouth compressed into a thin line, and he ran a hand through his hair before he turned and strode from the room.

He'd been gone less than a minute when her mind headed to a place she didn't want it to go. The constant ache between her thighs made it near impossible to ignore. The question shot through her mind then proceeded to pierce her heart with a force that belied the short time she'd known him.

How long before he came for her?

Eve hated herself for still wanting him.

It shouldn't, but the thought of possessing Lazarus, of being wholly possessed in return, felt right. Unfortunately, she was the only one who felt it.

Still staring at the door after him, she made herself turn, and rubbing the gooseflesh from her arms, walked to the bathroom.

She didn't have a claim over him, never would, and he sure as hell didn't own her. How could he?

He didn't even want her.

She needed a shower, needed to wash off his scent, his touch...his kiss.

The reminders of what they'd done the night before lingered. A tangible thing, crowding the room, almost like he was seared into her skin and, God help her, her soul.

Nineteen

Lazarus shut the door behind him and sucked in a ragged breath.

He'd circled the pits of Hell, had barely resisted the darkness calling him home, and had never believed it possible to sink lower than he had when he lost Scarlet. But at that moment, he despised himself with a fierceness of emotion he thought impossible.

He'd made his decision, but nothing had changed. He still wanted Eve, and he had to get away before he took her, for no other reason than he wanted to feel her body wrapped around his. He didn't need to make her his mate, didn't need to tie her to him for eternity. He should be pleased.

Instead, Eve's reaction to being set free from the life sentence stirred unwanted emotion and a feeling of such overwhelming possessiveness he was surprised his molars hadn't disintegrated to dust attempting to conceal the strength of his reaction.

He never expected to feel anything for her, and relinquishing his claim to her, shit, felt beyond wrong. It felt unnatural.

He mentally flinched, remembering the disgust covering her face and lacing her words. *"No, you're right, this is extremely good news. So how does this whole thing work? You start to lose control of your demon, and I—what? Jump on your dick and make it better?"*

The fact she didn't want him touching her, and because of the situation she found herself in, that she might be forced to have sex with him anyway, made his stomach roil.

Oh, physically she responded to his touch, but their connection removed a certain amount of control over her body's reaction to him.

Acid burned the back of his throat. Fuck, he was going to be sick.

Lazarus pounded down the stairs and out through the club's fire exit. If he was about to empty the contents of his stomach, he didn't want an audience. Palms pressed against the cool, rough brick, he sucked back oxygen trying to fight the nausea, but the stench in the alley only made it worse.

Staying away from her would help. The more time they spent together, the stronger their bond would become, and he couldn't risk growing any more attached to her than he already was. His demon clawed at his mind as soon as the notion crossed it. Silas had made it clear that bond was necessary to protect her, but he couldn't do it, not until this was all over. Not until Tobias was dealt with. And not until he was stable again.

Finding your mate should be a joyous occasion, ending a long and lonely life. Finally gaining the balance his kind fought to maintain their entire lives—the missing half of their soul returned, complete.

It was a rare thing, something he should have cherished and nurtured, not disrespected, and avoided. With the shitty way he'd handled this whole thing, he'd singlehandedly destroyed their one shot at happiness. He would never know the feeling of completing their bond. The exhilaration of fusing their life forces for eternity, or the euphoric surge as their powers increased and grew.

No, he would never know her the way he longed to.

After Scarlet's death, he'd been determined to avoid such a union. He'd barely survived the crippling grief of her loss, but after seeing the suffering of her mate followed by his slow descent into darkness, his own pain paled in comparison.

What if I fail Eve as well?

If something happened to her because of him...fuck, he couldn't think about that. As hard as it was to fight his instincts to claim her, it was for the best.

How could he force Eve to tie herself to someone like him? He didn't deserve her. Not after what he'd done.

Scarlet wrapped her arms around his waist and smiled up at him. That amazing knock-the-wind-from-your-lungs smile he knew so well. The one that reminded him of the little girl he'd found all those years ago.

"Thank you," she said.

"Why are you thanking me, sweet girl?"

She squeezed him tighter and glanced over at Tobias standing across the room. "I found my mate because of you. I have a family because you found me." She went up onto her tiptoes and kissed his cheek. "Lazarus, I owe you everything."

He groaned, the memory hitting hard, the pain accompanying it a knife to the heart.

As soon as this was over, he would deliver Eve to the compound, then he'd leave. He'd watch over her from a distance. His pain was nothing he didn't deserve. All that mattered was her happiness. And if that meant watching her move on, watching her...fall in love with someone else, that's the way it had to be. All that mattered was keeping her safe. Safe from Diemos. Safe from his demons.

And safe from Lazarus himself.

Lazarus punched the cushions again and propped his arm behind his head, unfolding his big body on the too-short couch. He'd had another shitty night with absolutely no sleep whatsoever.

Another week had passed, a week of searching for Tobias and of lying scrunched up on this fucking couch.

A week of Eve avoiding him.

He fucking hated it. Last night had been no different from the previous torturous ones. He'd spent every second trying not to go into that damn bedroom. He wanted to go in there and beg her forgiveness. Spend hours with his face buried between those soft, creamy thighs, apologizing for the pain he'd caused her. He wanted to slide into that sweet pussy and take his time fucking her like he'd promised in that airport storage room.

Christ, it had only been a matter of weeks, but it felt so long ago now.

He rubbed his hands over his face.

Now she could barely look at him.

Still, when he'd gotten back from searching the city last night, another night spent looking for Tobias, he'd done what he did every night. He opened her door and watched the subtle rise and fall of her chest as she slept.

And like every night, his desperate need for her freaked him out so much he'd kicked his own ass back to the couch.

The woman's taste still lingered in his memory, branded into his senses. The more time he spent with her, the more he felt. He didn't like it, didn't want to deal with the tender feelings that stirred inside him. He didn't know how to handle them. This was completely beyond his scope of knowledge.

Thankfully, things had settled down some at the compound now the autumnal equinox had come and gone, and with the amulet in Eve's possession, she was at least safe from those who would hunt her.

Now he just needed to find Tobias. He was close, Lazarus could feel it. Then Eve would be free to do as she chose, without him.

He growled. Even the thought twisted him in knots. It was illogical, but during their short time together his feelings for her had become powerful, all-consuming. It scared him. If he let her, the voluptuous female would not only claim his body but make him believe he had a heart worth salvaging.

Weak.

Flawed.

He shook off the direction his thoughts were heading. He'd spent the last few hours twisting himself in knots already.

The stack of books sitting on the coffee table caught his eye again. All of them Eve's favorites, he knew because she'd shared her love of books with him back at the compound, and had told him the ones she reread all the time.

Many were copies of the books she'd been forced to leave behind. Brent brought them for her as a gift. The warm smile she'd given the other male when he'd presented them to her had turned Lazarus inside out with jealousy.

He'd seen the way she'd gazed at the large collection in her home as he'd ushered her out the front door for the last time, or the words she'd quietly spoken. *Some of them belonged to my mother.* He'd known how important they were to her.

He couldn't help but be annoyed that he hadn't thought of getting them for her first. Brent and Eve were sharing mealtimes, and it had become part of their routine to watch a movie before he went down to his club for the night. Lazarus didn't like it.

He hated that he was jealous. He had no right to be, not anymore.

He was lucky Brent was there for her. He'd grown up around humans and better understood human emotions.

His Scarlet, on the other hand, had been more demon than human. He'd recognized that from the moment he'd found her. Eve was a different creature entirely. Lazarus didn't have the first clue how to ease her pain and worry, and right then he wished he did.

The rustle of bedding drifted in from the other room, and he could imagine Eve shifting under the covers, stretching out across the white cotton sheets, all warm and rumpled and sleepy. The T-shirt she had on would cling to her, outlining her curves.

He groaned and squeezed his eyes shut, trying to force the images from his mind. He needed to get a hold of this yearning, this clawing, unending ache for her. But deep down he knew it would only get worse.

Reaching down, he shifted his massive erection, grunting at the contact. He'd go and take care of it himself, but it wouldn't do any good. Only one person could ease this unrelenting need, and she lay in the other room.

Fucking her wasn't all he wanted, though. No, he wanted so much more. He wanted her eyes on him, bright with happiness. He wanted her smiles, and goddammit, he wanted to be the one who had put them on her face. He wanted to talk to her for hours and learn every little thing about her.

He just wanted her. All of her.

You don't deserve her.

He curled his fingers into tight fists. Somehow, he'd managed to control his demon this long without the need to take her again, but it was getting tougher by the day. Harder to resist and harder to keep his demon riding shotgun and not shoving him out of the driver's seat.

But how could he ask her to let him taint her beautiful

body after all the pain he'd caused her? To let him have her when the idea disgusted her?

Throwing off the covers, he sat up, groaning as he stood.

His cell rang.

Snatching it from the coffee table, he checked it. *Unknown number*. Not unusual. It could be James calling from the compound with an update. Most of their phones had blocked caller ID.

He put the phone to his ear. "Yeah?"

Silence.

"James?"

When more silence greeted him, he curled his fingers into a tight fist. It didn't take a genius to work out who the mystery caller was. "Tobias."

"Laz," he said, voice cold, brittle.

Pain twisted in his chest, hearing his brother's voice, so sharp he felt like he'd taken a knife to the chest. "Tell me where you are," Lazarus said. "I promise I'll end it quick, brother. That has to better than the slow torture Diemos will take pleasure in handing out."

"Hey, I'm all for torture. Maybe I'll find out if that curvy little demi you have stashed enjoys being on the receiving end." Lazarus barely contained a growl at the mention of Eve. "I'm surprised you left her unprotected. Out in the open like that, anyone could have taken advantage."

He'd had spies here the night Eve worked in the club. Jesus, he could have lost her. She could have been taken from him. If she'd gone outside...

"Tobias—"

"Anyway, as tempting as your offer of a quick death is, I think I'll wait for you to find me," Tobias said, changing the subject back.

"Brother," Lazarus choked out. "You can't want this."

"I'm not your fucking brother."

Another slice of pain. No, he wasn't. He didn't know this male, didn't recognize the cruelty, the hate in his deep voice.

"We both know it's only a matter of time before you succumb," Tobias said, and there was no missing how much he was looking forward to that day.

"I won't let that happen."

An arctic chuckle traveled down the line. "Yeah? I'm not so sure. As it is, your screwed-up sense of honor makes you weak. Instead of spending every waking hour searching for me, you return to that little demi you're guarding. I can see why you'd want her around, of course. Her power is...impressive, and she is kind of hot. Tell me, have you fucked her yet, Laz?"

Red rage clouded his vision. His demon stirred then roared, clawing to be free, to destroy any threat to his female. "You do not touch her. You don't even think about her. Do you understand?"

Tobias's silence said more than words ever could. With his loss of control, he'd gifted his weakness to his enemy on a silver platter and thrown down a challenge all at the same time. But then, despite Tobias's casual mention of Eve and her power, Lazarus had no doubt he already wanted her for Diemos's army. Her ability to read minds would be a unique prize. And that was without knowing she had the power to open the portal. If he found out...

Yeah, that would be the whipped cream and cherry on top.

"Ah, she's that good?" Tobias said finally. "Will she please me, do you think?"

Lazarus remained silent, refusing to bite, but all the while he was roaring inside.

"You never could control your emotions, could you, Lazarus?" He laughed, the sound causing the hairs on the back of his neck to lift. "That was always your weakness. It seems you've developed tender feelings for your *mate*. How sweet." His voice dropped to a harsh whisper, full of promise and pure hatred. "You have no idea how much I'm going to enjoy taking her from you, asshole, like you took Scarlet from me."

"I loved Scarlet. I'd do anything to bring her back." Lazarus would never forgive himself for her death, and was powerless to stop his reaction. His demon reared inside him, pushed for release with a greater force than ever before.

"You took my mate from me and I'm going to make sure you know exactly what that feels like."

Lazarus gritted his teeth, fighting for control.

Tobias's voice was quiet and controlled when he spoke next. "Did you know as the connection strengthens between the two of you, your senses mesh? You will have the ability to feel what she's feeling."

Lazarus was barely hanging on to his sanity. He didn't want to hear any more.

"No matter where you are, you will feel her take her last breath. Hear her scream your name, knowing there is nothing you can do to save her as her life's blood drains from her used and broken body." Tobias took a shuddering breath. "That sound will haunt you every day for the rest of your life. Best you watch her closely, *brother*." Then the phone disconnected.

Lazarus stood there, in the middle of the room, fighting for control. When that failed, he roared and kicked the wooden coffee table in front of him across the room. It crashed into the wall and splintered into kindling. His demon continued to fight for release and he didn't know how much longer he could keep it at bay.

"Who's Scarlet?"

He turned sharply toward the bedroom door. He hadn't heard Eve come out. She stood in a pink T-shirt and boxers, her hair tousled. He wanted to bury his hands in her hair, shove her against the wall, and fuck her so hard the building shook around them.

He jerked his head to the side, unable to answer.

"What happened to her?" She took a step closer.

"Stay...stay back, Eve. I'm not...I'm not myself." When he looked up, her sharply indrawn breath said it all. His demon had risen to the surface and was looking at her through its soulless black eyes. It twisted and coiled around his mind. It wanted Eve, and this time there was no stopping it.

The restraint he'd been hanging on to by a thread snapped. His demon took control and forced his body to move toward her. Lazarus tried to regain control, but it was no use.

When he got to her, he would take her, and his demon wouldn't let him be gentle.

Nausea churned in his gut and his heated skin broke out in a cold sweat. This couldn't happen, he couldn't allow this to happen, wouldn't be able to live with himself if he hurt her.

Drawing on the last ounce of his strength, he forced his body to turn. His demon's control weakened momentarily with Eve out of sight, but only for a moment. Lazarus gained enough momentum to flee the room, and pounded down the stairs to the now-empty club.

A clinking sound drew his attention as he pushed into the bar. Brent was busy putting away glasses. "What's up?"

"Take me to a room," Lazarus choked.

Brent frowned. "What?"

"You need to restrain me. Now."

The guy didn't need to be told twice. Leaping over the bar, Brent rushed to one of the private rooms with Lazarus hot on his heels.

"Get on here. It's more than strong enough to hold you."

Every muscle strained as he fought to lie down on the rough wooden bench. Brent yanked Lazarus's arms over his head and secured heavy metal shackles around his wrists. Pulling the thick chains taut so he couldn't move them, he quickly and efficiently shackled down his legs as well, pinning him to the sturdy surface.

Now all he had to do was wait and hope like hell that this wasn't the end.

Twenty

Eve stared after Lazarus, stunned. *What just happened?*

His face had been contorted in agony, filled with rage. She'd seen him struggling with his demon before, but nothing like this. Something was terribly wrong.

Eve ran out of the apartment after him.

At the bottom of the stairs, she pushed open the door and entered the club. The room was dimly lit, empty. No leather, no half-naked bodies writhing on the dance floor. No Lazarus.

A moan had her whipping around to the left toward the private rooms. Before she could think better of it, she started toward the anguished sound.

She stopped in front of a glossy red door just as a low rumble vibrated from behind it, through it. That sound, God, it hit every nerve ending in her body, lifting goose bumps all over her skin. Her step faltered.

You can do this, Eve.

Taking a deep breath, she ignored her apprehension and pushed on, an unexplainable need to find Lazarus propelling her forward.

He needed her. Somehow, she knew he needed her.

The low rumble was constant now and deep enough to shake the heavy wood. It sounded like growling, like some kind of wild animal prowled on the other side, desperate to get out.

The logical part of her brain told her to turn around, to get the hell out of there, but Lazarus was on the other side of that door and the longer she stood out here the more he suffered.

Not knowing what she might walk in on, but desperate to get to Lazarus, she ignored her anxiety, gripped the handle, and opened the door.

A roar rent the air and froze her to the spot before she'd barely taken a step. The room was small. Several wooden and iron structures filled the limited space, but the largest piece was a heavy wooden table.

That's where she found Lazarus, or what had been Lazarus, stretched out on its hard surface.

His wrists and ankles were chained down by some kind of metal cuffs, and a thick leather strap circled his middle, restraining him further. Teeth gritted, he thrashed and snarled, fighting against his bonds.

The shredded remains of his clothes lay scattered on the floor, half covered by his large charcoal wings that had sprouted from under his back. They draped over the sides of the bench, taking up most of the floor space. The wall-mounted lights caught the tiny flecks of silver that appeared to be threaded through each of one of his dark feathers. But most shocking of all was his body's complete transformation. His skin was leathery and deep crimson. Horns protruded from his head, just above his hairline, and his lips were curled back, revealing large fangs that extended halfway down his chin. He looked like a gargoyle from the top of one of those gothic-style buildings.

A movement had her gaze slicing to the other side of the room. Brent stood there, his eyes locked on Lazarus.

"How? What...what's wrong with him?" she choked out.

Lazarus stilled, his head turning on his thick neck toward her. Eve took a startled step back. His irises were huge, the whites of his eyes barely visible. Every bit of the emerald green color had been swallowed by midnight. He stared at her, eyes wide and unblinking as air hissed through his teeth in harsh, rapid exhales.

Brent grabbed her arm. "You need to leave."

An inhuman roar tore from Lazarus's throat. "Do not touch her." His voice echoed around the room in an eerie way that sent shivers across her entire body. His gaze tracked Brent and did not waver until he removed his hand and moved away from her.

"I won't touch her again." Brent lifted his hands in the air. "See, I'm not touching her."

Those midnight irises slid back to her and continued to stare with an intensity that was terrifying and made her feel as though he could see deep inside her. "What happened to him?"

"It's his demon. Lazarus has succumbed." Brent scrubbed his hands over his face. "This is all kinds of fucked up."

Oh God. This was her fault. He'd told her what he needed from her. But she'd been so busy nursing her own wounds, working hard to punish him for hurting her, she hadn't considered what could happen.

He hadn't come to her when he'd needed her help, trying to protect her from any more pain, and now his demon had taken him.

Brent slid his hands into his pockets. "If we can't bring him back"—he motioned to Lazarus's writhing form—"*this* will be permanent."

"We have to do something." Again, when she spoke,

Lazarus's thrashing ceased. She turned back as a wave of his intoxicating scent hit her, and sucked in a breath when light flickered behind his eyes, like a light bulb about to blow. Emerald sparks trying to break through the inky black of his irises.

"Say something else," Brent demanded.

She was frightened out of her mind, but this was Lazarus and he was suffering, so she forced herself to take a tentative step closer. "Lazarus, it's me. I'm here," she whispered.

This time the green held for a few seconds before being engulfed once more, sucked beneath those inky pools.

She took in his straining body, all of it, unable to miss the massive erection that lay against his defined, currently crimson stomach. His hips jerked at her scrutiny. Well, as much as they could against the thick leather band around his ribs. He groaned as if her gaze had caressed him, eased his hurt.

"I think it's helping," she said, glancing up at Brent.

Brent's eyebrows rose to meet his hairline. "So, it's true. You're Lazarus's mate?"

She nodded.

"Your voice is forcing back his demon." He waved her forward while keeping a safe distance himself. "Touching him might help. Just be careful."

If there was a small chance she could help him, she'd do whatever it took. Taking another step closer, careful not to step on his beautiful wings, she moved to the head of the table. Brent remained silent when she lifted a shaky hand to gently stroke his cheek.

The color of his eyes continued to flicker while he grunted and growled incoherently. Then it started, the purring sound she'd heard him make back at the compound, a deep rumble that vibrated from his chest. He pressed back as much as he could, rubbing his face against her hand.

She carried on stroking him and the sound got louder.

His horns were shiny black and she couldn't resist touching them as well, running her fingers over a glossy tip. His entire body jerked.

"Don't stop what you're doing," Brent whispered from his spot on the other side of the room.

She continued to speak to him, keeping her voice low and soothing. Then the black washed from his irises for several seconds, and though they were darker than their usual pale green, they were Lazarus's eyes, and the fear staring back at her broke her heart. Without thinking, she leaned down and kissed his forehead. His skin felt as leathery as it looked and cool against her lips.

"I'm here, Lazarus," she whispered.

A roar tore from his throat at her words and she staggered back. His body shook then torqued violently on the table. The tendons strained in his neck and across his chest and he jerked several times. Just like that, his body shifted back, besides the wings which still sprouted from his back and lay limp across the floor.

"Lazarus?"

"Don't stop now, he needs more," Brent said carefully.

"What should I do?"

Brent's gaze moved over Lazarus then lifted to hers. "I think you know what he needs, Eve." His eyes softened. "Will you give it to him?"

Still stroking his heated skin, she took in Lazarus's magnificent body, hard and straining. Yes, she knew what she had to do. Without looking up, she nodded. She'd do anything to help him, and deep in her heart, she knew he'd do the same for her.

"Don't stop." Lazarus's voice was a mixture of pleasure and pain. He'd responded to her touch, and her body heated, moisture rushing to her sex in reply.

"It's okay, Brent. I can take it from here." She couldn't

bring herself to meet his gaze.

"Are you sure?" He sounded reluctant to leave. "I can stay. I'll turn my back."

Nothing but concern filled his voice. For him, being in a room with others having sex was no big deal.

"Thank you, but I'll be okay. He won't hurt me." Lazarus would never purposely harm her, she knew that much.

"Don't untie him. The table's strong and can hold several people at once..." His gaze moved back to Lazarus's trussed-up form. "Just...be careful."

She nodded. "I will."

"I'll be right outside the door if you need me." Then he turned and left the room.

Running gentle fingers over his damp skin, Eve looked down at the pained expression on Lazarus's face. "What should I do?"

He was panting, eyes wild. "Eve...please...I need you." His body surged up again.

She didn't know if she really was Lazarus's mate, but she couldn't stand to see him this way, and if she could ease his pain she would. She wanted to be the one to help him.

She just wanted him.

The desperate, sounds coming from him sealed her fate. She left the head of the table and moved down his body.

"Don't leave me." The agony in his voice shredded her.

"I'm not going anywhere. I promise I won't leave you." She reached over and stroked his thigh, trying to comfort him.

His body went completely still, and she looked up. He watched her with those midnight eyes, now shot with sparks of emerald.

The knowledge of what caused that dark gaze sent a shiver down her spine. She pushed the fear to the back of her mind and refused to think about the demonic side of his nature, the side that wanted to dominate the man inside. Lazarus was fighting to regain control of his body and mind, and she would do whatever it took to help the male she cared about far more than she had a right to.

His cock was thick, veins lining his heavy shaft, and she had the sudden urge to bend down and run her tongue along each one, tracing them to the glistening tip.

He writhed under her heated gaze. "Touch me," he pleaded.

She wrapped her fingers around him, fisted the silky length, and began to stroke him slow and easy, not entirely sure how to proceed. Their gazes locked and the midnight turned to deep green again. He hissed and bucked.

Gasping, he panted out, "Take off your shorts."

She nodded, unable to speak, and slid them down her legs. His nostrils flared as the cotton pooled at her feet. Then his gaze traveled up her bare legs and zeroed in on her panties. "Take those off as well."

Her sex clenched, slick from the blatant lust on his face, the undisguised hunger altering his deep voice. It was pure gravel. Doing as he asked, she hooked her finger in the sides and slid the flimsy fabric down her legs.

The metal chains smacked into the wooden table as his big body jerked hard against his restraints. Without conscious thought, Eve took several startled steps back until she hit the wall, rattling the various chains, cuffs, and whips that hung there. His face contorted, but this time it wasn't physical. He looked tormented by her panicked reaction. He hated what he was doing to her, and the need to reassure him brought her back to his side, bolstering her courage.

"It's all right. I'm all right." She didn't know who she was trying to convince more.

He cursed repeatedly between panted breaths. "Climb up." The mix of pain and longing in his voice evaporated the last of her fear and replaced it with raw desire.

The table was wide enough for her to climb up beside him, and she straddled his hips. His breathing grew ragged as she moved up to position his engorged flesh. The head brushed her sex, and he hissed, rearing beneath her.

His heavy arms strained against the chains, the corded muscles bunching as he fought against his restraints.

Teeth gritted, chest pumping rapidly, he sucked back oxygen. "Fuck me, Eve. Please."

She didn't hesitate at his frantic plea and lowered her body, taking him inside her all the way. Her body stretched to accommodate his large size, the sensation almost too much. Lazarus moaned as her body gripped him tight.

"That's it. Take all of me, sweetheart." His foot thumped against the table. "Ah, fuck."

She bent down and brushed her lips against his, unable to stop herself, and he opened his mouth instantly, hungrily sliding his tongue against hers, deepening the kiss. It was desperate and needy. She felt it, too, and she gave him back what he needed.

Clutching his shoulders, she lifted her upper body slightly and began to move, up and back, trying to keep the pace measured. He went so deep with every stroke she could already feel her inner muscles beginning to ripple around him.

He tried to thrust up and growled in frustration. "Undo the band around my waist."

She reached down and unlatched the thick leather and it clattered to the floor. She wasn't afraid of him, not anymore. How could she be after the way he'd reacted to her touch? The chains attached to the manacles around his wrists and ankles appeared to be one length that ran below the table, and as he kicked out with his feet, his wrists slammed down hard against the top of the bench, pulling them down tight, causing the veins in his arms to bulge under the strain.

He kicked against the chains around his legs until he could

dig his heels in against the wood beneath and thrust his hips up powerfully to meet hers. She cried out as he repeatedly hit her right where she needed him, slammed their bodies together over and over in a desperate frenzy, racing toward release.

His massive charcoal wings, which up until now had lain unmoving against the floor, lifted. A cool breeze tickled her bare legs and stirred the loose strands of her hair as they moved, beating gently.

Lazarus snarled, the animalistic sound filling the small room before he thrust up, hitting her at an angle that sent stars exploding behind her lids and caused her inner muscles to clamp down hard, kicking off a powerful climax. She screamed his name while her body gripped him tight, clenching repeatedly around his thick length.

When the waves of pleasure receded, she collapsed against his chest, linked her arms beneath his powerful shoulders, and held on tight as he thrust up. A guttural sound tore from his throat when he found his own release, then those magnificent wings lifted, curling around them both, surrounding them in a dark, silken cocoon.

When she regained some of her composure, she took in his rugged face. He looked like the fierce warrior she knew him to be, despite the chains restraining him. It was hard to believe that she'd somehow helped him tame the demon fighting for dominance inside him.

His eyes were closed tight, and though she thought she knew, she couldn't be sure who had won this battle. Who it was that lay beneath her. Cautiously, she reached up and ran gentle fingers across his brow and down his cheek. "Lazarus?"

His lids fluttered open.

She gasped at the stunning beauty of his bright emerald gaze staring back at her.

"Thank you," he croaked.

She smiled. "I'm glad you're back."

"Is everything all right in there?" Brent's voice sounded muffled from the other side of the door.

"We're fine," she called, sitting up as Lazarus's beautiful wings unfurled from around their bodies. "Let me get you out of these shackles."

When he slipped from her body, she felt the loss instantly. She shook off the feeling and climbed to the floor to study his chains. "How the heck do I undo these things?"

"There's a key over there." He pointed to a hook on the wall.

The door opened a crack and a pair of jeans landed on the floor. "Thought you might need these," Brent said through the gap then shut the door again.

Retrieving the heavy key, Eve undid his wrists, followed by his ankles, and stepped back. Lazarus sat up and swung his legs over the side of the table. He stretched his limbs and flexed his stiff muscles. She stared in awe as those beautiful black shimmery wings folded in. He tagged the jeans from the floor and, without taking his eyes off her, pulled them on, not bothering to do them up. "As much as I want to keep you naked, you should probably get dressed."

"Oh...oh, right." She bent down and grabbed her shorts, but before she could pull them back on, he moved in behind her, pulled her up against his body, and wrapped his arms around her middle. He was shaking.

"I already want you again. I don't think I could ever get enough of you." He ground his already hardening length against her rear, even as his body continued to tremble in the aftermath of what he'd been through.

Her body flared to life, responding instantly.

"I'm sorry you've been dragged into all this. You have no idea how sorry I am," he said.

"It's okay. I'm glad I could...that I could help." She smiled, trying to reassure him as she turned in his arms and rested her hands on his chest. She traced the swirling design of his brand with her finger. The scar tissue was rough and slightly raised. "Let's get you upstairs."

He dropped his hands when she stepped back to pull on her underwear and shorts.

If it hadn't been for Lazarus, God only knew what would have happened to her. He'd saved her life, and she owed him the same in return. Being thrust into this new world was scary as hell, but she knew now she would give him whatever he needed, for as long as he needed it. She owed him that. Whatever was going on with him was bigger than her and her petty emotions.

When she lifted her head, she searched his body for any sign of the demon she'd seen moments ago, and sucked in a breath when he looked down at her again. His eyes were so bright, so startling a green they made it hard to focus on anything else when he was looking at her. His wings were gone now, his smooth back showing no trace of them ever being there, and his skin was once again tan and supple, not the leathery armor of his demon. There was also no sign of the horns that had protruded from his head, not a mark or a scar. Nothing. He was back to his former self. Powerful and raw. Terrifyingly beautiful.

Brent was waiting outside when she took Lazarus's hand and led him from the room. Concern lined his face. "You good?"

Lazarus nodded. "I owe you."

"You owe me nothing, brother," Brent said before he strode off.

Lazarus tightened his fingers around hers, and she led him back upstairs.

Twenty-One

It took everything Lazarus had not to fall on his ass. The shakes racking his entire body wouldn't let up. He'd never been that close to losing himself, had never stared through the eyes of his demon like that, feeling the darkness taking hold and knowing there was nothing he could do to stop it.

Eve continued to hold his hand, and somehow, despite how small and soft and so obviously weaker than his it was, it was that connection, her tight grip, that was holding him up. The only thing.

"You're burning up," she said and wrapped her arm around his waist.

She led him to the bedroom and he followed, struggling, trying desperately to find the words to tell her how he felt. How grateful he was. Christ, that she'd saved his life.

Eve pulled back the covers and turned back to him. She looked worried.

"I'm okay," he managed. "I'll be fine."

Her eyes were wide as she gently ushered him to the bed, making him lie down. "You need to rest."

She started to move away, but he grabbed her wrist, stopping her. "Will you stay with me?" Fuck, she was beautiful. And not just on the outside. Her inner beauty shone through so damn bright he felt the warmth of it soaking in deep, right down to his bones.

"I'm just getting you a drink. I'll be right back."

He tracked her as she left, couldn't bring himself to look away from the door until she was back. She handed him a glass of water and he drank it, then he held his hand out, asking her without words to climb in with him.

She didn't hesitate and slid in beside him, wrapping her arm around his waist. The heat of her skin soaking through her clothes, the weight of her body against him, was comforting. If he had the strength he'd pull her closer.

She tilted her head back looking at him. "I'm so sorry," she said. "This was my fault. You needed me. You needed me and didn't feel you could come to me. You almost lost yourself trying to protect me."

Lazarus stilled. *What?* "No, Eve. God, no. None of this was your fault. None of it. I fucked up. In every damn way I could have. Yeah, I was trying to protect you, because I'd hurt you and I was ashamed of myself."

She pressed a kiss to his shoulder. "I think we need to work on our communication skills. This, what's happening here, is new territory for both of us. I think that allows for mistakes."

He shook his head in awe of her. "I've never met anyone like you. Christ, you...you make me feel things that scare the shit out of me. Have me questioning everything...doubting things, things I thought I would never falter on." He felt her heart beating faster against his side as he buried his nose in her hair and breathed her in. The action, her scent, her warmth, soothed him instantly.

A vision of Tobias doing the same to Scarlet flashed through his mind, along with a large dose of pain. Because, fuck, he got it. If he hadn't before, he did now. The woman in his arms was the most important thing in his world and he'd do anything to protect her.

"What happens now?" she said softly.

"I don't know," he rasped.

Her finger traced one of his tattoos. "I don't either, and I think that's okay."

They were quiet again for several seconds.

"Eve?" he said into the silence.

"Hmm?"

He didn't know what happened next, how to get there, but he did know what he wanted. He also knew what taking it, keeping that happiness would cost him. He didn't deserve it, but right then, lying with Eve, he didn't think he had any other choice but to reach for it. "Hold me tighter, sweetheart," he said into her hair.

She didn't hesitate.

He'd never felt anything like it in his life. No one had ever taken care of him like Eve had, like she was now. He was a warrior. His brothers were warriors. All they knew was fighting and blood and pain.

The angels had screwed them over in so many ways. Except in this.

This was a reward. A gift.

And, God, he realized at that moment just how much he wanted to keep her.

"I want to show you something," Lazarus said as he led Eve up the stairs to the rooftop the next evening. They'd spent the day together and he wasn't ready for it to end. He'd have to go out and continue his search for Tobias soon, but first, he wanted to give Eve something in return for everything she'd given him.

He used his senses to feel for demons, for anything that

could cause Eve harm. The coast was clear. She was laughing by the time he pushed through the door to the roof, the sound high and breathy and one of the most beautiful things he'd ever heard.

"Wow, the view up here is...it's gorgeous," she said, beaming up at him when he pulled her to a stop. "Thank you for showing me."

"This isn't it," he said, a smile teasing his lips.

She searched the rooftop. "Where is it, then?"

He shook his head. "It's not down here. It's up there." He pointed to the sky above them.

Her eyes widened. "You mean..."

"You in the mood for some night flying?"

She bit her lip. "So you're going to..." She motioned to his back. "And we'll..."

"Yes," he said, chuckling. "You game?"

Her face lit up. "Um...*yes*, I'd love that."

Lazarus grinned, couldn't help himself. The look on her face was sheer delight. He tugged off his shirt, tucked it in his back pocket, and unfurled his wings.

Eve stepped toward him, her gaze moving over his charcoal wings. "Can I touch them?"

He had to swallow, his mouth suddenly dry. "Yeah, of course."

She moved around him slowly and the feel of her eyes on him had his skin feeling too tight for his body, had tingles sliding over his scalp.

And then he felt it, her hand moving over the inner arch of one of his wings. No one had ever touched him there, not once in his whole life, and he shuddered at the sheer pleasure the sensation shot through him. How it only intensified the more she touched them, petted them.

"The feathers, they're so soft," she said.

He shivered at the sound of her voice. It was like everything grew more sensitive while she touched them. Just her voice lifted goose bumps across his skin.

His cock pulsed hard against the zipper of his jeans.

"No one's ever..." He had to clear his throat. "No one's ever done that to me before," he said.

"Do you like it?" The little rasp to her voice said she already knew the answer to that question.

"Yeah, I like it." He reached back and tugged her around to his front before he disgraced himself, and kissed her, hard and deep, then he lifted her in his arms, spread his wings, and took flight.

Eve gasped, her arms tightening around his neck as he shot higher, carrying her over streets and rooftops until they were high enough to take in the whole of the city. Her arms were still tight around him and she'd pressed her cheek against his.

He wanted to see her face. "Do you like it?"

"Like it?" she whispered. "This is...it's..." She laughed, the sound so full of joy and happiness Lazarus's heart pounded harder. "There are no words. Thank you." She pressed a kiss to his cheek. "Thank you so much for this."

"Any time, sweetheart," he heard himself say.

They were up there for a while. He was reluctant to take her back. He loved the feel of her in his arms, the way her breathing quickened, her soft gasps, her laughter, as he flew through the sky at speed.

He wanted more of this. More nights like this. More nights with Eve...

Lazarus gasped, squeezing his eyes shut as a sharp pain sliced through his skull.

"*Fuck.*"

"What is it?" Eve asked, sounding panicked.

He kept hold of her and headed back to the club as fast as he could.

"It's Tobias," he said. "I can feel him." He'd sensed his

brother in this city many times since he'd been here, but he'd always covered his trail.

Tobias wasn't hiding now. He wanted Lazarus to find him.

It had to be a trap. Of course, it was. There was no other reason Tobias would open himself up like this. It didn't matter. This could be Lazarus's only chance.

They landed back on the roof and Lazarus rushed Eve to the safety of their apartment.

"What are you going to do?" she asked, watching him as he strapped on his weapons.

He met her blue eyes with his own. "End it."

Before he walked out the door she called his name. He turned back to her.

"Please. Be careful."

For the first time in a long time, there was someone he wanted to come home to. Someone who made all of it, his long life of nonstop fighting, of struggling, bearable. He rushed down to the club and found Brent, instructed him to watch Eve, but left out his destination. The guy would want to come, and right then it would be more helpful knowing Eve was safe. There was no way he could focus if he thought she was at risk.

He left Brent and headed out to the alley. The narrow space didn't allow much room, but managed to lift off without effort, taking to the skies.

Lazarus followed the invisible trail his brother was showing him. He felt it like a rope attached to his chest, reeling him in. He let it; didn't bother resisting its pull. He hovered above a building below, taking a few minutes to send out his senses, to gather his control.

Tobias was alone.

Not what he'd expected.

He tucked in his wings and dropped, gravel crunching

under the soles of his boots when he landed a little way back from the building.

He kept to the shadows and scanned the area. There had been several lights outside, but all were broken. The place was a rundown apartment complex, abandoned, unused, and according to the big sign nailed to one of the boarded-up windows, scheduled for demolition.

The front doors were boarded as well, so he made his way around the perimeter, searching for another way in. Several loud bangs came from the rear of the building, and on silent feet, he moved toward it. An open door swung on rusty hinges. A strong gust sent it crashing into the frame before swinging back once more.

Pulling the door wide, he entered the pitch-black interior. His eyes strained, trying to adjust to the inky darkness. Most demons had advanced sight. Laz was the only one among his brothers who hadn't inherited the ability from his demon father, though his other senses made up for the lack. Both facts Tobias knew.

What he assumed was broken glass crunched underfoot, and the only other sound was his own shallow breaths.

He followed the sense of dread prickling the back of his neck, a dark malevolence that turned his stomach and excited him all at once. A door to one of the ground floor apartments hung open, an obvious invitation to enter.

He stepped inside and tensed as a wave of hatred slammed into him, covering him like a thick shroud.

"Nice of you to pull your dick out of that demi long enough to stop by." Tobias's voice echoed through the gloom.

Lazarus swung around, trying to follow his brother's voice. It seemed to come from all directions and he couldn't pinpoint his location.

"You wanted me to find you," Lazarus said. "So let's get this over with."

Tobias's mirthless chuckle lifted the hair on the back of his neck. "You'll wish you hadn't."

He strained to see, trying to make out shapes in the darkness. "We were your family once, T. Doesn't that mean anything to you?" he called into nothingness, purposely using the nickname. Tobias's hiss and bellow of rage made it clear he'd hit his mark.

"My family is dead. You killed her," he roared back, his hatred echoing off the walls.

"Then hurt me, not the others. Why are you doing this, T?"

"Stop calling me that," he roared, his panted breaths harsh and raw. "And you know exactly why I'm doing this. I want you to suffer like I have suffered. I want you to watch everything that is important to you destroyed."

The pain in the other man's voice shook Lazarus to the core. With his demon in the driver's seat, he shouldn't be capable of feeling any emotion that didn't go hand in hand with hatred. "They were important to you once, too. Your brothers would have done anything for you. You loved them, T. Don't do this."

Images of Scarlet and her mate flooded his mind. The way they'd looked at each other, loved each other. Was that male truly gone?

This was his fault. Lazarus was the reason Tobias had chosen to succumb rather than continue to fight. His reason for living was gone. He got that now, more than ever. Lazarus had taken her from him.

"Shut up," Tobias seethed. "You're wrong. I only cared about Scarlet. She was my mate, my strength, and you couldn't fucking stand that. You couldn't handle that with us mated, I was stronger than you, my powers greater. So you took her from me."

"I was happy for you, and for Scarlet." Arms outstretched,

he began feeling his way along the wall, following Tobias's voice. His eyes had adjusted slightly, but it was still too dark to see much more than faint outlines.

"Bullshit."

Lights flashed on, blinding him for a few seconds. He blinked against the harsh brightness before he spotted Tobias a few yards from him. He wore jeans and a plain white T-shirt. His long blond hair was neatly tied back. His handsome face was smooth, showing no outward sign of emotion.

The only way he could tell this was no longer the male he'd once called brother was the large unwavering black irises staring back at him and the deep jagged scar on his forearm where he'd cut out his angel's brand.

Then he spotted the woman a short distance from Tobias. Tied to one of the building's exposed support beams, a young demi stood motionless. Her head was slumped forward. Rust-colored streaks of drying blood stained her clothing and smeared the length of her bare calves and feet.

The evil inside the male before him, a male he had once loved, still managed to rock him to his soul. "What have you done? Why would you do this?" He barely recognized his own agonized voice.

Tobias slid his fingers under the female's chin, lifted her head, and brushed back her blond hair to reveal her face. His nostrils flared and for a moment he looked as surprised as Lazarus by her features. She was so like Scarlet that her name whispered past Lazarus's lips.

Tobias's black eyes turned back to Lazarus, an expression on his brother's face he had no hope of reading.

Finally, he made a mirthless rusty sound that didn't hold a trace of humor. "Apparently, I've been searching for a replacement. Unfortunately, it looks like this one didn't make the cut." He paused, taking in the deep slices marring the petite female's pale skin. "Or maybe she did. Just not in the way either of us hoped."

Lazarus couldn't believe what he was hearing. "Scarlet wouldn't want this. She would despise what you've become."

"Do not speak her name. You know fuck all about that female and what she would want."

Lazarus took in Tobias's cold expression, the blood of an innocent demi drying on his hands, and fought to stay upright. He was so close to falling to his knees under the crushing weight of pain and regret pressing down on him. He'd grieved the loss of this male, a male who had once been his brother. Deep down, he'd held the smallest grain of hope that maybe he wasn't completely lost to them.

That hope shattered the minute the lights came on. Tobias had succumbed to his demon long ago, and though Laz wished otherwise, was beyond help.

Lazarus fought to maintain control as his demon howled for release. He held on with everything he had, and keeping Eve at the forefront of his mind helped. He had to keep her safe.

"Maybe I want my power fully restored," Tobias said. "The kind I can only get from another mate. The kind you..." His gaze bored into Lazarus then his head tilted to the side as if he were focusing on something. He barked a harsh laugh. "You haven't taken her as your mate yet. Still a fucking coward, then?"

And just like that, calm settled over Tobias. The easy grin he flashed Lazarus offered a painful glimpse of the male he'd once been.

"I have to go now, Laz, but we will catch up again soon, yeah? I promise you that." He motioned to the lifeless female at his side. "I'm kinda busy at the moment. I hope you don't mind cleaning up."

The lights went out again, followed by Tobias's

retreating footsteps. Lazarus tried to follow, but he was too late. Tobias had vanished into the night, once again covering his trail.

With his demon clawing at his psyche, Lazarus used what was left of his dwindling power to incinerate the demi's limp, lifeless body, unable to summon the strength to do anything else for her.

His control had all but disintegrated, and there was no stopping it at this point.

He needed Eve.

Wanted her.

God help anyone who tried to get in his way.

He sprinted from the building and took flight.

By the time he reached the club, he was barely hanging on by a thread. He rushed in, snarling and growling, shoving people aside to get to her.

His knees went weak as a rush of energy hit him. *Fuck*, he could feel her.

Close.

She was under his skin. Pumping through his veins.

So close.

Lazarus pounded up the stairs. He just had to hang on a little longer.

He used his powers to unlock the door, and it swung open with a bang. The small living room was dark. The only light was flickering from the television, casting a colorful wash over a surprised Eve.

She sat on the couch dressed in an oversized T-shirt, her smooth legs bare, and Christ, he got a tantalizing glimpse of pale blue panties.

She shot to her feet. "Thank God you're okay. I was worried out of my mind."

He couldn't answer.

She stared at him wide-eyed, her pupils enlarged as she

strained to see him clearly through the dim light, trying to see the condition he was in.

"Lazarus?" she whispered. "Are you...is everything all right?"

"Come here," he choked.

"What's going on?"

"Now," he ordered.

Her breath hitched and she took a step closer.

That was when he got a trace of something, something that tightened his already hard cock to painful proportions. Even in the dim light he could see her face darken with desire —there was no mistaking it. He just hoped like fuck there wasn't fear there as well.

His demon senses came alive. He could hear her heart racing behind her ribs, the way each exhale rushed from between her parted lips. Smell the intoxicating scent of her arousal. Her body seemed to be responding to his need.

Thank fuck.

He stalked over to her, chest pumping with every labored breath, and gripped the hem of her shirt, pulling it over her head.

She gasped.

"I can't stop," he choked.

Her tongue darted out, licking her plump lower lip. "It's all right. I'm here." She pressed a soft hand to his chest. "Take it, Lazarus. Take what you need."

He growled at her shakily spoken words, the unmistakable need in her voice, and fisting a handful of her sexy, tousled curls, he hauled her up against him and took her mouth in a hard kiss. He nipped and sucked the tender plump flesh, demanding entrance, and she opened for him without resistance or hesitation. Her heart thudded against his chest, and he moaned at the sweet taste of her, the exquisite sensation of her mouth under his.

He wanted more, so much more.

Lazarus pulled back and spun her around, holding her back flush against his chest, her ass nestled against his hard cock. He walked her forward until they reached the small dining table in front of the windows overlooking the busy city below.

He wrapped his fingers around the back of her neck and bent her forward over the wooden surface then ran his palms down the smooth expanse of her bare back. The feel of her warm skin soothed his demon somewhat, but not enough.

The urge to taste her was overpowering, and he dropped to his knees, unwilling to deny himself any longer. Gripping the sides of her underwear, he tore through the fabric. Her startled cry drew his gaze to hers, had him freezing in place, terrified that he'd frightened her. She watched him over her shoulder, but there was no fear there, only need, hot and intoxicating. Sexy as fuck.

She wanted this just as much as him.

"Open for me," he forced out past the lump in his throat.

She didn't hesitate and spread her legs farther apart. Her scent hit him hard, and he groaned. He'd been craving her, desperate to taste her again.

He parted her tender flesh, and the sight of her glistening and ready nearly unmanned him. He leaned in to taste her fully, lapped at her arousal greedily, drinking her down. She tasted fucking amazing.

Eve gasped and pushed her ass back in an attempt to get closer. Uninhibited, needy. And her sexy little moans had him growling his approval.

He worked her clit with his fingers, fucking her with his tongue, and he didn't let up until her body spasmed and she cried out. She came hard against his mouth, but he wasn't finished. Not slowing, Lazarus continued to lick her and didn't stop until he'd wrung every last bit of pleasure from her trembling body.

When she collapsed on the table, he stood and ripped open the front of his jeans, freeing his cock. "Hang onto the edge," he said, voice raw with lust.

He fisted his shaft, and skimming past the full cheeks of her lovely ass, plunged into her hot, wet pussy.

She cried out, and for a split second he worried that he might have hurt her, but then she pushed back, trying to take him deeper, and any worry disintegrated under a red haze of lust.

He gripped her hip and pulled out inch by painstaking inch, tormenting them both. Loving the way his cock glistened with her juices, proof of her desire for him.

The tiny thread of control he'd been hanging on to for all he was worth snapped, and he thrust home, taking her like a man possessed. Which wasn't far from the truth at that point.

The table scraped against the tiled floor as his brutal thrusts drove it forward. Eve arched her back and cried out when her second climax took hold, squeezing repeatedly around his cock, driving him damn near insane.

"Shit." He panted hard. He didn't want to come yet, wanted to take her over the edge once more. He *needed* to make this good for her. He'd fucked everything else up. He wanted to at least do this right.

The silvery thread was right there, calling to him, crying out for him to make Eve his mate, but he forced himself to ignore it.

Sweat slicked his skin from the effort of resisting, from holding off his own release. God, he wanted to fill the female writhing beneath him with his seed, mark her with his scent. Reaching around her body, he began to circle her clit with firm, even strokes.

"Oh God. I...I can't," she whimpered.

"You can," he growled, his voice desperate even to his own ears.

Then the first ripples of her orgasm began teasing his cock. He gritted his teeth and held onto her hips tight, thrusting hard, fucking her with short, deep strokes. Eve screamed as she went over moments later, and he exploded, going with her, gripped by the most powerful release of his long life.

When he was wrung dry, he collapsed, resting his forehead against her back. "I'm sorry, Eve," he panted over and over.

After a few minutes, she whispered, "Please, don't be."

He barely registered her words, but didn't miss the hurt in her tone. His cock was still achingly hard, his hunger for her not even close to being sated. He reluctantly pulled out of her warmth and standing her up, eased her around to face him.

He brushed the hair back from her face and cupped her chin, lifting it so her gaze met his. He leaned in and captured her mouth with his own.

The kiss was slow, claiming, and when he finally pulled back, she looked up at him, flushed and sexy as all hell.

He ran his thumb across her swollen bottom lip. "I'm going to carry you to that room and I'm going to have you again, not because I need you to quiet my demon, but because I want you again so bad I can't think straight. Because every part of me craves every part of you."

It was all he could manage before he lifted her off the ground and strode to the bedroom.

Twenty-Two

Morning light streamed in from the edge of the curtains and blanketed the room in a muted gold. It made the small space feel cozy.

Eve's soft, warm body still lay pressed tightly against Lazarus, her scent all over his skin. He'd slept well past morning, but at that moment couldn't bring himself to care. His cock was nestled against her round ass, and the temptation to slide into her from behind was driving him fucking crazy.

Nuzzling the back of her neck, he drew in more of her sweet, heady scent. This felt right, more than right. She belonged right where she was.

The woman in his arms had managed something he never thought possible: she'd broken down his carefully constructed walls. Last night she had given herself to him without reservation; not once did she hold back any part of herself. She'd smashed down his defenses, again and again, uncovering feelings he'd tried to keep on lockdown.

He still felt raw, exposed.

He'd taken Eve repeatedly through the night, and he'd told her the truth—it hadn't been about pacifying his demon, it had been about a male and his unquenchable need for his female. An undeniable, soul-deep yearning he felt even now.

It hadn't been enough.

He would never get enough of her.

Eve stirred, her body moving against his in a maddening way as she stretched and rolled to her back in his arms. The thick sweep of her dark lashes quivered then fluttered open, and his stomach clenched when heavy-lidded sapphire pools stared up at him drowsily.

She was so damn beautiful. She took his breath away.

He bent down and took her mouth in a soft kiss. When he pulled back, her cheeks turned a pretty shade of pink. Damn, he loved the way she blushed so easily.

"Morning," he said, voice still rough from sleep.

"Morning." Her gaze searched his. "Are you okay?"

"Yeah. Thanks to you."

Her hand slid up his biceps. "What happened with Tobias?"

"He got away." Seeing Tobias like that, seeing what he'd done to that demi, it cut to the bone.

"I'm sorry," she said.

"Me, too." Despite the conversation, he loved this, just the two of them, lying there, talking. His stomach rumbled.

Her mouth curled up on one side. "How about I make us breakfast?" She tried to roll away.

No way was he ready to let her go. He hadn't finished savoring the snug way her body fit perfectly against his. "Wait." He grabbed her hip, and she gasped in pain. He let go like her skin was molten beneath his hand. "What's wrong?"

"Nothing."

He tried to pull back the sheet, but she clung to the covers.

"Let me see." He loosened her fingers to reveal her waist, then farther until her hip and ass were on full display. A dark bruise marred her pale skin. A perfect handprint. "I did this to you?"

"You didn't mean to, and it didn't hurt at the time. Please, don't worry about it."

Even now she was trying to reassure him. *Protect him*.

"I fucking hurt you?" He looked down at his hands in disgust.

"I'm fine, really." She touched his arm to get his attention.

"Hurting you is the last thing I ever wanted."

She brushed light fingers across his jaw and the action warmed the center of his chest. "I know this isn't easy on you. I can't imagine what it's like having your body force you to do something you don't want."

He assumed she was talking about his demon's constant fight for dominance. She'd have an up-close and personal understanding of that kind of loss of control. "Yeah, but you'd know exactly what that feels like," he said carefully.

Her brow scrunched. "What do you mean?"

"Every time I come for you, your body is forced to respond to me because of our connection," he tried to explain.

Last night had been a prime example of what their connection could do. Her body had readied for him as soon as he'd walked through the door.

A blush crept down her neck to the tops of her full breasts. "That's not what's happening, not now anyway. I think I'd know the difference."

"What are you saying?"

She toyed with the sheet. "I know I could lose a few pounds, that I'm not the kind of woman a lot of men usually find attractive. And I know you only want me...*that way* because of the mate thing. But that's not what's happening to me. That's not why I...respond to you." Her gaze darted away. "I'm attracted to you. And I, I...care about you."

She cared?

He never hoped...he never imagined she could care for him in return. When he'd learned of her existence, that was the last thing he'd wanted. But now...

Before he could get too worked up about that astonishing admission, the rest of what she'd said, the way she'd put herself down, sunk in. A growl ripped from his throat before he could hold it back. "I don't want to hear you talk about yourself that way, not ever again. Do you understand?"

"It's okay. You don't need to—"

"You're beautiful, inside and out. You're the most caring person I've ever met." He threaded his fingers in her hair and held her wide gaze. "And you drive me fucking wild. I've never craved another being the way I crave you, and not just because of the mate thing," he said using the same words she had. Her breath quickened and his pulse skipped a beat in response. "I told you, Eve, you make me...want things..."

She licked her lips. "What do you want?"

He shook his head.

"Tell me," she said. "Please."

He held her gaze. "I'm not good for you."

"I don't believe that. I've never met anyone like you. I've never felt the way I do when I'm with you." Those words cost her, and it made him want her all the more.

"You don't know me, Eve. You don't know what I've done," he forced out.

She reached up and ran her thumb over his brow. "Then tell me."

For some reason, he wanted to. Perhaps once she learned the truth she'd leave on her own, saving him all this torment. She'd understand why he would never be good enough to be her mate.

The words spilled from his lips in one ragged exhale. "I failed her. She trusted me and I fucking failed her."

Eve frowned. "Who?"

He sucked in a shallow breath, struggling to take in oxygen. "Scarlet." Her name felt wrenched from his chest. "She's dead because of me. I may as well have buried the knife in her heart myself."

She stared at him for a moment then shook her head and moved to cup his face in her small, soft hands. No scorn or disgust twisted her beautiful face, only concern. "Tell me about her. Tell me what happened," she said.

Removing her hands, he sat up and swung his legs over the side of the bed, resting his elbows on his knees. He couldn't get through this with her looking at him like that.

"It was close to fifty years ago now. That's when I first sensed her, a demi new to her powers. I went to retrieve her, tracked her to an abandoned warehouse. She was homeless, living on the streets. She was only fourteen years old. The youngest demi to ever come into their powers. She was all alone and scared as hell. I took her with me. She became important to me, and I to her. She looked up to me, thought of me as her savior, I guess. I loved her like a father loves his child, and she loved me in return. As she grew older, grew into her powers, we discovered she possessed an amazing physical and mental strength. She was a warrior, had a way with people, too. They were drawn to her, trusted her. We also learned that she was Tobias's mate.

"We decided to use her in the field. Chaos didn't think Tobias working with her was a good idea so she worked with me." He held her gaze. "T trusted me to take care of her. He *trusted* me."

He sucked in an agonized breath. Eve gently glided her hand over his back, reassuring him, like she sensed his pain. He didn't deserve her comfort.

"We were on retrieval together. She'd usually go in first, do the talking." He glanced back at her. "In case you hadn't noticed, tact isn't one of my strong qualities."

Eve actually smiled at that, and his heart thumped in response. Now she'd brought the once dead organ back to life, the thing was liable to put him into cardiac arrest with all the jumping around it was doing.

The tender way she stared at him twisted him inside. He was about to shatter that soft look on her lovely face. He carried on before he could change his mind. "After she'd done her thing, I went in. The guy wasn't taking the news well. I was busy trying to get him out of the house, while Scarlet tried to talk sense into him. I told her to just let me get him out. I didn't care if he kicked and screamed the whole way."

He shook his head. "We always had each other's backs." He rubbed a hand over his face and shook his head. "I failed her that day, failed both of them. I'm ruled by my emotions, usually anger. When that happens, my senses dim, which means I can't pick up on the enemy as easily. She'd tell me to cut the shit, pull my head out of my ass, and get on with it."

Eve remained quiet beside him.

Weak.

Flawed.

"I was getting pissed, totally focused on the male fighting me, stopping us from getting him to safety. I let emotion take over...like I did when I met you." Eve's features changed, showing her surprise. "I didn't notice or even sense the Orthon that had followed us. It killed her before I'd even worked out it was in the house."

Twenty-Three

Eve ached for the male sitting beside her, not the one who literally carried the weight of the world on his shoulders, but a father who had lost his daughter.

Throat tightening, she struggled for breath as the truth of her feelings hit like a battering ram to the chest. She loved him. Loved him with her entire heart and soul.

As much as it hurt to keep her feelings locked inside, she would. Lazarus didn't need or want to hear it, not now, maybe not ever. He had more pressing matters to worry about. His feelings for her weren't the same, and telling him would only add to his guilt when it was time for them to part.

Not knowing what else to do, she pushed her sadness and anger aside and reached for him. "I'm sorry, Lazarus." It was all she could say. No amount of words would help at this point. So, climbing to her knees, she wrapped her arms around his shoulders and pressed her lips to the tattoo snaking up the side of his neck.

He froze, his large body going statue still. "What are you doing?"

"Kissing you."

"I thought...I thought you wouldn't..."

"What? You thought I'd get up and leave? That I'd think less of you? You loved her." She gripped his chin and turned his head. Their eyes met. "It was a terrible thing that happened, but it was an accident."

He shook his head, but she kept hold of him. "An accident," she repeated, and before he could say anything more, she leaned in and brushed her lips across his.

He pulled away, breathing heavily. "Eve...I'm not—"

"Don't," she whispered, and leaned in, pushed for more. Her lips were an inch from his when he turned away and stood abruptly.

Rejection, cold and sharp, hit her between the ribs, knocking the wind from her lungs. She scooted back on the bed and dipped her chin so her hair fell forward, covering the humiliation heating her face. *Stupid, stupid, stupid.* She should have known better by now.

Before she could scramble off the other side and escape, he gripped her upper arms and hauled her to her feet. With her standing on the bed in front of him they were nearly eye level.

Lazarus brushed her hair away from her face and cupped her cheek. His thumb stroked her jaw then he tilted her head back and stared into her eyes. "Don't ever hide from me. I can't bear it." His hand moved down to the side of her throat in a grip that was firm yet gentle. His thumb continued to stroke her skin and she wanted to lean in, seek more of his touch. The possessiveness of it was undeniable. "I've never known anyone like you, Eve, as good as you."

Before she could reply to that, he nuzzled her throat with a tenderness that should have been impossible for the massive demon warrior. The vulnerability and desperation in that one action tore her heart in two. The soft silk of his hair slid across her palm as she held him to her, as he kissed a path to her mouth, taking her lips in an achingly gentle kiss. The intensity of his mouth and his tongue against hers began a slow burn that turned her insides molten. The sound he made against her mouth was one of longing, of anguish, of hunger.

Eve wanted to love him like he deserved, and suspected he desperately needed. She wanted to show him how wonderful he was. This wasn't about the demon fighting for freedom inside him. It was about Lazarus and nothing more.

"Lie down," she whispered against his mouth.

"Eve..."

She shook her head. "Let me take care of you. Just this once."

He squeezed his eyes shut, going through some kind of internal struggle, but he needed this, needed to let go.

His eyes fluttered open when she took his hand. The vulnerability that stared back at her caused her chest to tighten. He came to her then, his body still deliciously naked and magnificently aroused. Doing as she asked, he lay back on the bed and Eve took a minute to admire his powerful body, hard and defined. Magnificent.

The beautiful symbols that marked his arm and the side of his neck fascinated her. She wanted to trace them with her tongue, and she would because right then, at that moment, he was hers and hers alone.

He was built like a weapon of mass destruction. It was all there, lethal power, unbelievable strength, all at her mercy. She drank him in, his powerful thighs, the hard length of his straining erection against cut abs. Those impressive pecs, then up to his face, a face that would be harsh if it wasn't for those sensual lips. His tongue darted out and he licked the full lower one. She couldn't help mimic the action, hungry for a taste of him. Their eyes met and the primal need there stole her breath.

She crawled over and straddled his hips, and his gaze traveled over her curves as she did. She forced herself to leave her body bared to him, resisting the urge to cover herself. Lazarus liked the way she looked. How could she doubt it with the way he was looking at her?

His big hands gripped her thighs, smoothing up to her hips to softly massage and caress the bruised skin there.

"I hate that I hurt you."

"You didn't." She leaned forward and kissed his whiskered jaw. "I enjoyed every minute of it." She kissed him slowly, licking and nipping his lips like he had hers earlier.

When he reached up to hold her in place, attempting to deepen the kiss, she gripped his wrists and pushed them back against the mattress. He let her. Lazarus could overpower her easily if he chose to, but he let her have her way.

His breathing quickened as she pressed a trail of hot, wet kisses over his jaw then moved down to nibble and suck his throat, following the ink over his shoulder. She continued her exploration and moved to his hard chest. Her breasts grazed his abs while she dragged her tongue over a flat nipple before catching it between her teeth and biting down gently.

He panted and bucked beneath her. "You're killing me, sweetheart."

Encouraged, she tormented the other nipple for a while before carrying on down to trace the deep ridges of his abs. As she moved lower, he threaded his fingers through her hair. She glanced up, holding his dark, hungry gaze then leaned in, licking away the salty bead gathered at the tip of his cock.

He groaned. "*Fuck.*"

Desperate for more, she kissed him where she'd just licked, an open-mouthed sucking kiss that had his hips lifting off the mattress. Still, she didn't take him fully into her mouth, and instead took her time to slowly lick and nibble every inch of his thick shaft.

His fingers flexed in her hair, forcing her to look up at him. "Eve." Her name rumbled from his chest in a growling purr that intensified the throb between her thighs. "Take me into your mouth, sweetheart. Please, suck me."

She grinned and gripped him tighter, running her tongue around the ridge one more time, lapping at the tiny slit.

He hissed in a breath through his teeth then growled again. His chest heaving, every muscle straining, locked up tight. "Please, baby."

His plea melted her, and right then she wanted nothing more than to tell him how much she loved him, how amazing he was. Instead, she said, "Since you asked so nicely."

Cupping his balls, she closed her lips over the head of his cock and took in as much of him as she could, moving up and down the velvety shaft with sucking pulls.

He lifted his hips like he had no control, thrusting into her mouth, and all the while he groaned out hot, tender, filthy things that had her squeezing her legs together to relieve the deep ache inside.

The musky, dark scent of him was driving her wild and then he fisted her hair tighter, his groans increasing. She moaned around him, loving how out of control he was.

He stilled suddenly, his spine torqued, muscles bunching. His massive body shook then he released a shout, her name groaning past his lips over and over. She didn't let go when he tried to pull away and swallowed down everything he had.

Finally, she released his cock and looked up at him with a grin. His large body was trembling, and when his gaze captured hers, burned into her, her grin disappeared. She still held him in her hand, and he hadn't softened at all. Her inner muscles clenched.

"Come here," he rasped.

Eve crawled up his body, beyond desperate to have him inside her, and straddled his hips. He reached down, brushing his thumb over her clit. "Ride me, Eve."

Her gaze darted up to meet his. Clear, pale green stared

back and her heart soared. She rose up, unable to wait another second, and sank down, taking him to the hilt. God, he made her so full. She moaned, her head falling back.

"Eve...*fuck*."

His big body shook beneath her while his thumb continued to work between her thighs as she rode him slow and easy.

Eve was lost to sensation, the feel of him deep inside, the sound of skin meeting skin, the harsh sounds of their panted breaths. He thrust up, silently demanding she increase the pace, and, whimpering, Eve gave him what he needed, what they both needed.

The tension inside her built in delicious waves, and she slammed down hard, taking him as deep as he could go. He hissed and held her to him, grinding up.

Light exploded behind her eyes, and she held on tight. Lazarus's fingers dug into her ass, holding on to her, and he thrust up harder. "That's it, come for me." His voice was nothing but a growl.

Pleasure lit up every nerve ending in her body and she threw her head back and screamed, vaguely aware of Lazarus stiffening beneath her.

The last thing she remembered after collapsing on top of him, and before sleep dragged her under, was of Lazarus wrapping his big, warm body around hers and holding her close.

Eve woke feeling warm and snug, and a little groggy.

The warmth was radiating from the big male pressed to her side. His features were smooth and relaxed in sleep, lacking the tortured expression he often wore like a fierce mask. A state that would disappear as soon as he woke and headed back out in search of Tobias.

He was wrapped around her, cocooning her in his arms. A large palm rested against her belly, his face buried in her hair at her neck, his legs tangled with hers. He'd pulled her in tighter during sleep, and the entire length of his body was pressed against her.

An ache started in the center of her chest. Being with him like this felt good, too good. How would she move on without him when the time came?

Her stomach growled so loud she was surprised she didn't wake him. Lazarus didn't stir. Her empty belly was no doubt the reason she'd woken, and as much as she wanted to ignore it and stay under the covers surrounded by Lazarus, he'd would no doubt need to refuel as well when he woke.

Lifting his hand carefully from around her waist, she slipped from beneath the covers and quickly dressed.

She headed to the kitchen, and after making enough sandwiches for the two of them, she headed downstairs to the bar to grab a couple of Cokes for a much-needed sugar hit.

A *buzz* came from the delivery door, stopping her in her tracks. She waited, not sure what to do. Then Brent, muttering to himself, pounded down the stairs. The buzzer went off again and he cursed.

"Hang on, I'm coming," he called, followed by the sound of numerous locks disengaging.

Eve didn't hang around and headed toward the stairs. She hit the first landing when a sharp cry rang out, followed by a heavy thump. Putting the drinks on the ground, she raced back down the steps.

Brent lay prone on the ground, his motionless body propping the delivery door open. There was a deep gash across his temple, leaking blood onto the mat. "Brent!"

She rushed over and crouched down beside him, feeling for his pulse. Still alive. He wasn't moving, was barely conscious, but she could hear his thoughts loud and clear.

Demon. Demon. Demon.

Oh God. She had to get him away from the open door.

In a panic, she grabbed Brent's arm and tried to drag him in enough so she could shut it. This place was warded, Lazarus and Brent had both told her that. She just needed to get Brent out of striking distance and he'd be safe.

A man stepped into view and Eve scrambled back, terror tightening her vocal cords, making it impossible to scream. His gaze lifted to hers and he smiled. Dread slithered up her spine and she stumbled back farther when he shoved the door wider and thrust his hand inside.

The screech he let loose lifted goose bumps all over her skin when he broke through the protective ward surrounding the building then yanked the hand back out quickly.

Demon.

It couldn't get through the wards, not without injuring, maybe even killing itself. But Brent was at an odd angle, and he'd slipped down the wall, God, so close to falling outside. The demon would kill him if he got the chance, she had no doubt about that.

There was no time to get Lazarus, so ignoring her terror, she grabbed Brent's arm and tried to drag him away from the door again.

The demon hissed with rage. Brent was heavy and she tugged harder on his arm. As he finally fell toward her, one of his legs straightened and his foot slid outside. The demon dove for it. Eve fell forward, grabbed hold of his leg, and jerked it out of reach.

The demon's eyes were milky white, locked on her. Eve scrambled back, but it shoved its hand inside again, over Brent's unconscious body, shrieking in pain but not pulling back this time.

The skin peeled from its arm like it'd dipped it in acid, exposing raw flesh.

Eve froze in horror. Everything around her seemed to move in slow motion. She realized too late that she was in striking distance and there was no way she could get back out of its reach in time. The demon grabbed her by the hair and yanked her hard. She fell onto Brent's legs, and the impact knocked the wind from her lungs. Right then, she was struggling to take in a breath, let alone scream for help.

She reached up and tried to loosen its grip, but her fingers slipped against blood and gore. It hissed in pain but didn't let go, and dragged her through the door, hauling her to her feet. She sucked in a breath to scream, but the demon slapped its uninjured hand over her mouth, stifling the scream she was about to let loose.

Still holding her tight, it began to vibrate. Its body shuddered and began to change, taking its Orthon form.

No. Oh God, no.

A gray claw was clasped around her wrist like a manacle, and it hauled her toward the mouth of the alleyway.

She turned back to the open door of the club a few short feet away. Brent was struggling to stand, but he'd taken a serious blow and collapsed to the ground again. She glanced up to the second-story windows. Lazarus was up there, but he might as well have been on the other side of the world.

Eve tore at its gray flesh with her fingernails, fighting with everything she had. But no matter how hard she fought, she couldn't break loose, couldn't make a sound.

The creature's cold fingers pressed against her lips and she shook her head trying to free her mouth, but it held tight. She bit down as hard as she could, and the demon hissed, striking her across the face.

Pain exploded through her head, her skin stinging from the long claws that had cut into her flesh. She ignored the pain and tried to pull free, to run.

It caught her back up and kept moving, dragging her with it.

A long silver car pulled to a stop in front of her. The creature beside her shifted forms again and was back to looking like a human male.

It yanked the door open, forced her inside, and closed her in. She grabbed for the handle and tugged at it, but it wouldn't open no matter how hard she tried. The car began to ease from the curb.

She cried out and pounded on the window as the club, and Lazarus, got farther and farther away.

"You must be Eve," a rough voice said.

Eve spun around. She hadn't even noticed anyone else in the car with her, too desperate to escape. A man sat beside her, and as he leaned forward, the sunlight streaming through the window highlighted his features. He was striking, chiseled, almost too good looking. Not as hard as Lazarus, but there was an unmistakable cruelty behind his unearthly coal-black eyes.

Definitely not human.

"What do you want with me?" she said, panic clear in her voice.

"I'm Tobias," he said. "You may have heard of me?" He grinned. "Nice to finally meet you."

He searched her face, for what she didn't know, before he said, "I look forward to getting to know you a lot better."

She opened her mouth to tell him to go to hell...but everything went black.

Twenty-Four

Lazarus came awake with a start and automatically reached out, searching for Eve, only to find the sheet still warm from her body but the space beside him empty. He tensed then shook his head at his behavior, forcing his muscles to relax.

She couldn't even go to the bathroom without him worrying...missing her.

Shit, Lazarus had lain himself bare before her last night, and instead of turning her back on him, she'd embraced him, kissed him...loved him.

Eve had opened herself to him while they'd made love, had given herself over so sweetly. Fighting the link that would bind them together forever had been so damn hard, but he had, because he wanted Eve to know exactly what was happening when they took it there. He wanted her to experience it with him, every moment.

Now he just had to figure out how to ask her. Did he go the human route: romantic dinner? Eve had believed herself to be human for most of her life. Is that what she'd want? Should he get down on one knee and give her a piece of jewelry? Fucked if he knew, but he wanted it to be special.

He rubbed his hands over his face and let out a shaky breath. He'd get down on his goddamn knees and beg her to accept him if he had to. After losing Scarlet, he'd believed he didn't deserve happiness, that he deserved the pain of losing his own mate just like Tobias, and maybe that was still true, but in punishing himself he was hurting Eve as well.

He couldn't do that. He wouldn't. She was all that mattered.

She was everything.

Screw romantic dinners and human traditions. As soon as she returned he'd ask her to be his. He would make her his.

He lay there for several minutes more, getting impatient. His hearing was exceptional and he closed her eyes and used his senses to search her out. Nothing. Silence.

Heavy, empty silence.

Ripping the covers back, he practically flew out of bed.

Something was wrong. He knew it, felt it.

After yanking on his jeans, he pounded down the stairs to the bar, and nearly tripped over a couple of drinks sitting on one of the lower steps. He picked up one of the cans. Ice cold.

She'd been down here, and something had disturbed her before she made it back to him.

Brent stumbled into view, clutching his bleeding head. "I'm sorry, Laz. Jesus, I'm so sorry," he gasped.

"Eve," he barked out.

"Gone," Brent choked.

"No." He grabbed the other male. "Where is she? Where the fuck is she?"

"They took her. They fucking took her."

The delivery entrance door hung open and Lazarus ran out into the alley. This couldn't be happening. He instantly picked up the familiar lingering scent, the unmistakable stench of Orthon, foul and evil.

A roar ripped from his throat, and he clung to the wall. It was either that or fall to his knees. He had failed her. She was in the hands of his enemy, at the mercy of beings that didn't know the meaning of the word.

Forcing oxygen back into his lungs, he tried to calm himself enough to think. He pushed through the door, pounded back up the stairs to their room, and strapped on his blades.

He had to believe she would be okay; that he would get to her in time. Anything else was unacceptable. Tobias had taken Eve, an innocent in all this. The bastard wouldn't care, too far gone for rational thought. Revenge was all Tobias cared about. He wanted to take Eve from him permanently.

Rising panic took over. His demon wanted blood, screamed out for Eve, fought to take over Lazarus, but his rage helped fight his demon back. The bond, now stronger than ever, between him and Eve helped him keep control, the male desperate to find his mate.

Brent was waiting for him when he came back down. "I've called the others." He was leaning heavily on the doorframe.

Laz didn't answer, couldn't even if he wanted to. He nodded and headed down to the alleyway. Cool air and the stench of garbage mixed with the lingering scent of Orthon hit him. With her still wearing the amulet, he couldn't track her, couldn't sense her power. He had no fucking clue where to start.

Not knowing what the fuck to do, he called for Silas. He called the fucker until his voice was raw. The angel never came.

In the end, not knowing what else to do, Lazarus took to the skies, circling, desperate for anything, any sign of Eve or Tobias.

He was standing on top of an apartment building, with no

idea how much time had passed, when the *thud* of boots hitting concrete had Lazarus looking up from the streets below.

Gunner, Rocco, Zenon, and Chaos stood there, wings tucked into their backs, crowding the rooftop.

"Fuck, Laz," Rocco said, strain clear in his voice.

Lazarus didn't want sympathy. He wanted to find Eve.

"You sure it was Tobias?" Gunner asked.

Chaos stepped forward. "It had to be."

Lazarus shoved his fingers through his hair. "Where the fuck would he take her?"

That's when it sunk in: the real reason Silas chose not to fill him in on what Eve was, why he kept it a secret. He'd used her as bait. Diemos had felt her, too, when she came into her powers. Of course he did. The daughter of a handmaid, a way to release all the horrors of Hell on Earth, and a true escape for the demon after being unable to leave for centuries.

The angel knew Diemos would send Tobias after Eve.

Bringing him right to Lazarus. Making it easier for him to kill his brother.

Well, Silas's plan had fucking backfired, and Lazarus was going to end the fucker when he saw him next.

"Do you have something with her scent on it?" Gunner said. "We can take it to Warrick."

Warrick was a friend of Gunner's and a ranking hellhound in his pack. He was also one of the best trackers the hounds had.

Lazarus went back to the club, to their room. The entire apartment was filled with her scent, sweet and delicate. He picked up her shirt, the one she'd been wearing last night, and he held it to his nose, breathing in deeply. His demon cried out, wanted to maim, to kill.

For once they were in full accord.

The hounds had set up in Linville, New Jersey, population 3007. Now they ran the place. People here thought they were just another motorcycle club. They had no clue about the monsters they had on their doorstep. The hounds owned the local bar and ran a garage out of the old factory they'd moved into when they liberated themselves from Hell.

They hired themselves out as mercenaries. Loyal to no one. Lazarus didn't blame them, not after the way they were treated by Diemos and his brethren.

It took two hours to reach the clubhouse. Flying made the trip shorter, but coming here still meant losing time they didn't have.

The place was huge. On the surface, it looked like what it was: a run-down factory, and with their patch painted on one of the outside walls, a motorcycle club. But inside, underground, there was a whole lot more.

The pack was big, and that was made more obvious by the number of bikes lined up outside the main doors.

Lazarus landed first, his brothers close behind. Gunner moved ahead, leading them toward the entrance of the clubhouse. A snarl came from behind them, so loud and deep it seemed to vibrate through their feet. Then another from the side.

In moments, they were surrounded by the hounds. They were in their human forms, no claws or massive jaws on display, but that didn't make the large males and several females any less dangerous.

"We're here to see Warrick," Gunner said.

One of the males broke away and moved closer. "You know better than to come here like this, Gunner," he growled. "You use wings to breach our clubhouse without an invite, you get them torn off."

Zenon growled as well, his yellow eyes near glowing, fury radiating off him. "Fucking try it," he rumbled.

"Rein it in," Chaos said to Zenon.

"You know I have respect for the pack," Gunner said. "But we need Warrick's help and we're running out of time." He motioned to Lazarus. "His mate was taken by Diemos. We need to track her before it's too late."

More growls and vicious curses rang out around them. They hated Diemos almost as much as the knights did. After Lucifer was overthrown, leaving Diemos in charge, he had treated the hounds like shit, had used them, forced them to do a lot of things they sure as hell didn't like, which was why they'd finally left as soon as they got the chance.

The knights had agreed to their terms, had given them sanctuary, and they'd agreed not to harm humans, and to help them out on occasion. An understanding had formed between them, a truce. If tentative.

"I need something to scent."

Warrick's voice echoed across the lots as he strode toward them. Lower-ranking pack members backed up, getting out of his way as the huge male joined them.

Lazarus pulled Eve's shirt from the waistband of his jeans where he'd tucked it during the flight, and handed it to Warrick.

The other male put it to his nose and sniffed, drawing her scent in deep, eyes closing. Hellhounds weren't like other canines; they were created in Hell by Lucifer himself, which meant they had their own powers. Warrick was an alpha, would more than likely run the pack one day, and his powers were stronger than most. He didn't need to physically follow Eve's sent. He saw it in his mind, would be able to pinpoint her location from that shirt in moments.

His eyes snapped open, and they were glowing red for several moments before changing back to normal. He pulled his phone from his back pocket, clicked open an app with *maps* written under it, tapped something out, and zoomed in on a location before holding it up to Lazarus.

"She's here."

Every one of Lazarus's muscles was tensed, ready to take flight. "I owe you."

With no time to waste, he stood back, making room for the massive span of his unfurling wings. Charcoal and silver-flecked feathers glittered in the light, and with each lift and pull he caught the air and lifted off with all the power and speed he could muster, his brothers close behind.

Moving at speed, Lazarus rose above the cloud bank.

Urgency, along with guilt reached up and gripped him by the throat. Now he understood what it would mean to lose her, to lose the person that you loved absolutely.

The emotion defied definition.

I love her.

The realization settled over him like a gentle caress, and for once he didn't try to fight it. He loved her. How could he not? If he was honest, he'd been hers from the moment he spotted her up that ladder in her little store, despite how hard he tried to deny his feelings.

Tobias had suffered the overwhelming sorrow of losing his mate, and it had changed him, had destroyed a once fierce and loyal warrior. He was lost forever, and though it pained Laz, he had to end this today. His brother didn't exist anymore. Eve was all that mattered. It was too late for Tobias.

God, Heaven, the fucking uppity angels that resided there, he'd never asked them for anything, not a damn thing, but he prayed now. He prayed for Eve to still be alive. He begged the Fates to keep her safe until he could reach her.

Twenty minutes later he had passed over buildings and skyscrapers and kept going until he flew over large yards and even larger houses. She was close.

"There," he growled to Chaos who flew at his side.

The house was huge, like the others in the area, with a silver car parked in the driveway. There wasn't much in the way of security from what he could see, but then Tobias wouldn't be expecting him. His brother thought he was untouchable.

As much as he wanted to swoop in, kill anything that moved, and take Eve home, he had to play it safe. One wrong move and Tobias would kill her, or worse—because Eve would suffer a million painful deaths at his hands—deliver her to Diemos. If he knew what she was, what she was capable of...

Fuck.

Lazarus circled the outer perimeter several times, pinpointing entry points and guard positions. His best option would be one of the unguarded doors on a second-floor balcony.

"I'm going in," Laz said to Chaos. "It's too dangerous for all of us to go in at once. If Tobias knows we're here, he'll kill her before I can get to her. Give me time to find her and assess the situation before you follow."

Chaos's jaw tightened, but he didn't try to convince him otherwise because he'd be wasting his breath. "Be careful," he said.

Laz dipped his chin, and letting his powerful wings do the work, slowed his momentum and landed effortlessly on the closest balcony.

The room beyond was silent, empty, and he easily broke the lock. A thick layer of dust covered the furniture and the room smelled musty. The décor was not Tobias's usual taste—lace and ruffles adorned the feminine room.

Eve was in the house, suddenly he could feel her, which meant Tobias had more than likely found the amulet and removed it.

He gritted his teeth.

Fuck. Stay focused.

Yeah, he could sense her power loud and clear now.

The buzzing awareness of her grew stronger, spiking. It turned his veins to ice, abrading his nerves like coarse sandpaper.

Something was wrong.

He had to get to her. Now.

He listened for movement beyond the wooden door that led from the room into the main house. Silence greeted him.

Easing it open, he moved into the hall, the plush carpet muting his footfalls. As he passed the next room, the smell of death, stale and sickly sweet, wafted from under the closed door. A human. More than likely the owner or owners of the house. Another victim in Tobias's quest for revenge.

The blood on Lazarus's hands grew thicker by the day in the fallout from his carelessness.

He had to stop this now. Eve would not be the next victim. He shook his head, stopping the thought before it sent rage and fear pulsing through his veins and weakened him.

He cursed under his breath at the sound and smell of more than one demon pounding up the stairs, heading in his direction. Stepping back into the room, he waited for them to get closer.

As soon as they were in striking distance, Lazarus stepped out, removing the head of the first with his short sword, then spun, nailing the second in the heart. Quickly dragging the bodies out of the hall, he removed the second demons head then shut them in the room, concealing them before they could ash out and draw unwanted attention.

Making sure the way was clear, Lazarus headed to the lower level via a rear staircase. The buzz of Eve's power grew even stronger, drawing him deeper. She was in the basement.

He came to a small landing that turned abruptly. Bingo. Golden light ghosted from the deep recesses.

Lazarus's every muscle strained to breaking point with the tension it took to make himself move at a slow pace.

Red rage almost blinded him, but he called on every bit of self-control. All that mattered was getting to Eve.

But before he could make it to the basement, more demons, Orthon, were approaching in front and behind him. This time he had nowhere to go.

He pulled his sword free and prepared to fight.

Twenty-Five

Eve wanted to scream, the agony pounding through her skull so severe it felt like her head would explode.

The demon stood too close, his rancid breath skittering across her cheek.

"Well, demi?" Tobias asked from his position a short distance from her, the amulet she'd worn around her neck dangling from his fingers.

He wanted her to read the creature's mind, like some screwed-up lie detector for his own entertainment, to confirm yet another loyal servant. For the most part, she had lied. All but a few hated his guts. She'd told him his minions loved him, were devoted to only him.

When, in actual fact, they wanted to rip his head off and... well, eat him.

She shuddered at the disgusting thoughts coming from the Orthon standing beside her. His face was only an inch from hers, staring down at her with cold, soulless eyes, all but daring her to tell the truth.

She panted through the pain. "He is loyal to you."

Once Tobias took the amulet, she'd only been able to

maintain her block for a short time; there were just too many of them. Now the strain of having every thought and disgusting image in the room bang around in her brain had become too much and she cried out in agony and frustration.

The demon sneered. Lifting its gray hand, it ran a yellow nail down the side of her face. Not hard enough to break the skin, but enough to leave a mark beside the bloody scratches she already had. It whispered something to her in a language she didn't, or at least shouldn't, understand. But a translator wasn't necessary because the words filtered into her mind in perfect English.

She would be dessert.

"Don't touch her." Tobias kicked the creature, sending him sprawling. "She's more important than you know. Isn't that right, Eve?"

The Orthon hissed.

Tobias laughed. "Leave us," he barked at the demons surrounding them from above. He'd chained her to the wall of a concrete pit in the basement. The creature eyed her as it scrambled from the floor and climbed out. The rest followed in its wake.

Tobias would soon find himself with a full-blown revolt on his hands, and after they'd feasted on him, she would be next, but not before they had used her in other disgusting ways.

Tobias moved toward her, a sneer distorting his beautiful face into something cruel and evil. And like Lazarus, she couldn't hear his thoughts.

"I can see why Lazarus wanted to keep you around. You're a very tempting female. How many times did he fuck you, demi?"

Keeping her eyes locked on his, she refused to give him what he wanted and rise to the bait. Instead, she pressed her lips together, refusing to answer.

"It doesn't really matter," his deep voice echoed in the confined space. "He didn't mate with you, and that's all that matters. I kind of wish he had. I would have loved for him to feel your pain, your fear the moment you give up and stop fighting. If I'd had my way, I would have delivered your used and broken body to him and taken pleasure in watching him succumb to his demon." He rubbed a lock of her hair between his fingers. "But fate has other plans for you. You know what you are, don't you, Eve?"

Terror made her limbs weak and her heart pound, but she tried to keep her expression blank.

"I may not be able to kill you, but I see I'll have a lot of fun breaking you." He cupped her cheek, letting his fingers trail down her face until he gripped her throat.

She had nowhere to go. Her back was hard against the wall of the deep pit. Leaning forward, he caught her mouth in a hard, bruising kiss. He pressed his fingers into her jaw and forced it open, trying to thrust his tongue into her mouth.

Wrenching her head to the side, she loosened his grip and took advantage by biting down hard on his lip.

"Bitch," he hissed and backhanded her so hard her vision blinked in and out. Her head rang for a few minutes, the force of the blow nearly rendering her unconscious. When Tobias's face came back into focus, the bastard was grinning. The metallic tang of blood filled her mouth and she blinked back the tears she refused to let fall.

His eyes flashed. "Oh yeah, we're going to have some fun." He turned away from her, moved to a small table set up on the other side of the pit, and picked something up.

"What is that? What are you going to do?" she said, terror almost choking her.

He turned to her. In his hands was what looked like a small leather package, brown and worn. He peeled back one side then the other, his black eyes focused on what he was uncovering.

"It's going to help you do what you were born to," he said without looking up at her.

Finally, he took something from the center, something yellowing, long and thin and pointed, and dropped the leather to the table.

"What the hell is that?" she choked.

"It's a bone. A very old and very powerful bone." He placed it in a crude wooden bowl and walked toward her. "As long as you're alive and your blood covers this bone, Diemos will have control over the hell's gate. He will be able to open and close it at will." He was breathing heavily. "Can you imagine, sweet Eve, what your Earth will be like then? With demons free to do what they like, more than the knights will ever be able to contain."

She shook her head. "No...no, please...you can't..."

Tobias ignored her, placed the bowl on the stone floor, and grabbed her wrist. "Time to take you to your new home. Diemos is eager to meet you."

He took the short sword, one that looked almost identical to Lazarus's, from the sheath strapped to his thigh and drew it across her skin without warning or hesitation.

She gasped in pain and watched in horror as Tobias held her arm above the wooden bowl, catching her blood, covering the bone he'd placed inside it.

Crying out, she kicked at it, trying to knock it over, but the chains around her ankles restricted her movements.

Tobias gripped a fistful of hair painfully, holding her still. The bone was soon covered and Tobias leaned in, lapping at her blood, at the open wound in her flesh. She tried to pull away, but he held her too tight.

"You want to stop bleeding, don't you? It won't do for

you to bleed out and die. That would ruin all our plans," he said.

Her mind started to shut down, her psyche throwing up walls to protect her sanity.

This can't be happening. It can't be real.

She would never see Lazarus again.

One voice, an Orthon's, rose, cutting through her own thoughts. Its distress penetrated the chaos of her mind and broke past the other voices in the room. Nothing she could put together, though, because its thoughts were far too jumbled.

Then it cut off abruptly, its mind suddenly silent.

More followed.

Their minds screaming, then nothing.

Tobias stood back, and beside her something flashed. A bright light. It was working. *Oh God*, the gate was opening.

She tried to fight her restraints, but it was no good. Her limbs felt weak from loss of blood and she was close to collapsing.

"They're coming," Tobias said, voice filled with excitement.

Her vision dimmed, the colors darkening. Eve blinked several times, positive she was about to pass out. A large shadow had descended over Tobias, half his face eclipsed by darkness. Her eyes were playing tricks on her.

She blinked again, looking up.

Her breath seized in her lungs.

Lazarus stood there, towering over them.

His face was in shadow. She couldn't see his expression, but the glow from the wall-mounted lights illuminated him from behind like a golden halo.

Tobias came forward, grabbing hold of her biceps, his grip painfully tight.

"Get your hands off her," Lazarus said, his voice echoing

around the confined space, full of fury and promising death and suffering to the male beside her.

Tobias's black eyes widened briefly before he chuckled darkly. "You found us, then?" He made a tutting sound. "Pity you're too late. You really should have mated her, Laz, and all this could have been prevented."

Lazarus hissed.

Tobias leaned in and breathed deeply. "She reeks of you." He grinned. "I'm glad she's yours. You have no idea how glad. That I'll be depriving you of your mate...fuck yeah, it made this so much sweeter."

"Don't fucking touch her," Lazarus said, his disembodied voice bouncing off the brick walls.

The portal beside them that had started as a small spark, a flash of light, was swirling, growing in size.

Tobias laughed then gripped her jaw and lifted a knife, placing it against her face. "You're too late. It's done. You've lost, and you've lost her."

Eve struggled, and the tears she'd fought blazed a heated trail down her cheeks. Her reaction seemed to excite Tobias more, and he drew the blade slowly across her flesh. She screamed and felt her blood bubble to the surface of her skin. Its warmth ran down her neck and the inside of her shirt.

"Stop," Lazarus roared.

Tobias leaned in and licked the rivulet from her neck. "Mmm, the taste of power. One of the handmaids' blood runs through her veins. Diemos has been looking for someone like her for centuries, and it'll be me who delivers her to him."

"Do you think he'll reward you? He's using you, Tobias," Lazarus said. "You think he'll pat you on the back, welcome you into Hell with open arms? You spent as many centuries stopping him from reaching his ultimate goal. Once you deliver her, he will turn on you."

The hell's gate pulsed, still growing.

Tobias had stilled at her side. "You're wrong," he roared.

"You know I'm not," Laz said back. "You know it."

Snarling echoed off the stone walls and filled the basement. Tobias pulled Eve in closer to him. "They're coming to welcome us home. Do you hear them?"

Light flashed so bright it blinded her for several seconds. Eve blinked, tears streaming down her face, and when she could see again she cried out in horror. Demons were crawling out of the portal.

Lazarus stepped closer.

"Take another step and I'll take a piece out of her," Tobias said.

Lazarus growled as demons edged toward him from all directions. He drew his sword a moment before they launched at him.

Eve screamed as he roared and tried to fight them off, but more poured out of the hell's gate, coming at him, taking their place instantly.

No matter how many he killed, more came.

"Lazarus!" she cried.

Something was wrong.

Tobias leaned in. "You see, a male's physical strength is irrelevant if he is weak of mind. As I suspected, seeing you bleed has caused his loss of control."

Please, God, no.

Tobias worked on her chains and had her free in moments, then started pulling her toward the hell's gate.

"No." She tried to fight but it was useless.

She cried out, trying to get Lazarus's attention, and hoped like hell she didn't distract him from his fight and get him injured even more. But she needed to do something.

His body stiffened, just a fraction. He'd heard her. She called his name again and he turned to her. Their gazes collided and held. His body went rigid.

Tobias hissed and clapped a hand over her mouth.

Lazarus snarled, the sound inhuman. He roared, his body seeming to grow and contort. He shook his head from side to side like an angry bull.

He called her name—

And exploded into his demon form, throwing off the demons that had covered him. His chest heaved, light glinting off his crimson skin and glossy black horns. His huge charcoal wings were spread wide, the silver flecks shimmering and dancing across each individual feather as they moved—causing a delicious spicy breeze to surround her, ruffling her hair.

The demons only stayed back a moment then dove at him, attaching themselves to his big body. Their teeth flashed as they bit and tore at his skin and wings with their claws. He peeled them off, but he was bleeding, his beautiful wings damaged.

He didn't seem to notice, and continued to fight in a mindless rage. The audible crunch of bone made her stomach lurch as he dispatched them one after another.

Tobias stilled beside her, releasing a shuddering breath. "His demon has taken him. It's done. It's over."

She shook her head. *Oh God. I can't lose him now.*

The demons still covered Lazarus, tearing at his flesh, and more tears broke free, tracking down her face.

They're going to kill him.

Lazarus was in there. He had to be. He wasn't gone. She refused to believe it. She'd brought him back the last time he lost control of his demon, and she could do it again. She twisted her head, and Tobias was distracted enough by what was going on in front of them that she managed to get her mouth free of his hand. At least long enough for her to call Lazarus one more time.

Lazarus stilled completely and looked down at them. "Let her go," he roared at Tobias. He didn't take his eyes off them as he again methodically peeled demons from his body, until he was free of them and holding back the horde with his sword.

Blood dripped from his wounded body and pooled at his feet. His nostrils flared and his chest heaved as he took a threatening step toward the edge of the pit.

He didn't seem to be struggling against his demon. The two of them seemed to be working together to protect her.

Tobias cursed and lifted his blade to her again. Lazarus froze. This was it. She was about to die without ever telling him she loved him.

Lazarus roared, the animalistic sound ripped from his throat.

She wasn't letting Tobias take her to Hell, no matter the cost. She wouldn't be the cause of these creatures invading her world, or what that would mean for Lazarus.

The bowl filled with her blood was still on the floor, just out of reach. Eve found enough strength to jerk to the side and kick out. She braced for the pain that was coming, as the knife that Tobias held was forced into her flesh with the movement, sinking deep into her shoulder.

The bowl toppled over, her blood splashed out onto the stone floor, and the gate flickered and closed, faster than it came.

Agony burned through her and knocked her legs out from underneath her. Tobias's hold on her vanished...then Lazarus was there.

A battle cry echoed around the brick walls, filled with so much hatred it lifted the hair on the back of Eve's neck. Lazarus's brothers were there. The massive males were fighting the demons that had escaped with brutal and lethal grace.

"I've got you," Lazarus said, chest heaving.

He cupped her face in his large, leathery, crimson hand. He was in his demon form, but his eyes weren't black; they were bright green. He was savagely beautiful.

His gaze dropped, zeroed in on the blood covering the front of her shirt, and he stilled. Fear, stark and violent, twisted his hard features and his eyes turned wild. "Oh, fuck." He made an agonized sound. "Where is it? Where were you cut? Don't leave me, sweetheart. You can't leave me."

Eve gripped his wide wrist. "I'm all right. I'm not going anywhere," she choked. She didn't think he heard her. His gaze focused solely on the growing patch of blood staining her shirt.

"Lazarus? Look at me." Agony lined his face. "I won't leave you. I promise I'll never leave you."

He shuddered, seemed to collect himself, and covered her wound with his big hand, applying pressure.

She hissed.

"You're okay. You're going to be okay," he said.

She got the impression he needed to convince himself as much as her. Eve cupped his face, fighting unconsciousness. "Yes, I am, because of you. You found me." Her voice sounded croaky, barely audible.

"I'm sorry I took so long," he choked. She didn't think he was aware of the tears running down his fierce and beautiful face.

"I knew you'd come for me."

Lazarus gently kissed her lips. "Let's get you out of here."

"He's getting away," Chaos yelled.

They looked up in time to see Tobias heading for the stairs. The other knights were engaged in battle, unable to fight their way to him.

Tobias paused at the foot of the stairs and gripped his head, his gaze sliding to Lazarus. His eyes changed, the black giving way to cool pale blue.

Lazarus sucked in a sharp breath, stiffening, and an anguished sound escaped his throat that broke Eve's heart. Tobias spun away, stumbling as he ran up the stairs.

Eve clung to Lazarus as he lifted them from the pit. Demons surrounded them, watching them with eager, hungry eyes.

But then Lazarus's brothers were there, cutting them back, creating a clear path.

Lazarus didn't turn back, trusting his brothers had his back, and carried her toward the stairs as well. They moved through the house and out onto the yard. Tobias was long gone, and Lazarus took flight, still managing to fly even with his wings as damaged as they were.

Eve clung to him and she was never letting go.

Twenty-Six

When Eve woke, it took several minutes for the fog of sleep to lift. She was in Lazarus's bed, in his room at the compound.

Warm.

Safe.

Home.

She lay cocooned by a mountain of pillows. The big room felt cozy with the lights dimmed. She tried to sit up, but could barely move her arms with the duvet pulled up high and tucked around her securely.

It took a moment for the confusion to clear and her memories to come flooding back. She struggled to get free of the covers again, and pain shot through her shoulder.

Lazarus?

The familiar scent of her mate surrounded her, enveloped her in warmth, and the panic subsided. He was safe.

The door cracked open and his wide shoulders filled the narrow space. With his feet bare and wearing only a pair of black jeans that sat low on his hips, she took the opportunity to search the hard planes of his bare chest, looking for any sign of injury. All that remained of the vicious wounds he'd received from the demon attack were fading pink marks, now barely visible on his smooth skin.

He carried a tray laden with food, and when he glanced up, he offered her a wide smile. "You're awake." He sat on the bed beside her. "You've been asleep so long I was getting worried. How are you feeling? Are you hungry?"

All she wanted to do was touch him, convince herself that he was unhurt, that he was really here with her, that this wasn't just some beautiful dream. "I think so."

"I wasn't sure what you'd feel like. So, I, ah"—he glanced down at the overflowing tray—"yeah, I got some of everything." He seemed unsure of himself, nervous.

"A drink would be good to start with." She gave in and rested a hand on his thigh. The heat and hard muscle beneath her palm reassured her like nothing else could.

He handed her a glass of juice and studied her face, searching her gaze for what she didn't know, but his uncertainty shone through. Her chest squeezed.

She lifted her hand to her throat. The weight of the gold disk she'd worn around her neck for weeks was noticeable in its absence. "The amulet?"

"Chaos found it where Tobias...where he had you... chained." His voice had grown deeper, rougher.

"What will happen to Tobias?" she asked.

"We can't feel him anymore. For the first time in centuries." His jaw bunched. "Diemos wouldn't have been happy with his failure." His eyes met hers.

"You think he's dead?"

Lazarus nodded.

Even after everything, it still hurt him. "I'm sorry."

He squeezed her hand still resting on his thigh and cleared his throat. His eyes searched hers. "When...when I first came for you, the idea of making you mine, shit, it scared the fuck out of me. I didn't want it, what you represented, what it meant for both of us." The muscle in his jaw bunched. "I didn't feel worthy of you."

Eve shook her head. "Laz—"

"I never planned to stay once I'd made you mine. I was going to leave, Eve."

Her pulse stuttered, raced faster. "You were?" she whispered.

Pain distorted his features. "I don't deserve you, Eve. And truthfully, I never will. I should give you back the amulet. I should leave. Let you find someone worthy of you." His voice was nothing but a broken growl.

She shook her head, unable to speak. She wanted to tell him she couldn't live without him, but her throat constricted, choking off her words.

He leaned forward and stopped her distress with a hard kiss, claiming and possessive. Finally, he pulled back. "But I can't. I won't. I'm too selfish. I want you to be mine, Eve. My mate. Will you?"

She swallowed the lump in her throat. "Yes. There's nowhere else I'd rather be than here with you."

He released a rough breath. "Really? You will?"

"Yes. I want that more than anything."

He cupped her face in his large hands. "I'm never letting you out of my sight, not ever again." He ran his knuckles down the uninjured side of her face. "When I saw you... Tobias's hands on you, bleeding..." His voice broke.

She reached up and grabbed his fingers, threading them with hers. "I'm all right now."

The pain remained, and seeing Tobias like that had to have hurt him greatly. She wanted to ease his pain and she wanted... she just wanted him. She untucked the covers and pulled them back.

Lazarus frowned. "What are you doing?"

"Climb in with me."

"Eve..."

She shook her head, stopping whatever protest he was going to make. "I don't want to wait, Lazarus. Please, make me yours."

His nostrils flared and the green of his eyes flickered dark then light. "Are you sure?"

"I've never been so sure about anything in my whole life."

He stood abruptly, his hands dropping to the front of his jeans and he quickly undid them and shoved them off.

Eve sucked in a breath at the sight of him standing there naked. "You're so beautiful."

He climbed in beside her, that big body shaking with need. "And you take my goddamn breath way, female."

Lazarus stared into Eve's eyes. His mate. *His*. He could barely believe this was happening. That he could feel this happy. That he could trust another being so fully. She held his heart and soul in her hands. This female, so beautiful inside and out, gave his existence meaning. She gave him a reason to keep fighting.

No, he never believed he deserved this, not after losing Scarlet and Tobias, but turning his back on her now was an impossibility. Leaving her was not something he could even contemplate.

One of her arms, the one not injured, curled around his neck and her fingers threaded in his hair at his nape. "I love you, Lazarus."

His heart squeezed and burst into a rapid-fire beat at her softly spoken words. He trembled harder. "And I love you."

He gently pressed his lips to hers and kissed her slow and deep. He was already hard and aching for her, his body demanding he take her, but he had to be gentle. Not easy with the way her thighs had spread wider, hugging his hips, her bare pussy hot and slick against his cock.

He groaned. "You're ready for me now, aren't you, sweetheart?"

Her hips lifted and she rubbed herself against him. "Yes. Now, Lazarus. Please."

A growl crawled up his throat, his demon twisting and snarling, as desperate for the connection as Lazarus was. "I'm gonna take this slow, okay? You're still recovering." He pressed the head of his cock to her opening. "Ready?" he choked out.

She bit her lip and nodded.

Lazarus kissed her then lifted to his elbows, needing to see her face when he slid home. He pressed forward, and they both moaned as he filled her. He made love to her then, both of them shaking from the beauty of it, the desperate need for one another, a need that would never wane or falter. The kind of love and connection flowing between them he'd never even dared to dream about.

It was hard, but he kept the pace slow, thrusting deep.

Oh fuck. There it was. He could see it. The thread that would bind them.

Eve gasped and her entire body bowed as a surge of power moved through her, turning her entire body into a live wire. He knew because he felt it, too. What looked like a full-body orgasm hit her and she cried out, trembling uncontrollably.

Lazarus watched in awe, clenching his fists, gripping the sheet as the link intensified.

He reached for it and grabbed on. His hips snapped forward, staying deep inside Eve. And like a tree sending out tender new roots, the connection thickened and grew, burying deep. Something wrenched deep inside him, the exquisite pleasure drawing out their bliss.

She was his, now and forever. Nothing but death could

ever rip them apart, and he'd spend eternity making sure that never happened. He felt it in his heart and soul, and he embraced the euphoric sensation with open arms.

Eve was his mate.

They lay there for the longest time, just holding each other.

Finally, he lifted his head and stared into her glistening blue eyes. "Thank you."

She touched his face, her thumb brushing over his whiskered jaw. "You don't need to thank me."

"You don't realize what you've done, sweetheart. I've fought an internal battle for centuries." He grinned. "I don't... I don't need to fight it anymore. My demon is finally leashed," he whispered then swallowed hard. "Because of you, because you gave yourself to me."

She smiled so wide his stomach clenched.

"I'd fight it again, no matter how many centuries it took, as long as I knew you were waiting for me at the other end," he choked out.

Her eyes grew brighter. "We make a pretty good team, huh?"

"Yeah, sweetheart, we do," he said.

She looked over his shoulder and he knew the moment she spotted it. The large bookshelf full of books, her mother's books, worn and well-read, and precious to her. Her gaze moved around the room, spotting other bits and pieces scattered about, little things. Her things.

She blinked up at him. "You got my books?"

"This is your home now. I want you to be happy here."

She looked around, flabbergasted. "How did you get them here so fast?"

Christ, she was cute. "Wing power, baby. Fastest way to fly." He chuckled at the way her eyes grew wider.

"Really? You did that...for me?" she said, voice raspy with emotion.

Lazarus brushed back a strand hair from her face. "I'd do anything for you. Anything."

A tear streaked down her face and he brushed that away as well.

"Though, in this instance, I can't take all the credit. I sent the others as well, got them to collect as much as they could carry. I'll have the bigger stuff shipped."

More tears slid down her cheeks. "This is...you have no idea how much this means to me."

"I did it for purely selfish reasons. I want you to love it here. I want you to feel at home, to never regret—"

She pressed a finger to his lips, stopping him mid-sentence. "I can live without my things, Lazarus. At the end of the day, it's all just stuff. God, because of you, I've finally found my home, the place I belong. A place I know I will always be loved and cherished. I don't want to live without you. I can't. I love you," she said simply.

Something tickled his cheek and when he swiped at it, his fingers came away wet. This female, what she did to him. "I'm yours, Eve, now and forever." His face darkened with hunger before he bent forward and kissed her again. "God, I love you so much," he whispered against her lips.

It was her turn to wipe his tears away, and then she wrapped her arms around him.

Lazarus buried his face against her neck, breathing in his female.

His mate.

She smelled like home.

Epilogue

Three months later

Eve walked down the hall, arm linked with Meredith's, both ready to do battle.

Meredith squeezed her hand. "I can't believe Chaos went for it. You know, since the guy's completely allergic to fun."

Wasn't that the truth. But Eve had been determined, and in the end, he'd relented. The guys had been fighting a lot, especially with the way the demons in the city had been behaving. They all knew something was seriously off and Eve knew how worried they were. She just wanted a night where they could relax, laugh. "You know we have to beat Chaos now, right? At everything, or we'll never hear the end of it."

Meredith laughed as Eve pushed open the door to the control room. "We'll have to join forces..."

"Go long!" Kryos called and tossed a ball across the room and out the balcony doors. Rocco sprinted after it, jumped to the railing, and dove off the side, shifting into his demon form midair. His clothes disintegrated, falling from his body then he disappeared from view.

Lazarus strode over to her and tugged her into his side. Eve looked up at her grinning mate. "Um…this wasn't the kind of games night we had in mind."

He smirked. "No?"

A heavy *thud* against the balcony floor had them all turning back to the open doors. Rocco, ball in hand, and completely naked, strode back in.

Kryos growled and put his hands over Meredith's eyes, and Lazarus curled his hand around the back of Eve's head and smooshed her face against his chest.

"Put it away, asshole," Lazarus growled.

"Bother, seriously. No one wants to see that," Kryos added.

Rocco chuckled. "Feeling threatened are we, boys?"

Kryos snorted. "As if."

Eve tried to move, but Lazarus wouldn't let her lift her head. "Really?" she bit out.

"I'm sorry, sweetheart," Lazarus said. "But it's just not done. A male does not flash his jewels at another male's mate."

"And if he does, he gets his ass kicked," Kryos said. He sounded like he was gritting his teeth.

"Can I lift my head now?" Eve asked.

"No."

"Okay, let's all calm down," Rocco said. "Instead of kicking my ass, how about you Kryos and Gunner, play me, Chaos and Zen…out there. First to miss a pass loses."

"Loses what?" Chaos said, obviously now joining the ridiculous conversation.

"Their dignity," Rocco said.

Meredith cursed. "You males are so juvenile."

"This *really* isn't what we had in mind for tonight," Eve added.

"You're on," Lazarus said, ignoring her completely.

"Whatever," Meredith muttered. "I just want my eyesight back."

Lazarus tipped Eve's head back and she blinked up at him. "You want to watch me play?"

His hopeful expression made her giggle. "Sure."

"Teams are going to be uneven. Gunner's AWOL," Chaos said.

Lazarus frowned and Eve knew the guys were worried about him. He'd told her Gunner hadn't been himself for weeks.

"I'm out," Zenon said.

Eve hadn't even realized he was in the room.

The male was so closed off, spent so much time alone, she hated that he was leaving. She reached out to touch his arms as he walked by, about to try and convince him to stay, but he jerked back like she'd stabbed him.

"I'm...I'm sorry, I didn't mean to..." What? She wasn't sure how to finish her sentence.

Zenon dropped his chin, letting his hair fall forward, covering his face, and strode from the room.

Lazarus curled his fingers around the side of her neck, drawing her attention back to him. "It's not you," he said. "He just...Zenon doesn't like to be touched."

What had happened to him to make him react like that? She hated to think. Out of all the knights, Zenon was the most distant, the one she wished she could figure out. But she got the feeling there was no getting through to him and that made her heart hurt.

"You ready?" Rocco called.

"I was born ready," Kryos said as he stripped off, shifted, and dove off the side of the balcony.

"Nice work, Eve," Rocco said. "Games night rocks." He winked at her and shifted as well, joining Kryos and Chaos who were already passing the ball to each other high in the air, their massive wings working to hold them at the same height, five floors above the ground.

"Will you be here when I'm done?" Lazarus said, grinning down at her. "When I return victorious and ready to claim my spoils."

Eve grinned back. "I told you, I'm not going anywhere. Not ever."

His eyes softened and he tugged her close, kissing her slow and deep.

"Enough with the sucking face," Rocco called out. "Your stalling tactics won't save you."

Lazarus lifted his head. "Oh, it's on."

Eve watched her mate shift into his demon form and join the others, the thunder of heavy bodies colliding and the ball being thrown hard, following soon after.

Meredith sighed and plonked down on a seat beside her. "Maybe we can get them to play Monopoly next week?"

A window smashed somewhere followed by hoots and cheers.

They both burst out laughing.

Eve wiped her eyes. "Yeah, I'm not liking our chances."

Zenon was torn from his sleep as a wave of...fuck, he didn't know what it was, sliced through him. He gritted his teeth, frozen in place as it smashed through him a second time.

Something he couldn't name pumped through his veins, Christ, sank into his bones. His spine torqued and his eyes rolled back as the feeling grew and grew...then finally, released him.

He collapsed back on the bed, covered in sweat, heart pounding, mind racing.

Zenon knew pain, it was his constant companion, what

he'd just experienced couldn't be described as pain, though, it had almost felt, fuck, it had almost felt...*good*.

He shoved his long hair away from his face and stared up at the ceiling as it slipped away, leaving his limbs loose and warm, and a sense of...*knowing* filled him, like there was this thing, this big, important fucking thing, in the back of his mind, just out of reach. Something he needed to remember or know, but couldn't get to.

Another wave moved through him, softer this time, like an aftershock after a colossal earthquake.

A demi.

He could feel one, new to their powers.

What the fuck? He'd never reacted like that before.

With a growl, he shoved the covers back and climbed out of bed, and as he dressed, as he headed to the control room, that feeling inside him pushed forward again causing tingles to dance along his spine, making his head tingle and fucking goosebumps to lift all over his skin.

It was that feeling that had him walking straight up to Chaos and insisting that he send Zenon on the retrieval—something he never did. Ever.

Chaos finally, reluctantly, agreed, then Zenon forced himself to stay calm while he waited for Roc and Gunner so they could leave.

Standing back from everyone, he ignored the worried glances his brothers sent his way.

"You'll let Roc do the talking?" Chaos said again.

Zenon didn't even bother replying. Of course, he would, because when he got close, when he tried to talk to people, they got uncomfortable. Another reason he shouldn't go.

Chaos sighed and walked away. Yeah, he thought Zenon would fuck this up, and he was probably right. But Zen couldn't make himself stay behind, not when that *thing* he'd woken with was pushing him on, when this sense of urgency was driving him forward.

Laz was about to head off on patrol, and Zenon tried not to watch as his brother leaned in and kissed his mate goodbye, but he couldn't make himself turn away. It was a soft kiss. They kissed a lot. Sometimes hard and urgent, sometimes soft like now. So did Kryos and Meredith.

The affection they had for each other flowed from them, so visceral it had those tingles moving up and down Zenon's spine up their efforts. Eve's arms wrapped around her mate, her dainty hands against Laz's broad back, her hold gentle, light brushes, soothing rubs.

That weird feeling gripped Zen's gut tighter.

What would that be like? To be touched that way? Gentle. Not to cause pain or to humiliate. Not to control.

A growl tried to crawl up his throat.

"Yo, Zen, you ready?" Rocco called.

Zenon jolted, humiliation heating his face at being caught acting like a fucking creeper. He quickly dipped his head lower and nodded.

Yeah, he was more than ready to go.

Whoever this demi was, they were affecting him in a way he didn't understand, a way he didn't fucking like or want.

And he was going to find out why.

KNIGHT'S SALVATION

KNIGHTS OF HELL, BOOK 2

Demon hunter Zenon lives with a dark secret. When he escaped Hell, he didn't leave alone—and he'll do anything to keep the shameful reason hidden. But when an intoxicating demi-demon, new to her powers, has him breaking all his own rules just to be near her, he knows he's in serious trouble.

Painfully aware of being different, Mia Westbrook has always kept herself apart from others. Yet her new demon life comes with strings attached, namely one scarred and broodingly seductive knight who storms into her world—and her heart—and may just be her perfect match.

But a formidable evil has been watching, and is determined to tear them apart. They want Zenon is back in Hell, with them, where he belongs...

Also by Sherilee Gray

Hell On Wheels

Bad Demon

Blood Moon Brides:

Blood Moon Bound

The Thornheart Trials:

A Curse in Darkness

A Vow of Ruin

A Trial by Blood

An Oath at Midnight

A Promise of Ashes

A Bond in Flames

Knights of Hell:

Knight's Seduction

Knight's Redemption

Knight's Salvation

Demon's Temptation

Knight's Dominion

Knight's Absolution

Knight's Retribution

Rocktown Ink:

Beg For You

Sin For You

Meant For you

Bad For You

All For You

Just for You

The Smith Brothers:

Mountain Man

Wild Man

Solitary Man

Lawless Kings:

Shattered King

Broken Rebel

Beautiful Killer

Ruthless Protector

Glorious Sinner

Merciless King

Boosted Hearts:

Swerve

Spin

Slide

Spark

Axle Alley Vipers:

Crashed

Revved

Wrecked

Black Hills Pack:

Lone Wolf's Captive

A Wolf's Deception

Stand Alone Novels:

Breaking Him

While You Sleep

About the Author

Sherilee Gray is a kiwi girl and lives in beautiful New Zealand with her husband and their two children. When she isn't writing sexy contemporary or paranormal romance, searching for her next alpha hero on Pinterest, or fueling her voracious book addiction, she can be found dreaming of far off places with a mug of tea in one hand and a bar of chocolate in the other.

To find out about new releases, giveaways, events and other cool stuff, sign up for my newsletter!

www.sherileegray.com

Printed in Dunstable, United Kingdom

81580248R10167